FALL OUT BOY

FALL OUT BOY

OUR LAWYERS MADE US CHANGE THE NAME OF THIS BOOK SO WE WOULDN'T GET SUED

BEN WELCH

Published by Music Press Books
an imprint of John Blake Publishing
2.25, The Plaza,
535 Kings Road,
Chelsea Harbour,
London, SW10 0SZ

www.johnblakebooks.co.uk

www.facebook.com/johnblakebooks
twitter.com/jblakebooks

First published in paperback in 2016

ISBN: 978 1 78606 125 6

British Library Cataloguing-in-Publication Data:

A catalogue record for this book is available from the British Library.

Design by www.envydesign.co.uk

Printed and bound in Great Britain by Clays Ltd, Elcograf S.p.A.

3 5 7 9 10 8 6 4 2

Papers used by John Blake Publishing are natural, recyclable products made from wood grown in sustainable forests. The manufacturing processes conform to the environmental regulations of the country of origin.

John Blake Publishing is an imprint of Bonnier Books UK
www.bonnierbooks.co.uk

CONTENTS

INTRODUCTION

On a humid summer's night in July 1979, fifty thousand people descended on Comiskey Park in Chicago, Illinois, to witness something extraordinary. Comiskey Park was the home of the White Sox and 'The Baseball Palace of the World', but this mob wasn't out for a ball game. They were rock fans, and tonight they wanted fire and noise. For the previous couple of years the infectious grooves of disco had been spreading over the airwaves, converting rock radio stations and displacing DJs as it went. Steve Dahl had been fired from local station WDAI, but he sensed that rock fans were ready for a fightback; under the rallying call of 'disco sucks', he organised an audacious spectacle to coincide with a game between the White Sox and the Detroit Tigers. It was a twilight-night double-header, and in between the two games he planned to blow up a pile of disco records in the middle of the field. All were welcome to contribute vinyl for the musical bonfire. He christened the stunt 'Disco Demolition Night'.

But the event's organisers had misjudged the depth of feeling. Thousands more arrived than could fit in the stadium so people started breaking in, and the security team were overwhelmed; they were powerless to stop records being thrown on the pitch during the game, cutting through the hot air and jutting out of the grass like landmines. When Dahl finally arrived, clad in military fatigues and lapping the stands in a jeep, the atmosphere had reached boiling point. With the detonation of the explosion thousands poured onto the field and gathered around the blaze, cheering and punching the air. 'Long live rock and roll', read one banner. It was a remarkable outpouring of anger from one set of music fans to another, from the all-American machismo of rock 'n' roll to the fashion and flamboyance of disco.

Thirty-three years, six months and twenty-three days later, a Chicago band would stage their own miniature parody of Disco Demolition Night. In a snowy field with just a photographer present for posterity, they burnt their own records on a modest fire. But this was not a rejection of what had come before. This was a rebirth. They had returned to save rock 'n' roll – just not as we knew it.

CHAPTER ONE

HOLDEN CAULFIELD WITH A BASS GUITAR

Head north out of downtown Chicago, along the shore of the vast expanse of Lake Michigan, and in about forty minutes you will reach Wilmette. It's a pleasant and well-to-do suburb, one of the so-called North Shore communities that cluster at the western edge of the lake, a village of tree-lined residential streets and well-manicured front gardens. It was in Wilmette that on 5 June 1979 Peter Lewis Kingston Wentz III was born. His mother, Dale, had family ties to Jamaica and was related to Colin Powell, who became the US Secretary of State from 2001 to 2005. His father was the second Pete Wentz, and the two had met whilst working for Democrat Joe Biden in the seventies. They were a liberal island in the sea of Wilmette's conservatism, values that would have a great impact on the younger Wentz's outlook in later years. Dale worked as an admissions dean for a local private school and Wentz II was in the legal profession. For the most part, home life was a picture of suburban normality: his dad spent a lot of time working, while his mum was 'in the kitchen baking stuff'. It was, as he told *The Independent*, 'very non-exceptional'. As a kid, he loved *ThunderCats* and had a crush on spotted-haired Cheetara; he enjoyed many a happy dinner eating burgers at local diner the Chuck Wagon in Wilmette; and he spent one blissful summer at the age of four visiting his aunt in Switzerland. But his early years were not without their troubles. On his sixth birthday his parents separated, and though they would reunite a few months later, he would hate birthdays from that day on.

His first memory of music is a vague and hazy one, sitting in the middle back seat of his dad's car and listening to Otis Redding's '(Sittin' On) The Dock of the Bay' on AM radio. But it was a chance encounter with the King of Pop whilst watching the Calgary Winter Olympics on TV in 1988 that really left a deep impression on him. He saw German ice skater Katarina Witt perform a routine to Michael Jackson's 1987 smash 'Bad', and something stirred in him. I want to make music, he thought, no doubt spurred on by the sight of a leather jacket-clad Witt high-kicking and moonwalking across the ice (Witt would win the gold that year). A fascination with Jackson and his genre-hopping futurism soon followed, but as his teenage years beckoned, his tastes would turn to music with a nastier edge.

First came a chance encounter with Guns N' Roses. Extravagant, brawny, larger-than-life and with more killer riffs and catchy choruses than any one band has a right to, Guns N' Roses are the ultimate gateway band to rock 'n' roll – the kind of act that changes the minds of impressionable kids forever. And when Wentz saw Axl Rose stepping off the bus in the 'Welcome to the Jungle' video, his vague desire to make music became a burning obsession. 'It made me want to be in Guns N' Roses or something,' he said to BPM TV. 'I think that Axl Rose walking off the bus is an epic moment in rock 'n' roll history.' Metallica's 'Enter Sandman' was another defining moment because the song was so big that it reached every sleepy corner of America, even well-heeled Wilmette. 'I remember being in the back of my parents' station wagon and blasting "Enter Sandman" and it was cool because it was like "this is my music",' he told *NME*. '"Enter Sandman" was so pervasive because it was played on this radio station in Chicago called B96, which usually played more urban music, but they played "Enter Sandman" because everyone had to play it because it was such a big song. There was something about it that made me be like, "I can make music, [this is] the kind of music that I want to make."' When he was old enough to have money of his own to spend, he made his first pilgrimage to a local record store called Coconut Records and bagged himself a copy of Slayer's *Decade of Aggression*. Wentz hadn't realised that it was a double live album, but his friend was into Slayer and he knew a few of the songs listed, enough to convince him to part with his cash.

But there was still one more left turn that he needed to take in his musical development, and it came when someone handed him a Minor Threat tape. Minor Threat were a Washington DC-based punk band active for a short period in the early eighties, but during just a few years of putting out material they would have an immeasurably big impact on the development of punk rock. In the mid to late seventies punk had moved from its brash and rebellious origins into more experimental territory, with post-punk bands like Television and Talking Heads in the States, and Joy Division and Gang of Four in the UK. Meanwhile, other first-wave punk acts were moving closer to the world of pop, formulating a sound that would later come to be known as new wave. But a third new branch of punk emerged, doubling down on the aggression and abrasiveness whilst upping the tempos. This new form would come to be called hardcore, and Minor Threat were one of its driving forces. In contrast to the art-school sensibilities of post-punk and the mainstream flirtation of new wave, hardcore was fiercely political and anti-establishment, and Minor Threat went one step further by disavowing the excesses of some parts of the rock and punk world. 'Straight Edge', from their first EP, laid their philosophy on substance-abuse bare: 'I'm a person just like you / But I've got better things to do / Than sit around and fuck my head / Hang out with the living dead / Snort white shit up my nose / Pass out at the shows,' barked icon-to-be Ian MacKaye, and the straight edge movement was born. Wentz's love for punk rock soon grew to include everything from the pop punk of Green Day to the more melodic hardcore of Gorilla Biscuits, as well Metallica's thrash metal and Earth Crisis's hybrid of metal and hardcore. Wentz's tastes were becoming omnivorous. As long as it was fast and loud, he'd listen. 'I was basically into fireworks and skateboarding,' he told *FasterLouder*. 'I needed a soundtrack to vandalism, basically.' At the age of fourteen he scratched his first tattoo, a black 'x', into his ankle with Indian ink. Wentz now had the mark of a punk rocker.

But while he was finding a love of music Wentz was also

struggling to find his place in the world. He was a student at New Trier High School in Wilmette, but by his freshman year he had started skipping class and would also be diagnosed with attention deficit hyperactivity disorder, a condition marked by difficulties in focusing and controlling one's behaviour. He would sneak out late at night through a window to the basement of his house. When his dad found out he screwed the window shut, but Wentz would simply undo the screws or kick the window out. Eventually it was decided that something had to be done. A guidance counsellor recommended that his parents send him away to a boot camp to shock him out of his misbehaviour, but the long two months he spent there would have a traumatic effect on the young Wentz. 'Every kid there was so much more fucked up than me – demented, satanic kids,' he explained to *Rolling Stone*. 'I got beat up a couple of times. I'd call my parents every day, crying and saying I wanted to come home. I would beg. I felt isolated. It created these dependency and attachment issues.' He thinks that the experience made him emotionally withdrawn, prone to suppressing and bottling up his feelings. But it would also push him towards music as a cathartic outlet for the things he couldn't otherwise express.

Wentz moved to a private school and also began escaping the suburban bubble of Wilmette for the lights and noise of Chicago. He became a regular face at punk rock shows at local venues like the Fireside Bowl and the Metro, the latter a one-thousand-capacity theatre on Clark Street that had been an essential part of the Chicago music scene since the eighties. Pop-punk bands like Screeching Weasel from Prospect Heights and Alkaline Trio from McHenry, towns close to Chicago, would come through the city on a regular basis and gave Wentz the chance to see the bands he loved first-hand. At the age of fifteen or sixteen he'd started playing the bass too. As a kid he'd taken piano lessons, though it had never really stuck, and had also dabbled on a normal six-string guitar before realising an instrument with a couple less strings might suit him better. His first bass was 'a cheap knockoff that said "Naugahyde" on the headstock,' he told *Premier Guitar*. 'I had never heard of it before – but I really don't think anyone has.' It was Duff McKagan who had the biggest influence on his playing, and it's no wonder. McKagan's role in Guns N' Roses was so much more than simply a support for the guitar work, weaving as it did in and out of the riffs and giving the songs melodic accents where you least expect them. Green Day's Mike Dirnt was another bassist he admired, with his lightning-fast right hand and brittle, metallic tone.

But music wasn't Pete's sole obsession; in another world Fall Out Boy might never have existed had Wentz pursued his other passion: soccer. As he moved towards graduation, Wentz had become something of a sporting ace in his school, claiming all-state honours and the captaincy of the school team. It's hard to imagine, but to Wentz a career in professional football represented the 'easier option' over music. 'If I hadn't become a musician I'm sure I could have carved out a decent career as a footballer,' he told the *Daily Mail*. 'I loved playing the sport and there was no feeling that came close to scoring a great goal or going on a great run down the right wing and putting over a perfect cross. Doing things with the ball was a natural instinct for me.' Chicago's DePaul University had offered him a soccer scholarship, and he had grand plans of heading over to Europe to launch a professional career there. But whatever sporting successes Wentz was enjoying on the field, he was still struggling to process his emotions. The image of the tortured artist channelling his pain into deeply moving work is an enduring one. But Wentz would later say that he's probably closer to a confused kid, more like the subject of JD Salinger's novel *The Catcher in the Rye* – Holden Caulfield with a bass guitar.

CHAPTER TWO

THE METAL DRUMMER AND THE BEAST

Beyond Wilmette, Chicago had its own very active hardcore scene, a truly DIY environment where musicians and fans would meet to play, listen and mosh. That scene would prove fertile soil, producing dozens and dozens of bands both short- and long-lived; some would dissolve with little by way of recordings with which to remember them and others would leave a lasting legacy. Some would even become global phenomena, whereas others were more interested in shocking and stirring up debate than getting a deal and breaking out of Chicago. One notorious example of the latter was Racetraitor. Superficially it's hard to imagine a band less likely to be an antecedent to Fall Out Boy. Look closer and you see that they had a big part to play in Fall Out Boy's development, and their relevance to the band as it exists today.

Racetraitor was formed around the core membership of Dan Binaei, Karl Hlavinka and Brent Decker, with Mani Mostofi – a former student of New Trier High School – on vocals. It began life in the power violence/grindcore tradition, delivering thunderous blasts of uncompromising noise over extremely short songs. And as the band's name suggests, they were a highly politically and socially aware group who used the platform of the hardcore scene to raise issues surrounding race and privilege in the US. 'There was a band before Racetraitor called Hinckley,' Mostofi explains when asked about the origins and aims of Racetraitor. 'I wasn't in that band, I put out their seven-inch – but Karl, Brent and Dan were in that band. Hinckley kinda just broke up, in the way that bands do, you know; members got in personal disputes and whatever. And they wanted to continue what Hinckley was doing but up the ante in terms of how political it was. And that's where the concept of Racetraitor came from.'

He goes on, 'Look at what a lot of people talk about in terms of US politics today: white privilege, the Black Lives Matter movement, mass incarceration and even wars of intervention. I'm following the US presidential debates and these are the things they're talking about. Well, that's everything that Racetraitor was fixated with twenty years ago. We were really angry and no one was talking about it, and we wanted an avenue to do that.'

Mostofi and his bandmates had been heavily influenced by a short-lived Chicago band called Anger House, as well as Los Crudos, a 'really dirty, raw hardcore band' that sang in Spanish and were also highly socially conscious. But they soon found themselves in the position of elders, mentoring younger musicians coming up through the scene.

Hlavinka was initially the drummer, but there was a decision made within the band that he should switch instruments. 'He was playing drums in Racetraitor but he was actually a guitar player, so we decided to have him move to guitar,' Mostofi explains. 'And he said, "I know this drummer." He called him "the metal drummer". He didn't have a name at first. He was just a kid, like fifteen years old. But he said, "You guys should check him out, he's really good, we should get him to play."' The 'metal drummer' was named Andy Hurley.

Hurley had grown up almost a hundred miles due north of Chicago in Menomonee Falls, Milwaukee, another city on the shore of Lake Michigan. Hurley was born on 31 May 1980 and raised by his mother, a nurse, as his father had passed away when he was five years old. He had first fallen in love with music, like so many others, through the titans of American thrash Metallica; the first albums he ever bought for himself were Metallica's *Ride the Lightning* and Van Halen's self-titled 1978 debut. But it was Slayer's Dave Lombardo, famous for his mastery of the double kick technique, who compelled him to want to sit on a drum stool. Hurley had first been a saxophone player, but by the time he was attending Menomonie High School he had switched to the drums and was already forging his reputation as a musician of note. He joined the marching band, where the emphasis was on technical ability and a solid knowledge of the rudiments; combined with his love of thrash, he was developing into a fearsome player. Unfortunately his mother was not, at first, so keen on his taste in music. As a boy he would put on a shirt and tie and dance with her to classical music, and now he was asking to go to Metallica concerts. To this day he hasn't quite got over missing his chance to see Metallica on the *And Justice for All* tour.

Hurley did not have the easiest childhood. Two years after

his father died his grandmother also passed away in his house, and around two years after that, his mother was diagnosed with breast cancer. His dad had been the father of nine children in total, but after his death Hurley's stepbrothers and sisters moved away from the area, leaving Hurley and his mother alone. The result of these traumatic experiences was, according to his mother, a very angry child. But Hurley was also starting to forge an identity through music. It was the discovery of the ultra-influential metallic hardcore band Earth Crisis that would give his life purpose and direction. The New York act had released *Destroy the Machines* in 1995, something of a landmark album which had combined the aggression and energy of hardcore punk with the musicianship and sinister atmosphere of metal, arguably giving birth to the metalcore genre in the process. But the band were known as much for their politics as their music. They were committed vegans and promoted animal rights through their music, as well as a straight edge lifestyle – the no drink, no drugs principles as laid out by Minor Threat. 'I used to like, smoke pot and drink when I was pretty young,' Hurley would later explain to the *Expansion Project Podcast*. 'But I kinda fractured my relationship with my mom, and she was really bummed out. [...] I think she was really nervous that she was losing me. And I was into hardcore and a lot of straight edge bands, but it wasn't until Earth Crisis [that I went straight edge] because that really solidified it and politicised it in a way that really spoke to me. I was like, "Yeah, fuck that, I don't need that stuff. Drugs are not more important to me than my relationship with my mother."'

Vegetarianism soon followed his decision to go straight edge, and later Hurley would switch to veganism: 'I can't pick and choose my ethics if I want to be an ethical person living in this world,' he explains. His mother has no doubts about the positive effect that discovering Earth Crisis and their contemporaries had on his life. 'Music saved his life,' she told *FranklinNOW*. 'Due to the influence of band people he met, and what they told him, he changed his lifestyle; he never veered from that, ever.'

From Metallica and Earth Crisis the teenage Hurley had naturally started to investigate the hardcore scene in his own backyard, and it was there that he had first encountered Racetraitor's then drummer and aspiring guitarist, Karl Hlavinka. Soon he found himself invited to rehearse with this controversial and confrontational Chicago band. 'Our lead guitar player Dan went up to Milwaukee, and Andy, Karl and Dan practised with each other,' Mostofi explains. 'And then they came to Chicago for another practice, and that was the first time that I met Andy. He was this tiny kid with a shaved head, very shy and wearing a huge hooded sweatshirt. He sets up his drums and barely says anything, but as soon as they start playing the first song, I just started laughing. I was like, "Where did this discovery come from, of this child prodigy?" He was amazing at drums. And that's really how I got to know him. He was recruited to join the band.'

Meeting Andy had changed Racetraitor's approach to music, as they realised that with this skilled player forming the backbone of the band they were able to take things to the next level. 'As soon as we got Andy we realised we had to have proper instrumentation across the board, and we essentially wrote a whole new set of songs,' Mostofi says. 'I remember our first show with him. There were people standing around the drums, like other drummers of Midwest hardcore straight-edge bands. They were all lined up around Andy with their jaws open, talking about how fast his double bass was and things like that. And we knew immediately we had a secret weapon.'

The position of bass, however, was less of a sure bet, with Mostofi describing it as more of a 'revolving door' situation. Fortunately the band were in touch with another young player who had attended New Trier High School a couple of years after Mostofi and who was quickly getting a reputation as one of the most active members of the scene. 'Pete Wentz was not only part of the Chicago scene but the subset of the Chicago scene, which was called the North Shore scene,' Mostofi explains – the North Shore encompasses the Chicago suburbs of Winnetka, Evanston, Wilmette and more. Wentz was in the same year as Mostofi's sister and he had developed from being a young kid that Mani would see at shows to someone who started hanging out more and more, until he was just another member of the crew. 'He sung in a couple of bands, played bass in a couple of bands,' Mostofi remembers. 'He had a nickname for a while: "The Beast". I don't know how he got that.' The Beast would do stints performing with Racetraitor, though his membership of the band was more fluid than Andy's, who was a full-time member.

This group of musicians was comprised of people from varied backgrounds, and speaking from a different perspective to the average hardcore band was a part of the vision. 'I'm from a Middle-Eastern background; I'm Iranian, and Dan's half Iranian,' Mostofi points out. 'Pete's half black. There was a sense in which we all looked at the hardcore scene as our home but maybe at the same time as a bit alien, because a part of our experience didn't have a voice there. We saw ourselves as kids from rich and privileged backgrounds, but with somewhat of an understanding of what it meant to be an outsider, so we wanted to do a band from that perspective.' While he stresses that the band wasn't *about* being Middle Eastern or mixed race as such, it was trying to highlight economic exploitation and systemic racism in the US and beyond. 'We were really angry about it, and our community was the hardcore community, so those were the people we could talk to,' he says. 'We used the band as a vehicle to talk to them, and to shock them, really. We weren't about just making friends as a band – we were really about sort of jilting people, and forcing people to have huge arguments that we thought might force an awakening.'

Mostofi thinks that Racetraitor's propensity to stir things up was part of the appeal for Wentz. 'He's experienced racism personally, and he looked up to Malcolm X and [black social reformer] Frederick Douglass, so he got what the band was about,' he offers. 'And plus Pete – more back in those days but even once he started Fall Out Boy – Pete likes to make trouble sometimes. He gets a kick out of it. And the mission of the band was to make trouble, so he saw an affinity there, I think.'

Unsurprisingly, being in Racetraitor was not always the smoothest ride. The band didn't antagonise people through carelessness; they were actively out to do it, and the crowd would often respond in kind. Mostofi acknowledges that the message wasn't always welcome, particularly since lots of the audience were working-class kids who considered themselves in opposition to the forces of oppression, be that society, the government or the cops. The hardcore scene was a safe space for these kids, and to be told by a hardcore band that they were in fact not the oppressed but the oppressors would often stoke ire. 'The singer from the hardcore band called Coalesce [...] was online this year in a conversation about Racetraitor on Facebook, and he said Racetraitor were trolls before we had a word for it,' Mostofi goes on. 'And that's kind of true. We were there to say outrageous things that were based in this core truth and force people to react.' And they often got what they were looking for. Shows would sometimes be forced to shut down before they ended, with the audience spontaneously erupting into arguments with one another and the band that completely disrupted the set. 'There's very few artistic endeavours I've ever done in my life where we strived for a specific goal and we achieved that goal exactly, as effectively as it could have been done.'

One particularly notorious Racetraitor gig went down in a convention for Anti Racist Action, a group that Mostofi describes as a 'bunch of anarchists and skinheads' who would disrupt and counter-protest groups that they considered to be racist. On paper you'd expect their beliefs to be more or less aligned with Racetraitor's, and sure enough they were booked to play a basement show in Columbus, Ohio, as the after-party band. But even Anti Racist Action were not safe from Racetraitor's critical gaze. 'Basically, we went in there and started calling out all of the anti-racist activists for not being anti-racist activist enough.' Mostofi laughs, with a hint of mischief in his voice. 'We said, "Why are you protesting the Klan? The problem in the

US is the prison system, that the economy is structured to keep black people down. Go and protest the White House, protest Wall Street, protest the cops." I think I said during the set that protesting the Klan is like swatting at the leaves, and you need to be cutting at the trunk of the tree to bring it down.'

Members of the crowd started to heckle Racetraitor, with one calling them out for being 'rich kids', a common challenge that the band would face. 'Our retort was always, "Exactly"; the point of the band was to speak from that perspective,' says Mostofi. 'It was called Racetraitor. The idea was to betray your race and your economic privileges.' However, on this occasion one of the band's friends spoke up on their behalf. It was Jody Minnoch, the former singer of Hinckley, who said that as the son of a bus driver and a librarian he was as working class as anyone could be and still supported what Racetraitor were saying. It was not, as Mostofi notes, a particularly inflammatory statement, but it was the spark that set the gig alight. 'Out of nowhere this skinbyrd [a female skinhead] lunges out of the crowd at Jody and starts basically clawing at him,' he says. 'She was clawing at his face, and then that erupted and the crowd started rushing forward. It was just a basement show, there was no real stage, and a couple of our crew started pushing people away. There was a bunch of pushing and yelling and profanities, and because this was just a basement show it was only lit by one light bulb hanging from the ceiling. That gets shattered, and this whole room goes black, and I'm basically hiding behind the bass amp laughing at the whole thing. Ideologically these people were our closest allies, but we turned it into a circus.'

Even if Racetraitor were trolls before the word existed,

Mostofi stands by the tactics that the band used to incite debate. The fact that people still talk about Racetraitor now, and the issues they highlighted, is evidence that their confrontational approach worked. Mostofi points to a song by the technical metalcore band Botch named 'C. Thomas Howell as the "Soul Man"'. *Soul Man* is a movie about a white man who pretends to be black to get into Harvard, and C. Thomas Howell is the actor who portrayed him; sample lyrics include: 'The worst music I've ever heard / Honesty that touches a nerve / The words fall onto the floor / Drive home with no lessons learned'. Mostofi was pretty sure that the title and lyrics were a criticism of Racetraitor and their approach, and whilst tour managing another band, he got the opportunity to meet Botch and ask them in person. 'They got into it and defended themselves, and said yeah, it was about us,' Mostofi recalls. 'Us and bands like us, but if you read the lyrics it was really about us. […] At this point it's like two or three years after we broke up. And we had a long discussion about why we did what we did, and what we saw as the main problems in this country, and it was an interesting discussion. But then I got an email from the bass player, saying after that they had a five-hour drive to the next show and the entire drive was a conversation about race. He had been in this band for however many years and they had never had a conversation about race before as a band. It was more validation that in the hardcore and punk scene, it wasn't something that got talked about until you put it out there.'

CHAPTER THREE

ARMA ANGELUS

While Pete Wentz was not a permanent fixture in Racetraitor, he would come to be one of the most high-profile members of the Chicago hardcore scene around the turn of the new millennium, and one man who was there by Pete's side for much of it was Christopher Gutierrez. He would also come to have his own special place in Fall Out Boy's history, but his journey into punk rock began long before that.

For Gutierrez, music, and punk in particular, offered sanctuary from a traumatic upbringing. 'I grew up in kinda like a broken home, a single-parent family,' he explains. 'My little brother and my grandfather were killed behind my house when I was young, and there was a lot of abuse – sexual abuse, drug abuse, alcoholism.' Unsurprisingly, this unstable home life led to behavioural problems. 'I have this lineage of a lot of either terrible people – sociopaths – or people who don't know how to make responsible and healthy decisions,' he explains. 'So what happened with that was it led to a confused child. When you grow up in these really kind of unstructured homes, and are around a lot of abuse, it tends to make for a lot of confusion. [...] My mom is a wonderful woman, but she was working two jobs and putting herself through school in order to raise my sister and I, and so I was left alone. And that is kinda of one of the worst things you can do to a kid with a head full of confusion, because the confusion turns to anger, and when you're young you project that confusion outwards.'

Run-ins with the principal and bullying from his classmates followed, but he was able to find his tribe through the other kids in his neighbourhood who skateboarded. 'Punk rock and skateboarding were one and the same during the eighties,' he explains, 'So that was when I discovered the Dead Kennedys, the Sex Pistols, T.S.O.L.'

Punk was not in regular rotation on the radio in late 1980s USA, particularly not on the stations available in suburban Chicago, so finding bands like these felt like the discovery of a real alternative to the grand and remote new wave that was presented as the alternative option on the radio. 'What you have to understand, and this is where I sound like the old guy, is that punk rock was so underground in the eighties,' says Gutierrez. 'On the radio your choices were like, U2, The Police, and INXS. That was weird – that was the weird stuff. And so for me when I heard songs like "Macho Insecurity" off the final Dead Kennedys record, *Bedtime for Democracy*, I was like, "Holy fuck!" The first line is "Name one thing on Earth lower than a tough guy." They're talking about getting bullied, and people projecting this macho aesthetic, and I get that. I understand what it's like to be weird and different and get beat up for who I am. So that was the first time I had ever felt like I had somebody on my side, like I had an identity.' The trifecta of lyrical themes that dominates the majority of pop music – 'love, money and sex', as Gutierrez figures it – were simply not relatable for him. 'As a kid who came from a broken home, a fucked up family with a lot of abuse, I can't identify with that. I'm not in love, I'm not banging anybody and I certainly don't have any money, so when I finally heard songs about feeling like an outcast, I was like "I get it! You motherfuckers, I've finally found my people!"'

His first show was in a 200-capacity club seeing the Insane War Tomatoes, a native Chicago act who combined a punk sensibility with the theatre and crudity of cock rock. At the moment that the giant tomato suspended from the ceiling shot a flame above the heads of the audience, Gutierrez was hooked, and from then he was coercing his mother into taking him to the city at every available opportunity to catch a punk rock show. Soon he decided that he wanted to be more than a spectator. 'That was the great thing about punk rock: it didn't make you feel like you couldn't be a part of it,' he says. 'I looked at somebody like the Misfits, who are still incredible musicians, but technically are unbelievably simple. And I was like, "I can do that!" I asked for a bass in 1989 for Christmas and I got one. [...] We managed to put together this shitty high school band, called Line Drive, and we were together from 1988 to 1992.'

After the demise of Line Drive, Gutierrez went on to play with other bands, including XshroudX and Restraint, and continued to be active in the Chicago hardcore community with the launch of a fanzine that would later lend its name to Gutierrez's publishing house, DeadxStop Publishing Company. It was in these years that his path would first cross with Pete Wentz, though the pair did not strike up an immediate friendship. 'You've been to a show and you see people, anywhere, and for some strange reason – it's so stupid and juvenile – but you're like, I don't even know you, but I already know that I hate you. And that was kind of how I felt about him. I'd never spoken a word to him but I hated him.' By this point Pete had been in a bunch of short-lived Chicago bands. Gutierrez: 'Anytime his bands would play, whatever vegan band he was in, I was like, "You're so obnoxious, put on some pants that fit." But I didn't know him.'

Although Chicago is a big city, the hardcore scene was composed of a small group of people: by Gutierrez's estimation, maybe just twenty-five who were regularly active at any one time. That made interaction with Wentz, who was a few years younger than Gutierrez, a foregone conclusion. 'One of my friends, Jim, was like, "Dude – you should hang out with me and Wentz sometime. You guys would get along a lot,"' Gutierrez remembers. 'I was like, "Fuck that kid! I don't want anything to do with him."' But the decision was taken out of his hands, and one day in 1996 Jim brought Pete round to Christopher's apartment where a group of people were hanging out. 'I was super-pissed,' he remembers. 'I still remember it vividly like it happened yesterday. He was a younger kid; I was definitely in my mid-twenties and he was probably not even twenty-one, and five years is a big difference at that age. Anyway, everyone sits down and there's nowhere for him to sit so he sits up against a wall. My friend Jim looks at me and he's like, "Dude, you should have Wentz tell you the story about how when he was at Northwestern [University] this weekend. He went to this frat party, and he pissed on all the coats in the coat room." And I was like, "For real? That's awesome!" [...] I sat down next to him and Jim was right, we got along ridiculously well. And from then on we hung out all of the time, and he was one of my best friends in the world.'

The seeds of a collaboration between the two on a musical project were sown one night when the pair were driving around the city. Wentz played Gutierrez some material from his new band, Novena, a group that featured ex-members of Racetraitor and another key Chicago band named Extinction. 'He put it in, and I thought it was just gonna be more screamy vegan stuff, but it wasn't. It sounded like [Washington DC metalcore act] Damnation crossed with [German thrash band] Despair, and I was like, "Holy shit, this is fucking good!" And I remember being jealous that I wasn't in that band.'

Novena was effectively the forerunner of another act who came to be known as Arma Angelus, a band composed of key figures from the Chicago hardcore scene. Though the line-up would see various changes, the first iteration of the band was Adam Bishop, a guitar player who had performed with Gutierrez in XshroudX, and in Extinction; Dan Binaei, the aforementioned guitar player who had performed with Wentz in the politically-charged Racetraitor, as well as a number of other bands; and drummer Tim, who was universally known as Morgan Renegade. Wentz took on vocal duties, and there was a quick succession of bass players before the band settled on Tim McIlrath. McIlrath had previously played in Baxter, a popular band from the Chicago scene, and had first met Pete when Pete was performing in an earlier band called First Born. To most of Arma Angelus, Pete included, Tim would simply be known as 'Baxter'.

But though McIlrath was the fifth or sixth bass player that the band had recruited, he too would depart the band to start his own project – initially known as Transistor Revolt, in 2001 the band would re-brand as Rise Against and record their debut for Fat Wreck Chords. (By 2004 the band had been signed to Geffen and would release the popular *Siren Song of the Counter Culture*, marking the beginning of a successful run of major label releases.) That left Arma Angelus without a bass player, and Christopher Gutierrez found himself first in line for the open position. 'Pete Wentz texted me and said, "Dude, what are you up to, and hey – would you want to play bass for Arma Angelus?" They had only started playing a handful of shows, and I was like, "Yes, I'd love to, 'cos your band's fucking awesome."'

Due to the tight-knit nature of the Chicago hardcore scene, Gutierrez was already close friends with the other members of the band, so no introductions were necessary, though getting to grips with the music did prove a challenge. 'I went in there and I remember Wentz gave me a tape and said, "Here, learn this." I was like, "I can't learn this! I need somebody to teach me! What number is that on the fretboard?" So we came to practise and they'd show me something and I'd copy it, and then they'd say, "Play it a bunch, 'cos that's what we're playing right now."' With a solid line-up in place, Arma Angelus was primed to start making waves outside of Chicago.

CHAPTER FOUR

A NIGHTMARE SCENARIO

Arma Angelus would ultimately put their name to two releases, the first a 2000 EP called *The Grave End of the Shovel* (Pete, as chief lyricist, was already displaying a penchant for wry titles). At this stage the band were bruising and unpolished, even on 'Victoria', a song which benefits from the more melodic vocals of McIlrath, who played bass on this release. Wentz's gnarled singing is hair-raising, an animalistic roar that butts heads with the guitar riffs for space in the mix, but the band displayed all the key elements of metalcore before it became a worldwide phenomenon: the sudden switches from melodic to atonal passages, the emotional friction, the brutal breakdowns.

After the release of *The Grave End of the Shovel*, there was some more line-up shuffling within Arma Angelus when Dan Binaei started dividing his time between California and Chicago, meaning the band needed a fill-in guitar player.

That fill-in was Jay Jancetic, and his appointment would soon become permanent. A native of Buffalo, NY, Jancetic had also started getting into punk and metal through skateboarding, and eventually picked up a guitar in the sophomore year of high school. 'As soon as I learned what a power chord was, it was all over,' he says. 'It was like someone had given me the key to punkdom, and everything just made more sense. I locked myself in my room and played along to Gorilla Biscuits for hours on end.' At the age of nineteen or twenty he had moved to Chicago, and it was there that he would become a central member of the hardcore group Extinction. Jancetic and Wentz's tenures in the band did not overlap for the most part. 'Pete actually joined the band later on, after I had left Extinction, and our then bass player Adam Bishop took my spot on guitar,' he explains. 'At that point, Pete was playing bass. But I was already friends with Pete as I knew him from his previous straight-edge band First Born, and he was also in Racetraitor.'

Getting to grips with the tangle of interwoven roots that is the membership of Chicago hardcore bands is no easy task, and Jancetic himself admits that the band's line-ups could be a confusing affair. 'Arma was formed from the ashes of both Extinction and Racetraitor, which were at the time two of the more integral hardcore bands in Chicago. But, it was all very incestuous and Arma always had members kind of coming and going,' he explains. 'For a time, we technically had three guitarists. Although we never performed live this way, we often practised and made road trips in this manner when Dan was in town. We'd rotate who was playing that night and there are some rare promo photos I have of Arma with all six of us that are funny to see now. It was a bit of a clusterfuck actually, but we made it work.'

Live shows were often a riotous affair, particularly for bassist Gutierrez. By his own admission not the most musical in the band, he saw them as an opportunity to cut loose. 'I knew that people couldn't hear me very well, so I got to play the Sid Vicious role,' he explains. As the most iconic of the two Sex Pistols bassists, Vicious's contemptuous onstage swagger gave the band much of their attitude and menace, though his bass skills were reportedly so lacking that he would often be unplugged from his amp by his bandmates. 'You just knew that there was a rumbling in the background, and that was good enough for me,' Gutierrez continues. 'If it's just a rumbling in the background that gives me the freedom to jump around, to stab people with my bass, to walk on people's faces and stuff. For me it was about having as much fun as possible with it.'

However, Gutierrez concedes that his attitude often left him at odds with Pete. 'Wentz really took that band seriously, surprisingly enough. Everybody else just liked to play – Adam, Dan, they were musicians, they loved playing. They would sit there all "No, stop touching me, I need to play this riff." And Wentz was being super-serious over here, and there's me, going, "Ah! Let's have fun!" It was always a point of tension between Wentz and me, because I didn't take it as seriously as I guess he wanted me to. I guess I came off as a fool a lot.'

According to Jancetic, though, Pete was not above prizing showmanship over musicality. Though they were not in Extinction at the same time for the most part, the pair had played together in the band for a couple of reunion shows around 1999, whilst Arma Angelus was also active. 'Pete didn't really do much "bass playing" per se,' Jancetic offers. 'It was more about jumping around and looking cool. But then... you could say that to some degree about all of us I guess.' Just as Arma Angelus knew how to put on a high-energy show, so did Extinction, and Jancetic's account for this book of their first reunion show paints a vivid picture of the live experience in the scene at this time:

> Extinction shows frequently ended with instruments getting smashed or band members bleeding. I told our drummer Jason Gagovski before we started the set that I was going to throw his drum set into the crowd. He thought I was joking, but during the last song I started grabbing pieces of his kit and tossing them into the frenzy of kids in the pit. He kept playing like a trooper as bits of his drums disappeared into the mosh abyss. Eventually, I remember one of his cymbals resurfaced from the crowed [and came] back towards the stage, and the cymbal had turned inside out. I just remember Jason grabbing it as we were finishing and throwing our guitars on the ground, and he made a point to show it to me while yelling at me. I couldn't hear him over the insanity, of course, and I just laughed. There was also a bottle of sparkling grape juice that another friend of ours had shaken and sprayed over us when this was all transpiring, so it was just complete chaos and a total mess of broken gear, feedback [and] drenched and exhausted people. Extinction was always more about the emotion of the live performance and I think that last show exemplified that.

Arma Angelus was making significant strides off the back of their first release and live shows, and would eventually sign a contract with Eulogy Recordings, a Floridian label that had backed influential metalcore bands such as Unearth and Walls of Jericho. For Gutierrez, much of the band's success can be attributed to Pete Wentz's drive. 'There was no secret that Wentz was the mastermind of that band,' Gutierrez offers. 'Everything was his call, it was all his lyrics, he wrote probably a good majority of the music, and he has this uncanny ability to make things happen that he really, really wants. And he's always been that way. Before he turned into *the* Pete Wentz, he always had that uncanny ability to make people like him, and make people want to do things for him. He was unbelievably persuasive.' To Gutierrez's surprise, Wentz was able to use his charms to secure the band a deal. 'So one day he came up to me and said, "Guess what, we've got a record deal. [...] I need you to sign these contracts. We just got signed to Eulogy Records." It was a big fucking deal, 'cos at that time they were a big label.'

The resulting album was recorded at Zing Studios in Boston, Massachusetts in September 2001, with Gutierrez and Jancetic both in the fold. Jancetic remembers the session as a highlight of his time with Arma Angelus. Whereas Extinction was a chance to 'get his feet wet', Arma was significantly more technical due to the skills of Dan Binaei and required Jancetic to push his playing to new levels. It was also his first time in a serious recording studio. The album was made with Adam Dutkiewicz, now best known as the lead guitarist in Killswitch Engage, and the sessions were unforgettable for a particularly tragic reason – they coincided with the September 11 attacks. 'It was nuts,'

Jancetic remembers. 'As you know, the whole world was glued to the TV for about three days straight. We were on a time constraint obviously, so the show had to go on. I remember sitting in the lounge at Adam's studio with Pete and Dan while Chris was recording bass tracks, watching the towers fall and watching the Pentagon blow up. We didn't know if the world was ending or what. It was complete chaos.' The situation was made all the more tense due to the fact that the band's drummer had departed from Logan airport – the same airport that the planes which ultimately struck the North and South towers had departed from, and on the same day. 'I remember for about twenty-four hours we couldn't get a hold of him to find out if he even made it home OK or not – this is before everyone had cell phones,' Jancetic recalls. 'And during those couple days, there was so much confusion about flights crashing, flights being grounded, more flights crashing, rumours of more flights crashing or headed towards the Sears Tower in Chicago … it was crazy because here we were finishing this recording and we didn't even know if our drummer was alive. Everyone always says they will never forget what they were doing during 9/11. I was recording an album with Pete Wentz.'

The resulting album was entitled *Where Sleeplessness Is Rest from Nightmares*, an appropriate title given the atmosphere of panic and despair that gripped the nation whilst it was being recorded. The record is a big evolutionary leap from *The Grave End of the Shovel*, not least in part down to the significantly improved recording quality; the snare cracks like a gunshot, the guitars sound thick but crisp, and there's plenty of headroom for Wentz's impressive scream. And this is no metallic hardcore by numbers. Arma Angelus are succinct, technically proficient and well aware of where to drop a breakdown to get a pit moving.

Opener 'An Anthem For Those Without Breath and Heart' creeps in with an almost machine-like hum of feedback before the walls crumble with the force of a wrecking ball of double kick drum and detuned riffs. Verbosity is what Wentz would later come to be known for, but 'An Anthem…' is decidedly laconic; 'Breathe their control, fuck their control' are the only lyrics in this ninety-second blast. There's no shortage of guitar fireworks on show either, most strikingly on the doom-laden 'Cold Pillows and Warm Blades', a track which has more than a hint of Damnation A.D. about it (Wentz would later admit to cribbing heavily from the DC stalwarts in Arma Angelus – 'we lifted a lot from Damnation AD,' he told AbsolutePunk, now listed as *chorus.fm*). Lyrically, the tone is as dark and heavy as the music. 'We Are the Pale Horse' rolls in like thunder before settling into a lurching groove for the verse as Wentz takes aim at faith and hammers home the inevitably of death. 'Suffocate in this belief, like nails driven through my feet,' goes the opening line, and the pale horse is a biblical reference to the steed that Death, one of the Four Horsemen of the Apocalypse, would ride at the end of days. 'For The Expatriates of Human Civilisation' is one of the songs Jancetic is most proud of, noting that it was 'mainly the result of Pete and my collaboration' and that 'Pete and I actually worked really well writing together'. Needless to say, it's a fair way away from pop punk.

Wentz did have his reasons to be angry with the world. As revealed in an interview with the website *AbsolutePunk*, prior to writing the album his aunt had passed away from lupus, an umbrella term for a number of autoimmune diseases which cause the body's immune system to start attacking healthy cells. He would channel the pain into album highlight 'Misanthrope 2.0', which rails against the medical establishment: 'They flood the margin to feed the treatment / A cure that will never come, she becomes a study,' he screams. 'I guess it was about my thought that it made more sense for companies and practices to treat people than to cure them,' Wentz explained to *AbsolutePunk*. 'This was all the "well-researched" eighteen-year-old's uneducated emotional perspective.' The band was not all misery and misanthropy, though. After the final throes of album closer 'I'm Every Broken Man' they throw in a curve ball with a cover of 'Surrender' by Cheap Trick, a classic American rock band also born of the fertile fields of Illinois.

The band had found themselves booked for larger and larger shows with major players in the genre, which Gutierrez once again attributes to Wentz's determination and talent for persuasion. 'First he was like, "Hey, we're going on tour with Throwdown. And Throwdown in the early nineties was a pretty big band. Then he was like, "Hey, we got this show with Hatebreed in Canada". And then he was like, "Hey, we're gonna play Hellfest this year."' Hellfest was a hardcore and metal festival in New York which became known as something of a tastemaker for heavy music, so scoring a slot on the bill was a big deal. 'We pulled off all this shit, and I don't know how in the fuck he pulled it off,' says Gutierrez. 'Through all the shit that we went through and the issues that we've had and the fact that we're not really friends any more, I still have to give him the credit. That dude can make pretty much anything happen.'

CHAPTER FIVE

THE OLDEST TRICK IN THE BOOKSHOP

It was as Arma Angelus were growing in renown that the seeds of Fall Out Boy were sown. Andy Hurley was already a fixture on the scene, owing to his work with Racetraitor, Killtheslavemaster, and pretty much any other band that needed a solid drummer. But the next piece of the puzzle was a Jewish kid called called Joe Trohman, who came into Pete Wentz's orbit by chance.

Trohman was born in Hollywood, Florida, but at the age of twelve would move to Ohio and then to Illinois, in the Chicago area. Joe's father was a cardiologist and more importantly a classic rock fan, and passed his love of music on to Joe. The junior Trohman started his love affair with music in a genteel fashion – with piano lessons, then on to the viola, and then on to the trombone. But almost as soon as he had begun playing the trombone, he was struck down by the power of another iconic rock 'n' roll moment from Guns N' Roses: not Axl jumping off the bus in 'Welcome to the Jungle', but Slash mounting a grand piano to rip through a solo in the video for 'November Rain'. At around the same time his (particularly cool) grandmother had bought him Metallica's *Live Shit: Binge & Purge* live album, and he was nurturing a newfound obsession with LA's undisputed kings of American thrash. There was no question about it: the trombone simply wouldn't do. 'I thought the guitar was really cool as far as just an aesthetic thing – like it aesthetically looked cool,' he said in an interview with *Fender.com*. 'The guys who were playing them looked cool. There was nothing cool about the viola, nothing cool about the trombone. Now as an adult, I would say there are incredibly cool things about those instruments. But no matter what, my head always goes back to seeing Slash in the "Welcome to the Jungle" video and especially the "November Rain" video, and how cool that looked.' So far, Guns N' Roses and Metallica had derailed two potentially promising careers: Pete Wentz the soccer player, and Joe Trohman the concert trombonist.

His first guitar was a ramshackle hand-me-down from his grandfather, with his dad promising him that if he could prove a commitment to learning the instrument he would buy Joe his own. Soon enough, the young Trohman was the owner of a Harmony/Barclay Bobkat, a common catalogue guitar in the States, and a complementary amp. He began lessons with a jazz bassist but the tutor's long thumbnail freaked Trohman out, so he sought another teacher through a guitar shop in the North Shore suburb of Evanston. There he was taken under the wing of the appropriately named Marshall, who taught him his first songs: 'Kick Out the Jams' by proto-punk pioneers MC5 and 'Purple Haze' by the inimitable Jimi Hendrix.

His first taste of punk came from Black Flag, a band from California who are often credited as the forefathers of hardcore punk. With breakneck tempos and barked dictums on rebellion and nonconformity, along with a strikingly no-nonsense aesthetic, they have had an almost immeasurable impact on the sound of punk rock and birthed an icon in the form of Henry Rollins. Trohman was first introduced to the band through a friend who lent him 1983's compilation album *The First Four Years.* He would later head to his local rental shop and loan out *The Decline of Western Civilisation*, a Penelope Spheeris documentary film about the LA punk scene, and his love for the band was cemented.

But Trohman wasn't solely fixated on metal and punk. He developed a special appreciation for the blues, spurred on by Chicago's special standing in the genre. Chicago blues is a sub-genre all of its own, where the electric guitar is considered the key component, and the city has produced an incredible amount of musical icons – including, but not limited to, Buddy Guy, Muddy Waters, Howlin' Wolf and Bo Diddley. Trohman would add to that list Texas's Freddie King and Johnny Winter as well as Carolina's Reverend Gary Davies, but just as he was heading back in time to discover the roots of rock 'n' roll, he was also studying the playing styles of those in punk and new wave. Both Black Flag's Greg Ginn and Depeche Mode's Martin Gore would have a huge influence on his style, alongside the iron-strong rhythm and lead guitar combination of James Hetfield and Kirk Hammett.

By the age of fifteen Trohman was well and truly into his rebellious phase. 'In '99 I was stealing smokes from the convenience store and drinking mixtures of wine, beer and vodka while listening to Kyuss, busy being the worst type of human ever: a teenager,' he remembered to the *Chicago Tribune*'s *RedEye*. It was at this time that he first started making his way into the city to catch hardcore shows, driven out of the suburbs by its lack of creative energy. 'They breed some intelligent people, but a lot of people determine themselves by their financial wealth,' he'd later comment to *The Salt Lake Tribune*. 'There weren't too many grounded people there.'

Though Joe was some five years Pete's junior, they had attended the same high school, New Trier in Winnetka. There he was already playing in his own hardcore band called Voices Still Heard. (According to their Bandcamp page, a grand total of sixteen cassette copies of a demo were made and distributed around New Trier by the bass player; one has survived and made its way into digital format.) As an ex-member of a list of high-profile Chicago hardcore bands and current frontman of a band signed to Eulogy, Wentz seemed like a local celebrity to the younger Trohman, who was a regular at the shows of Extinction, Racetraitor et al. By his own measure, he was also one of the youngest people at the shows. 'You're a shitty kid who goes to punk and hardcore shows,' Trohman explained in an oral history of Fall Out Boy's first years, compiled by Ryan Downey for *Alternative Press #303*. 'You see the other bands playing and you want to make friends with those guys because you want to play in bands, too.' But the fact that the pair had come from a similar area created a connection that grew into a friendship, and before he knew it, the sixteen-year-old Trohman was driving Pete all over town, as Wentz had had his licence suspended. Whilst in the car they would listen to plenty of hardcore, particularly the influential metalcore band Shai Hulud, but they would also indulge a shared love of pop punk.

It didn't take long before Trohman was getting called up for musical duties as well as chauffeuring. Arma Angelus were booked for a tour but Chris Gutierrez was unable to get the time off work, so Wentz asked Joe if he was able to fill in on bass. Wentz was required to use his famous powers of persuasion on Trohman's parents to convince them to let their teenage son on the road with a metal band in their twenties, but eventually they relented and Joe headed out as a member of Arma Angelus. The tour itself perhaps wasn't everything that Joe had imagined. As the youngest and newest member of the band he got more than his fair share of horseplay, and the rest of the band would rip his underwear off him every day. It would have been better, he later realised, to stop wearing underwear altogether. The performances weren't exactly a walk in the park either, and his inexperience began to show. 'I would kind of freeze a lot on stage,' he recalled to *Fender.com*. 'I would kind of just statue myself. I was young and worried about fucking up or being judged in general or looking stupid. I didn't have a sense of self. I would make myself nervous and be like a deer in headlights and freeze.'

Joe's stage fright was so severe that, according to Gutierrez, the rest of Arma Angelus called on him to fly out and replace Trohman for the second half of the tour. 'They flew me out and paid for my ticket, 'cos they were like, "Dude, he's not cutting it. You've gotta come out 'cos he is not cutting it." [...] So I flew out to Boston, or maybe New York, and played the rest of the tour while Joe basically just hung out and sold merch and stuff.'

While the tour wasn't exactly an out-and-out success for Trohman, it brought him and Wentz closer together and they began discussing the possibility of a new band, one that drew on their mutual love of pop punk. 'When you're playing hardcore music and you're screaming every night, it just grates on your ears, and at some point, the grass is always greener. You want to be doing something different,' Wentz reflected to *Today.com*. '[We] listened to the Descendents and Lifetime and bands like that growing up, so we wanted to play in a band like that.' It was here that fate stepped in to give Wentz and Trohman one almighty shove in the direction of an extraordinary future.

The story goes like this: Trohman was in the Borders bookstore in Wilmette's Eden Plaza with his friend Arthur, browsing through CDs (not the books, he has been clear on that) and talking about music. The pair were discussing Neurosis – the Californian band often dubbed 'post-metal' for their experimental take on the genre – and were trying to define the band. Suddenly, a complete stranger inserted himself into the conversation to correct the pair on their erroneous classification. That person was Patrick Martin Stumph.

Stumph's family had been in Chicago for 150 years, back to the time of the Great Chicago Fire which engulfed the city in 1871. (Stumph would later use the spelling 'Stump' for his public life to clear up any confusion around pronunciation.) His mother Patricia was an accountant, and prior to his birth his father David had been a folk singer, though later years would see him working in the corporate world. While David had long stopped performing by the time Patrick arrived, his musical background would have a profound impact on his son, who was the youngest of three children. He would sing songs around the house, and had an extensive record collection that hopped around genres, though when Patricia and David ultimately divorced the extensive record collection went with him. Patrick has said that he never really made the decision to 'become a musician'; playing music was simply something that you did. After his parents overheard him singing along to the radio, they gently teased him for sounding like Elvis Costello. There and then, Stump decided that he was a fan of Elvis Costello; the Londoner's music, with his tendency towards socially conscious lyrics and genre-blending eclecticism, would continue to influence Patrick throughout his life.

A musical education was not the only thing Stump had inherited from his father, who had also passed on his sense of ethics to his son. 'Civil rights was a huge thing in my family,' he remarked to *The New York Times*. 'It almost took the place of religion as far as morality, ethics, things like that.' At an early age he was also showing a natural predilection to performing. In the third grade he had a teacher named Mrs Sternberg who, in place of regular show and tell, had a period in her lessons called 'show time'. Students were welcome to perform skits, sing, dance, play music, whatever they felt they had to share. 'I totally rocked that so hard,' he would recall in a video interview with the Fueled By Ramen label. 'I used to do all sorts of dumb stuff, [like] lip-syncing to "Weird Al" Yankovic. [...] I did really well at show time.'

But lip-syncing to parody songs – even ones by the undisputed king of parody – can only take you so far, and Stump moved on to piano lessons to begin developing his musical chops. From there he began playing the guitar, his first instrument a black Epiphone lent to him by his stepbrother that was in bad condition but nonetheless playable. And his musical appetite was growing too, as he moved into his teenage years and starting consuming a whole range of different styles, from pop to punk and metal. He was a fan of the guitar playing of Prince, with his incredible technical ability, and of Pantera's Dimebag Darrell, who injected a low-slung groove into the thickset metal template. But Elvis Costello remained a fixture throughout this period of development. Costello allowed him to be comfortable with the idea of not being a 'shredder', a flashy guitarist who shows off his ability with lightning-fast lead parts. He was starting to hone his craft as a songwriter, where powerful chord changes and memorable melodies are the most valuable currency.

His teenage years were largely spent in his bedroom devouring whole catalogues of music, which by his own admission he did in place of chasing girls. But with his father's fire for activism within him, it was only natural that Stump found himself drawn to the highly political Chicago hardcore scene, where animal rights, race relations and civil-rights causes were every bit as important as exorcising some aggression in the pit. 'That's what attracted me to punk rock,' Stump explained to the *Chicago Tribune*'s *RedEye*. 'I was always one of the more political punk rock kids. I wasn't into it for moshing, I was into it for the statement.' By the time Stump had bumped into Trohman in Borders, drums had become his principal instrument and he was already playing in various bands like PDI (Public Display of Infection), Xgrinding processX and Patterson. Xgrinding processX had released a live split on cassette, and Patterson would go on to play a basement show with the newly formed Rise Against, featuring former

Arma Angelus bassist Tim McIlrath. Drumming had become Stump's main focus and he was determined to make his way into more high-profile bands but was regularly pipped to the post by a couple of other drummers in the local area.

As Stump and Trohman spoke in the store, the friend that Joe had arrived with was slowly getting pushed out of the conversation. The pair talked about music for an hour before Joe revealed that he was trying to put a band together with Pete Wentz. Stump was immediately intrigued. At the time he hadn't been playing music for a couple of months, and was dealing with the aftermath of a break-up. Though he'd seen the likes of Racetraitor and Extinction perform around Chicago, he'd never actually seen Wentz perform with them, only hearing talk of this magnetic band-hopping bass player. He felt the opportunity to try-out for a band with such a high-profile member of the scene was exciting, but not because he necessarily saw the band going anywhere. He fully expected to meet up with Wentz once and never see him again, as he had done with many other aborted projects. But it would be a story to tell nonetheless. Joe related that they needed a guitar player, a singer and a drummer, and Stump knew that with his varied musical ability he could be one of those things, though he was hoping that he could be the drummer. Trohman, however, had other ideas. He already had his sights set on Andy Hurley, the drummer of choice in the Chicago scene. And besides, Patrick had given him a link to a website that featured some MP3s of him singing along to an acoustic guitar, and Trohman had been impressed with what he'd heard of Stump's voice.

Patrick, Pete and Joe first met at Patrick's house, and Wentz remembers him answering the door in a crazy outfit, like a member of the emo band Endpoint – in shorts, socks and an argyle sweater. Stump was surprised at how short Wentz was. As the three sat down to start playing, Patrick was still determined that he'd be the band's drummer, but Joe encouraged him to sing for Pete, so Patrick took out an acoustic guitar and the pair sang songs from Saves the Day's *Through Being Cool.* Saves the Day were one of the main players of the mid-nineties emo movement, taking the well-established melodic hardcore sound but adding confessional lyrics and a more pop-friendly approach. Stump had been working at his high school's radio station when the record was first released, and though Saves the Day were a guilty pleasure at first, he grew unabashed in his love of *Through Being Cool.* It would be one of the key starting points for this new musical collaboration – Stump claims there would certainly have been no Fall Out Boy without the influence of Saves the Day – so Pete and Joe were delighted with what they heard. They had never been in a band with anyone that could sing like Patrick before. The decision was made, whether he liked it or not; Stump was going to be the frontman.

At this early stage, though, global superstardom was far from their minds. Pete was at college at DePaul University in Chicago, and Hurley either declined their offer of joining the band or was never asked. Wentz remembers that he asked Hurley a number of times and was rejected, a reflection of the fact that the band wasn't showing too much promise in the early days. Hurley, however, has stated that he was never even asked, given that he was already performing in three different bands and at college full-time studying anthropology and history. But nonetheless, Pete was convinced that he had found something special in Stump. 'Pete was basically like, "We found this guy,"' Mani Mostofi remembers. '"He thinks he's gonna play drums but he's gonna sing." That was basically the conversation. I think a lot like the way [Racetraitor] found Andy and felt that we had found this hidden treasure, Pete felt that way about Patrick.'

The world would have to wait. Joe, Pete and Patrick's first concern was conquering Chicago.

CHAPTER SIX

EVERYTHING'S COMING UP MILHOUSE

The band's first show was at Chicago's DePaul University, and they were booked on the strength of Pete Wentz's involvement, essentially billed as 'Pete Wentz's new band'. At the time they were a five-piece. A second guitar player named John Flamandan had been drafted in, and drum duties were handled by a player named Ben Rose. The show was in a cafeteria at the university and headlined by Stillwell, a post-hardcore band with technical leanings from the Chicago area. Another band on the bill simply played Black Sabbath's self-titled debut album in full. Pete, Joe and Patrick only had three songs at the time and played first, and Patrick was not in his element as a frontman. It was an inauspicious start. John Flamandan quit shortly after, and Stump was fairly sure that the band was on a short road to oblivion. But Trohman wasn't about to give in. He was determined to make the band work, going as far as picking up the other members in his car and delivering them to practice. With Flamandan out, Patrick filled in on guitar even though he didn't consider himself quite up to the task.

The band's second gig was another college show supporting The Killing Tree, the band that Arma Angelus's Tim McIlrath had gone on to form with Geoff Reu, formerly of Baxter, and Todd Mohney, who would go on to play in Rise Against. It was here that once again, just as chance had brought them together, chance would also gift them with a name. To an audience comprised of the other bands on the bill and a few friends, Pete introduced the band with whatever name they were going with at the time. But someone from the audience interrupted, shouting out that no, they were Fall Out Boy. The trio were huge fans of *The Simpsons*, often sparring with quotes from the show; Fallout Boy was the sidekick of Radioactive Man, a superhero from an in-universe comic book whom Milhouse is chosen to play on screen. They had previously shortlisted the name as a possible option, hence the heckling. And by the time The Killing Tree had thanked 'Fall Out Boy' for their set, it seemed like kismet. The name had stuck.

According to Mostofi, the band still had a lot to figure out at these early shows, but it was also clear to everyone watching that Fall Out Boy had something. 'Everyone was impressed with Patrick right away,' he says. 'Pete was really hyping up Patrick and at the first show that I saw them it was very evident that Patrick had the skill. I don't think that he had totally found his own style – it was a little bit of an imitation of Saves the Day at first – but he later sort of figured out what was going on. They were kind of really goofy. Patrick and Pete hadn't established a strict chemistry yet on how to run the live show, and there was a lot of really funny banter. But the songs were catchy and there was obviously something to them. We all knew that they had a lot of potential.'

A three-song demo was recorded in Ben Rose's basement to cassette tape, and one of the first people to hear it was Chris Gutierrez. His response to what he heard was immediate. 'I remember being in Arma Angelus's practice and Wentz was like, "Hey, I met these kids and they're playing these pop punk songs and I'm gonna start this band with them, and it's gonna sound like a cross between Lifetime and New Found Glory",' he explains. 'And I was like, "That's my shit! Everybody made fun of me for listening to that!" People didn't mix genres back then. Then [Pete] came into another practice wearing his Elvis sunglasses, and he said, "Dude, I got a fucking demo for this new band." [...] They were on tapes, which I still actually have, and I want to say they only made like fifty, maybe? I listened to it, and that was my thing – that was what I loved. I loved pop punk, and I heard it and I was blown away. I said, "Dude, this is for real fucking good. I'm not blowing smoke up your ass, but this is really fucking good." I remember saying, "I'm gonna ride this shit with you to TRL [Total Request Live]!"'

Wentz has always maintained that there were no ambitions in the early days for Fall Out Boy to get big; in his mind, Racetraitor and Extinction were 'big' bands, and Fall Out Boy was little more than a side project, a distraction. But Gutierrez sees it differently. 'At the time New Found Glory had this weird huge following, for their level,' he says. 'They were one of the first bands, and I know it's common now, but they were one of the first bands to be hardcore kids playing pop-punk music.' Chad Gilbert, who had joined the Floridian pop-punk band in the late nineties, had formerly been the vocalist for hardcore band Shai Hulud. New Found Glory had released their self-titled second album in 2000, and suddenly been thrust to the centre of the burgeoning pop-punk movement. 'Shai Hulud were a very pivotal band in hardcore in the late nineties,' Gutierrez continues. 'They made being melodic but heavy very popular. So when that record came out, that influenced Arma Angelus, and all we wanted to do was play with Shai Hulud, 'cos I think Wentz felt we could do really well with their audience and we could get bigger. His whole goal, whether he's willing to admit it or not, was that he wanted to be able to make this into something bigger than it was, to no fault – I went for that ride too, and who wouldn't want their band to be recognised on a bigger level?'

Gutierrez feels that early on, Wentz recognised the greater possibilities for success with a pop-punk band, as opposed to a heavier, more abrasive one. 'I think he saw that we didn't have as much potential as Arma Angelus as Fall Out Boy would,' he says. 'This hardcore thing was only gonna take us so far, but this Fall Out Boy thing...? There's no way even he could have predicted the level that they got to, but he saw it.'

Mani Mostofi also recalls a conversation he had with Wentz that shows how serious he was about finding success with the band. 'We were at this pop punk show and Pete had started going to them because he wanted to get a sense of who his audience was, because he knew that all the people from the hardcore scene weren't necessarily gonna come along with him,' he says. The very fact that Wentz was attending gigs as a kind of market research shows how focused he was on the business side of the band. 'He wanted to make friends and get a feel for that scene,' Mostofi continues. 'And he told me right away, "We're the next Blink-182." And where they were – like the quality of their songs, the professionalism of their live show, with a lead singer playing guitar who wasn't even a guitar player... it would've have been a crazy statement for someone to make, it would have come across totally egomaniacal, but I just thought, "Yeah." I thought that because, one, I think we recognised the raw material he was working with. But two, he was just totally locked in. He was never this super duper ambitious guy; he didn't really go to college, he didn't really pursue anything that intensely; with Racetraitor sometimes he was in it and sometimes he wasn't. With Arma Angelus he had started taking a band more seriously, but once he met Patrick, that was it.'

The next step for the band was to head to a real recording studio to lay down a more professional demo, but they suffered a setback when the band and Ben Rose decided to part ways. Stump told *Alternative Press* that he was the 'greatest guy', but musically something was not quite right. With recording time already booked, it was felt that Patrick should himself fill in on drums, but an alternative presented itself in the form of Jared Logan, the producer for the demo. Logan was the drummer in 7 Angels 7 Plagues, a fellow hardcore/metalcore act from Milwaukee that had been active in the Chicago scene alongside Arma Angelus. They were ferocious and technical, so Logan had exactly the kind of chops that could wind Fall Out Boy's spring-loaded pop punk tight.

The resulting demo featured three songs: 'Growing Up', 'Switchblades and Infidelity' and 'Moving Pictures'. The demo bears the imprint of the band's love of Descendents and Screeching Weasel, and Stump's confessional tales of suburban alienation and heartbreak are typical of turn-of-the-century pop punk. 'Growing Up' puts a plodding instrumental section amidst a breakneck verse and chorus, as Stump sings of getting over a failed relationship. It's simply growing up, he seems to admit in the chorus, though we learn in the last verse that he's not above a little puerile revenge ('I'll go out tonight and piss on her doorstep and listen to Misfits' "Where Eagles Dare"', he sings). 'Moving Pictures' opens with a strobing guitar part backed by some huge power chords in a section that could easily have come from the heyday of heavy metal, before diving headlong into another double-speed, self-lacerating exploration of a failed relationship. Even at this stage, the band's penchant for pop-culture references was beginning to show itself. 'Growing Up' mentions 1998 cult movie *Rushmore* as well as New Jersey's the Misfits, and 'Moving Pictures' revolves around the teenage tradition of stealing kisses from your date at the movies. Both are a snapshot of suburban American life. The demo's highlight, though, was 'Switchblades and Infidelity', a delightfully scrappy cut of angst-ridden hardcore-inflected punk. Stump had not yet developed the vocal range or soulful embellishments that would later come to set Fall Out Boy apart from the pack of pop-punk ankle biters, and the lyrics are decidedly on-the-nose, like passages from a diary that you'd rather not have read. But there's no question that an ember of potential burns at the heart of the demo. The songs are structured simply but effectively, the musicianship is rugged yet capable, and the choruses leap from the songs and lodge themselves in your subconscious.

With the demo in hand, Fall Out Boy set their minds to further building their local following. Pete and Joe would spend hours putting demos together, first heading to copy shop Kinko's to photocopy the liner notes then heading back to Joe's bedroom at his parent's house to cut them out, burn more CDs and package them together. The band had been joined by two new members: drummer Mike Pareskuwicz, who had formerly been in Subsist, and guitar player T.J. 'Racine' Kunasch. They were playing shows all over the suburbs of Chicago, at venues like the Knights of Columbus halls, sometimes twice a weekend. Since Joe and Patrick weren't yet twenty-one, they would play all-ages shows so their friends could get in, and they were always on hand with a stack of CDs and some flyers to hand out. 'When people see you putting in the work, you can at least get a cool local following,' Trohman said to online magazine *ModernGuitar*. 'You know, a lot of people have hometown pride, since that's where they're from. Chicago was ours.' One regular fixture at the shows was Chris Gutierrez, who was often in attendance to help hand out demos or sell merch, long before there was any reflected glory to bask in. 'I know how it sounds now, later on [...] but I really was their first fan,' he says. 'Regardless of whether five people or fifty people or five thousand people knew who they were, I thought, "These fucking songs are good", and I loved them.'

One person who was not interested in Pete's new band was Jay Jancetic, whose time with Arma Angelus had come to an end shortly after the recording of *Where Sleeplessness is Rest from Nightmares*. 'During my tenure in Arma, I was in the process of getting married, buying a house, and my daughter was a toddler at the time,' he explains. 'I felt exceptionally bad that I was so busy with "life stuff" while Arma was hitting our stride. [...] I actually at one point ended up flat out telling Pete that I was going to have to quit, because I felt like my responsibilities were going to hold back the band. Our heart-to heart-resulted in Pete convincing me to stay in the band.' After recording was wrapped up, Jancetic was unable to go on the subsequent tour due to his family commitments, and Joe Trohman was recruited to take Jay's place. 'I unwittingly volunteered to come to practice and teach and coach Joe on playing my parts, to songs I wrote or helped write,' Jancetic says. 'I had no idea I had volunteered to teach my [permanent] replacement for what I thought was for the greater good of the band. Within a week, I received a phone call that a decision was made to kick me out of the band due to my inability to tour and keep pace.' Jay feels that the move was a calculated one, and he confronted Wentz on that charge. 'I expressed to Pete that I really felt like it was a cop-out on his part, especially after our "heart to heart". Essentially I called him out on kicking me out of the band for the very reasons I had previously tried to quit, and for what I felt was a very calculated move on his part to keep me in the band in order to help finish writing and recording the album, yet kick me out for the very reasons he talked me off the ledge of quitting for [...] I lost a very good friend that day, all for the sake of ego and the taste of fame, and it all started with Arma Angelus.'

Jancetic is now the guitar player in Chicago hardcore band Harm's Way, who released the critically acclaimed album *Rust* on Deathwish Inc. in 2015, as well as a member of Buffalo straight-edge band Black X.

Arma Angelus was ultimately wrapped up in 2002, leaving

Pete free to focus on Fall Out Boy. They played their last show on 16 November, a birthday show for former Extinction frontman Jim Grimes. The line-up cribbed heavily from Fall Out Boy: Gutierrez and Wentz were joined by Trohman on guitar and Stump on drums. The line-up had only rehearsed for the show twice and in Gutierrez's own words they 'butchered their way through three songs' before Grimes joined them onstage to cover an Extinction song. Gutierrez has uploaded a video of the set online and the clip stands as a fantastic document of the scene at the time: 'If you're straight edge put your fucking fist in the air for this song,' Wentz says before the band tear into 'An Anthem for Those Without Breath and Heart', and the windmills duly start spinning in the pit.

Behind the scenes, Wentz had grown disillusioned with the hardcore scene. 'We stopped doing Arma after a while not because FOB got big (we hadn't at all),' he said to *AbsolutePunk*. 'But I think I got tired of screaming every night and I definitely got tired of a scene where there were a lot of people just yelling, "mosh you faggots" into a microphone.' His sentiments are shared by Stump. 'The hardcore scene always goes in waves,' he offered to Scuzz TV. 'And we just happened to hit this wave where… we had got into hardcore bands for a lot of the expression and some of us, the politics and stuff. And we hit this wave where those things weren't cool any more. There were a lot of big dudes fighting each other. And I know TV might add a bit of height as well as weight but we're not really built for that.'

Gutierrez offers a different perspective on the state of hardcore in Chicago around 2002. 'One thing that I think is the benefit of me being old is that I can see the different incarnations of each thing,' he laughs. 'I've been going to hardcore shows since the eighties, so I can see each wave come and go, you know. And the thing that everyone always says is, "It was cooler back in my day, and people didn't act like this back in my day". All this scene stealing, scene climbing, backstabbing… there's always been that, there's always been people who said all the wrong shit, there's been people who back-stabbed people or people who were scene climbers. But we don't see it when we're young. We're young and we're idealistic and we have our eyes wide. We're not seeing what goes on backstage because we don't have the ability to get back there yet. […] There's always been assholes, there's always been people who said the wrong thing. Did I see it? Of course I saw it, and I still see it, but it's always been like that.'

Whether the scene had gone rotten or not clearly depends on who you ask, but there's no doubt that it produced an uncanny amount of talent: not just the high profile careers of Fall Out Boy, Rise Against et al, but also a plethora of lesser-known acts who burned brightly away from the gaze of the general public. So what was it about Chicago that produced such a thriving community of fiercely determined musicians? Mani Mostofi thinks that the location of the city has a lot to do with it. 'I think Chicago kind of benefited from the general climate that existed in Midwest hardcore, that was I guess more thoughtful, more intellectual, less violent,' he says. 'The bands were less successful, so they just did it from the heart. Not to say that East or West coast bands weren't from the heart, but if you're a kid from the Midwest or Chicago or Louisville or Minneapolis, one of the really active scenes, you had to really want to do it. If you wanted to play a show you had to drive quite far, and if a band came to town it was a big deal. [...] It was really a true DIY scene and it was full of committed people.'

Chris Gutierrez agrees that being in the centre of the US made Chicago something of a magnet for creative people. 'The US is massive; it's fucking massive. All the cool shit is happening on the coasts, and we're in the middle. We're an island of diversity and culture and surrounding us in like a thousand miles in all directions is nothing – it's corn fields, rednecks and racism. And you'll find little pockets of punk rock here and there but overall Chicago is the spot in the middle of America.'

And Jay Jancetic, not a native Chicagoan, suggests it's a reflection of the city's hard-working heritage. 'Moving to Chicago as an outsider, one of the things that drew me here was the diversity in both the bands within the scene and the type of music that the people within the scene were into. I think that really came out in the kind of music we were (and are still) doing. [...] I also think there was and is a large concentration of both talent and people that are very driven in Chicago. City of broad shoulders, lunch pail and hard-hat mentality – all that cliché stuff, I guess.'

CHAPTER SEVEN

RECORDING *FALL OUT BOY'S EVENING OUT...*

Fall Out Boy's demo found its way into the hands of Sean Muttaqi, the owner of Uprising Records and the former singer of Vegan Reich, for whom Andy Hurley had done a stint as drummer in the late nineties. Uprising had previously worked with 7 Angels 7 Plagues and Racetraitor, and Muttaqi had an idea: to release the demo as a split with another new pop-punk band from Chicago called Project Rocket. Project Rocket had something of a friendly rivalry going with Fall Out Boy at the time, as they were also comprised of luminaries from the hardcore scene that had moved towards a pop-friendly approach. One of those luminaries was T.J. Minich, the former guitarist for Spitalfield; another was Andy Hurley. It was smart move from Uprising and Muttaqi, with Project Rocket's yearning rock sitting neatly alongside Fall Out Boy's more punk-influenced style. Soon Uprising Records was tabling an offer for Fall Out Boy to cut a whole album, an offer that few bands would be able to pass up. But it did not pan out as hoped.

The band headed back to Jared Logan's studio in Milwaukee to record what would be their first and only album for Uprising Records, but almost immediately bumps started to appear in the road. When Muttaqi had proposed the album to them, they still had only three songs complete and were in the process of figuring out who they were as a band. The recording session was booked over two days on a 'less than shoestring budget', as Patrick put it to Scuzz TV, and the rest of the material was hastily put together in time to get in the studio. Mike Pareskuwicz laid down his drum tracks first, and right away the rest of the band could see that the record wasn't going to turn out as they wanted. Mike had not played to a metronome – a click track that ensures strict timekeeping is kept – and the tempos for songs would wander throughout a take. Without time to go back and re-do the drums, the rest of the songs had to be built on these imperfect foundations. It wasn't just the technical side of things that weren't as the band wanted – the speed with which they had put together the remaining six songs left the band dissatisfied with the songs themselves. Even during the recording session the band were looking unfavourably on the material.

Dissatisfied or not, the album clearly shows a band developing fast, getting to grips with the tools of the songwriting trade. Opener 'Honourable Mention' has far more texture and variety than anything off the Project Rocket split, with rhythms that shift their weight at unexpected moments and a slow-building middle eight that opens out into a big double-time chorus. Stump's voice, too, had matured noticeably from earlier efforts. Here he sounds in complete command of his range, and has more of the soulful timbre that would later make him one of the most recognisable voices on the radio. Lyrically, the band were still tending towards self-eviscerating honesty, but this time spiked with wry humour. 'Maybe next time, I'll remember not to tell you something stupid like I'll never leave your side,' Stump sings on 'Honourable Mention', and it's a perfect encapsulation of the kind of spite that can develop at the end of a relationship.

While Descendents-esque pop punk still provided the template for the record, the songs recorded during these sessions also demonstrated ambitions beyond simply playing fast and furiously. 'Calm Before the Storm' has a genuinely affecting chorus carved out amongst the palm-muted by-the-numbers verses. These songs show a fascination with the sexual politics of courtships and relationships, something that would become a big part of the band's writing in the future, even though at this time Wentz and Stump were sharing duties on lyric writing (a more clear-cut division of labour would arise in the future). 'Pretty in Punk' features the line: 'The only girl who ever wanted my time was the one who only wanted five minutes of mine / knocking boots in the back, how degrading is that?' It's an observation as self-pitying as it is tongue-in-cheek.

They weren't merely becoming a more capable band, then; they were becoming more like Fall Out Boy. Take 'The World's Not Waiting (For Five Tired Boys in a Broken Down Van)'. It's a two-and-half-minute slice of melodic punk rock that builds to a satisfying sing-along final chorus, and there's nothing particularly unique in that. But the perspective that the song is sung from would be returned to again and again. The song is about the experience of Fall Out Boy as a band, hopping in their van to play shows around the Chicago area, well aware that they might be wasting their time but nonetheless perfectly content to be doing so whilst playing music in the company of their friends. 'We'll all take turns, not for the worst / We're all has-beens and never-weres / And we're all in the back singing "Roxanne" / Just watching life pass us by,' sings Stump, and it's like looking at a sun-bleached polaroid of the band from the era. It's an unusual thing for a rock band to do. So often artists will reveal deeply intimate and private thoughts through their lyrics, and occasionally they might address issues happening in the world at large, but it's rare to see this kind of account of a band's day-to-day life contained in a song. It feels like the barrier between musician and listener is being dissolved, like the moment in *The Wizard of Oz* when Toto pulls back the curtain that separates Dorothy from the mighty Wizard and exposes an ordinary man, frantically pulling levers to keep the illusion alive. 'Pay no attention to that man behind the curtain', most bands say: Fall Out Boy positively encourage us to peep. With that said, at this stage in the band's career what we were seeing was nothing particularly amazing; it's a pretty standard account of a broke band's touring life. But as their lives would become more and more remarkable in the coming years, Fall Out Boy would continue to show us the world behind the screen.

The album's not without its missteps. 'Short, Fast and Loud' is a makeweight track with little to mark it out from the rest of the songs recorded, apart from the refrain of 'Good God I wish I was tall', a lyric which Wentz regrets ever making it on to record. 'It just seems like it was a little bit too literal and a little bit too bad,' he said to *Gigwise*. 'I don't want to throw him under the bus, but I think Patrick may have written it... but then it could have maybe been me.' The collection of songs ends on a stronger note with 'Parker Lewis Can't Lose (But I'm Gonna Give It My Best Shot)', a track with a frantically melodic verse that opens out into a chorus that begs crowds to sing along. The title is a reference to the nineties sitcom of the same name, a show released essentially as an unofficial TV adaptation of eighties cult classic *Ferris Bueller's Day Off*. The film and pop-culture references come thick and fast throughout these songs, as they would continue to do throughout Fall Out Boy's career. Take, for example, the 'I can be your John Cusack' rally of 'Honourable Mention', probably in reference to the movie *Say Anything...* – most famous for the scene when Cusack serenades his estranged girlfriend with Peter Gabriel's 'In Your Eyes' coming from a boombox as he stands in her driveway. Any proper appreciation of Fall Out Boy lyrics also requires a knowledge of eighties cult films.

Regardless of the strides made in recording this new material, the band weren't happy with the results, and that wasn't the only challenge they had to contend with. The relationship with additional guitar player T.J. 'Racine' Kunasch fell apart. In the *Alternative Press* retrospective, Joe Trohman described him as 'the guy who showed up to a show without a guitar', a nice guy who couldn't quite get it right. One day, apropos of nothing, he turned up unannounced at Joe's parents' house to collect some gear whilst Joe was sleeping. He found his way into Joe's bedroom, who didn't appreciate being woken up, and was fired from the band on the spot. But just as Kunasch was departing, two separate incidents would shape Fall Out Boy as it exists today.

The first was a request from a friend to do a split EP with a band called 504 Plan. The record would never see the light of day, but nonetheless the band headed to Smart Studios in Wisconsin with producer Sean O'Keefe to lay down three new songs. Incumbent drummer Mike Pareskuwicz was unable to get time off from his job to make it to the sessions, so the band asked Andy Hurley to fill in. Hurley was currently playing in a band called The Kill Pill, an act featuring Mani Mostofi. 'The Kill Pill basically started up at about the exact same time as Fall Out Boy did,' Mostofi explains. 'The Kill Pill lyrically was very much in the same vein as Racetraitor, but The Kill Pill was a little bit broader politically – it was more positive I guess. It really came out of a desire for Andy and I to do something that felt more rock 'n' roll.' The Kill Pill had a recording session booked in on the same day in Chicago, so Hurley agreed on the proviso that that he was able to make it from the city to Madison, where Smart Studios is located, in time to lay down his tracks. 'Pete was needing a drummer,' Mostofi explains. 'For a while Fall Out Boy didn't really have a steady drummer, and Andy was an old friend, a good friend, and the best drummer that Pete knows. So it made sense that Pete asked. Andy had to finish all of his parts in a day or two so he could get to Madison to track for Fall Out Boy, and if he couldn't then Patrick was gonna do it.'

Hurley arrived as Patrick was setting up the drums with O'Keefe, under the assumption that he would have to play them. 'We were literally about to start my first take of "Dead On Arrival" when in walked Andy,' Patrick would remember in a post on his website. 'I guess in a lot of ways, in walked the actual beginning of Fall Out Boy as well; from that point onward, Joe, Andy, Pete and I were a proper band. The three songs we recorded in what felt like two days [...] would go on to become three of our most enduring, and certainly the first time any of us heard ourselves in speakers and went "Huh! We definitely don't suck!"' It was an eye-opener for the band, and O'Keefe made his feelings known, too – that they needed to get Andy in the band.

The second factor was a two-week tour that was booked with Spitalfield, the local band who shared members with Project Rocket (Spitalfield had also worked with Sean O'Keefe on their debut album for Victory Records, *Remember Right Now*). Once again, Pareskuwicz couldn't make the tour due to work commitments, so the band asked Hurley to fill in, and he once again agreed.

A string of guitarists had also come and gone since Kunasch was dismissed from the band from Trohman's bedside. The first, Brandon Hamm, was never an official member but filled in on a temporary basis. He quit whilst the band were practising a new song called 'Saturday'. The second was Chris Envy, singer and guitarist of Showoff, another Chicago-based pop-punk band. Showoff had released a self-titled album in 1999 on Maverick, Madonna's personal imprint of Warner Brothers. Showoff had since split up, and Pete had managed to convince Envy to join, which felt like a major coup – after all, he had been a major-label artist. Envy rehearsed for the tour but quit two days before it was due to begin. With no time left to recruit another replacement, Patrick was forced to step up to the plate. He borrowed a guitar from Joe and headed out on the road as Fall Out Boy's singer and rhythm guitar player.

The tour with Spitalfield was far from a raging success. Many of the shows were cancelled, and turnout was so low that Fall Out Boy would often be playing to just the other bands on the bill. But something had fallen into place. Hurley was having a blast playing with the band, after acknowledging during the recording sessions in Madison that this was some of the best songwriting that he had ever been a part of. 'He came back really thrilled about the process of recording with them,' Mostofi says. 'I remember him specifically talking about how insane Patrick's vocals were in a couple of parts.' Those sessions had been a huge deal for Wentz too, who had a feeling that getting a great drummer on a permanent basis was going to make or break the band. Seeing the way Hurley played, and the way he was able to communicate and understand the rhythmic writing of fellow drummer Stump, had convinced Pete that Andy was the man for the job. He'd been in Trohman and Wentz's sights since Joe first met Patrick in Borders, but he formally asked Andy to join the band. 'Andy called me and he basically asked for permission,' Mostofi says. 'I don't think he really felt like he needed permission, but I think it was like a sign of respect, you know. He was a friend and maybe at that time I was still an older brother figure, so he said, "Can I do this thing and be in both bands?"'

At the time Mostofi was shortly due to be heading to graduate school, and the plan was to continue with The Kill Pill from the three different cities that the band would now be located across. 'I knew that Andy's dream in life was to be a professional musician, and he was definitely the most talented guy in our friends,' Mostofi says. 'Patrick was sort of in our group of friends too, but we'd only known him for about a year really from the time that Joe had discovered him in a book store. He wasn't one of us the way that Andy was. So when Andy asked 'cos he didn't want to betray The Kill Pill, to be polite and kind, I encouraged him to do it.' It was decided: Andy was going to join Fall Out Boy. The Kill Pill, meanwhile, would eventually run out of steam, and only wrote one song and played one show after Mani moved away.

CHAPTER EIGHT

GRAND THEFT RAMEN

Early on in the band's development, they made an agreement amongst themselves about the distribution of profits that might come the band's way. In music publishing, there is one cut of royalties set aside for the songwriter – the person or people that compose the melodies – and another for the lyricist. But Fall Out Boy had decided to split everything equally amongst the members. 'Real early on we decided that, regardless of who wrote what, we'd split everything four ways,' Stump told *Rolling Stone*. 'There are records where I've done a whole song or Joe has written an entire music bed, but we all get the same credit. If there's four of us onstage, the four of us are receiving the same amount of credit, the same amount of money and the same amount of everything.'

Clearly the band's hardcore sensibilities had not left them, nor had the scene turned its back on them. In these early days the band would regularly play on hardcore bills, and found that the response there was far more welcoming, if somewhat sedate, than on bills with other bands that might be considered their contemporaries. 'The proper pop punk infrastructure of bands around town didn't really want to mess with us,' Stump commented to Scuzz TV. 'Our hardcore fans would put us on shows, they were really supportive, but it was just like, "Eh, we just wanna mosh, we don't really wanna see you guys sing".' While the term 'emo' would go on to be broad-brush definition to mark a whole range of bands, including Fall Out Boy, at the time it was a more specific term most commonly applied to the likes of Jimmy Eat World, The Get Up Kids and The Promise Ring. 'At the time there was this emo thing in the Midwest, and the Midwest emo thing hated us. That scene didn't want anything to do with us.'

Being from a hardcore background and then performing at so many hardcore shows with a pop-punk act both had a big effect on the way the band would play live. These were not crowds that it paid to be coy in front of; wallflowers were not welcome on stage. The audience's respect had to be bought with sweat and commitment. 'What they did was put on a live show like a hardcore band would do, where you're just throwing around your instruments, constantly stage diving, going absolutely crazy,' Mani Mostofi remembers of these early shows. 'Pop punk bands and emo bands, they didn't go as crazy as hardcore bands. It wasn't part of the live aesthetic. Fall Out Boy brought that to those shows and it was Andy that allowed them to do it, because Andy and Patrick could stay in place and play the songs, and then Joe and Pete would go actually bonkers.' Mani agrees with Pete that Andy was the missing component in the band, the glue that stuck the whole sound together. 'Once Andy was in the band, then there was no question that Pete's ambition was matched by what they were producing,' he says. 'Andy was basically the best musician in the band. Patrick was a good singer and a natural songwriter, but Andy was the only one who actually had chops at that point. So once they had him everything fell into place.'

While some of the band were at college during this period, Fall Out Boy had become a major focus for them – so much so that three members of the band had moved out of their respective parents' places and moved in together to an apartment in central Chicago. 'They were living in an apartment about five or ten minutes from where I live now, in Roscoe Village,' explains Chris Gutierrez. 'It was Joe, Patrick, Pete and two other dudes, one of whom kind of lived in Wentz's closet. It was the second floor, and it was above an ice cream shop, I think. We would all go over there all the time and watch movies, and everybody would bring their girlfriends and there'd be twenty people just sitting around talking shit and hanging out.'

Since the split EP with 504 Plan never came to pass, the band had three professionally recorded songs in their possession to use as a demo, and they started knocking at the doors of other record labels. Their first choice was Drive-Thru Records, and for good reason; Drive-Thru was the label that had released New Found Glory's self-titled debut and their 2002 follow-up, *Sticks and Stones*. Both were certified Gold in the US. Run by sibling duo Richard and Stefanie Reines, all bands on the label were agreed upon by both brother and sister – so when Richard was considerably more keen than Stefanie, the pair agreed to go and see the band perform live. They didn't consider the live show up to scratch (a criticism that would crop up a few times in the early part of Fall Out Boy's career), and as a compromise offered the band a place on Rushmore Records – a subsidiary of Drive-Thru. Fall Out Boy declined.

As local following grew, more labels started to take an interest in the band, including California's Militia Group and Chicago's own Victory, sometime home of Damnation A.D., Earth Crisis, Hatebreed, Madball, Refused, and Fall Out Boy's close buddies Spitalfield. On paper, it seemed like a dream offer, but still the band resisted. They had been strongly advised by Militia Group to seek management before signing any contracts, and were recommended Crush Management; while the first representative of Crush wasn't interested, the second was. His name was Bob McLynn, who had himself been the bassist and singer in alt-metal band The Step Kings. He and Wentz clicked immediately, and the band signed on the dotted line with Crush Management – a relationship they maintain to this day.

It was whilst different labels were vying for Fall Out Boy's attention that they first caught the eye of John Janick. Janick was the founder of Fueled By Ramen, a label he had started during his time as a student in Florida alongside Vinnie Fiorello, the drummer of ska band Less Than Jake. At this time Fueled By Ramen was a small affair, with only a few breakthrough successes to its name, most notably Jimmy Eat World and Yellowcard. But Janick had seen their name on fliers and was intrigued, so he called a Chicago-based band called August Premier that was currently on his roster to ask what they were like. August Premier gave him the thumbs up, so he went in search of more info. On hearing a song online, he knew immediately that he wanted Fall

Out Boy for Fueled By Ramen. He got hold of the number for the apartment where Patrick, Joe and Pete lived and made an unannounced call. Janick wanted to buy the three songs that the band already had recorded and offered them money to go and record more. Wentz, meanwhile, was attracted to the idea of signing to Fueled By Ramen precisely because they weren't as established as some of the other labels they were talking to; with typical foresight, he saw that there was less risk of getting lost on the roster. There was also an additional sweetener to the deal with Fueled By Ramen. As part of the deal Fall Out Boy received $40,000 dollars from Island Records – a division of Universal Music Group, one of the largest record labels in the world. In exchange for the funding to make the album, Island would have first refusal on any Fall Out Boy album following their record for Fueled By Ramen. It was the best of both worlds. They had the credibility of being associated with an independent label married with the support of a major. Wentz has been clear, though, that Island's involvement in their debut stopped there. 'They gave us like $40,000 for our record and allowed us to make the record how we wanted to make it, kind of no strings attached,' he told *AbsolutePunk*. 'We've never been shy about saying that Island was there and had a very hands-off approach with us.'

Added to the three songs that had been recorded a year prior – 'Dead on Arrival', 'Saturday', and 'Homesick at Space Camp' – the band also had two more songs recorded with O'Keefe in a separate session: 'Grand Theft Autumn / Where Is Your Boy' and 'Grenade Jumper'. With the support from Fueled By Ramen the band were able to work in earnest on finishing a record with Sean O'Keefe. They were back at Smart Studios, a recording facility owned by legendary producer Butch Vig, most famous for his work on Nirvana's *Nevermind* in 1990. It would later become the hub for Vig's band Garbage, as well as hosting grunge and alternative heavyweights like Smashing Pumpkins. It was a serious studio with a serious amount of heritage: the *Nevermind* plaque hung on the wall, and the band got to see the microphone that Kurt Cobain used to track his vocals. Together, they recorded seven songs in nine days, as well as re-recording vocals for 'Saturday' and adding some guitars to 'Where Is Your Boy'.

But Fall Out Boy weren't living like rock stars yet. In fact, the budget was stretched so thin that they couldn't even afford accommodation, and were sleeping on the floor of an apartment belonging to a girl they had met shortly after arriving in Madison. Even eating was a challenge. The studio would provide two six-packs of soda every day for the band, who requested that they buy a loaf of bread and some peanut butter and jelly instead, so they could at least get something in their stomachs. The studio managers obliged.

Relationships within the band were straining, too. Prior to recording the record Pete had tried to quit, announcing to the other members that he wanted to leave whilst in the car with them, and then heading back to his parents' house rather than the apartment that they all shared. He had only been coaxed back into the band by Patrick, who called him up that night and told him that the band would not go on without him in it. Wentz was back in the fold, and seemed to commit to the band with a whole new level of energy, but his desire to be heavily involved with the lyrics caused tension between him and Patrick.

Stump has admitted that he wasn't taking duties as a lyric writer particularly seriously, and it was frustrating Wentz. Stump was more interested in the musical effect of the words: the rhythms, the sounds of the syllables and the way that lines would flow from one to the next. Wentz, however, was all about the meaning of the words. He started to assert himself by giving Patrick notes, but the constant back-and-forth caused friction. Stump eventually declared, half out of irritation, that Wentz should just write the lyrics himself. So that's what he did. Whole songs that had been written with Stump's lyrics would be replaced by Pete's, which Stump would then fine-tune to be more musically gratifying. Wentz would then come back and gripe that the effect of his words had been diluted. The process was slow and frustrating, and it almost split the band up various times during the recording of the album. The only thing that kept them together was knowing that when they finally found the middle ground, the song was better. The end was justifying the means.

CHAPTER NINE

AS LOUD AS THE GRAVE

The record was in the can, and the band starting gearing up for its release. A major part of its legacy would later be associated with its cover, and true to form, Pete Wentz made sure he was involved in the process of shooting it. But like so many elements of Fall Out Boy's early steps into the limelight, chance had as much a part to play as foresight and intuition.

The cover was shot by a photographer named Ryan Bakerink. He and Wentz were vacillating between two ideas for it: the first was a portrait of the band, and the second was a mocked-up bedroom scene. The shoot took place at the apartment where Wentz, Stump and Trohman were living in Chicago's Roscoe Village, where Pete's room was first stripped and then props were collected from around the apartment to stage the scene. The accoutrements arranged around the bed consisted of a tableau of the influences that meant so much to the band: posters, toys from the eighties, an Elvis Costello record sleeve here and an Earth Crisis sleeve there. The bedroom shoot went on way into the night before Wentz and Bakerink agreed on a shot of a girl lying face down in the bed, asleep or exhausted among the chaos. Shots of the band were almost an afterthought, taken in the early hours of the morning. Bakerink arranged the band on a broken futon in front of a bare brick wall and then took individual portraits, with the intention of using them for the back cover. But the intended cover photo could not be used because of the amount of copyrighted images contained within it, so at the last minute the band decided to run with one of the shots of the band sitting on the couch. Blue colouration was added in homage to Blue Note Records, a jazz label that had put out albums by the likes of John Coltrane and Sonny Rollins with the same warm, mysterious colouration. The listing of the band's names on the front was inspired by the same source, and it was here that Stumph first made the decision to be known as Stump.

But just as circumstances can conspire to make big things happen, so they can put obstacles in your path. Just two months before the release of the new record, Uprising Records decided to release the album that had been recorded in a few short days with Jared Logan, back when the band were still a five-piece. The album was to be titled *Fall Out Boy's Evening Out with Your Girlfriend*, and Fall Out Boy were not at all happy that the album was seeing the light of day. It was felt that it would create a confusing situation for potential fans, with two records coming out within a short period of time, and from a band with a markedly different line-up. More importantly, Fall Out Boy didn't like the songs. Both Uprising owner Sean Muttaqi and Fall Out Boy discussed with *Alternative Press* the implications of the release and the friction it caused. Muttaqi explained that he had invested money in the record and that he did not deliberately time the release of *Fall Out Boy's Evening Out with Your Girlfriend* to piggyback on the new album. The band, meanwhile, refused to discuss or promote the album. The feud has reportedly since been put to bed, but Wentz still finds it hard to listen to the album. 'You know when you go through an awkward time in your life and take a weird picture?' Wentz remarked to *NME*. 'You look back at that picture and you're like, "Wow, I was so weird". Making some strange decisions with my hair and my clothes and stuff... This is like having an album worth of that. It's cool and it got us to where we are and stuff, but it's really hard to have that awkward time memorialised forever.' While it's an important part of the band's history, most do not consider *Fall Out Boy's Evening Out with Your Girlfriend* to be the band's true debut – Wentz included.

The new album, entitled *Take This To Your Grave*, was released on 6 May 2003 with a launch party at the Metro in Chicago. 'Honestly, literally my only goal with the band was that I wanted to play Metro,' Stump would later tell the *A. V. Club*. 'All my other little bands had never gotten to play there, and I had really just wanted to play Metro.' It was, therefore, a fitting place to begin Fall Out Boy's assault on the mainstream. The album's title was a late decision taken over second choice *To My Favorite Liar*, and though the band didn't know it at the time, they couldn't have selected a better one. *Take This To Your Grave* would become a seminal album for a whole generation of fans, a record they will likely carry with them throughout their lives.

The first ten seconds of *Take This To Your Grave* perfectly set the tone for what's about to follow. The first thing we hear is a dial tone, as if a phone call has just ended or we have just been hung up on. It's almost as if an intimate conversation has just ended, and we've found ourselves alone in a private place; the rest of the record almost seems to exist in this confessional, intimate frame of mind where anything can be admitted or exposed. Then 'Tell That Mick He Just Made My List of Things to Do Today' comes careering in, a pummelling wall of glittering guitars tethered to galloping drums like a chariot. It was Sean O'Keefe's idea that the record should come in immediately, so Stump composed an intro inspired by The Who, who would often layer guitars and synths into attention-grabbing introductions. The title is yet another reference to Wes Anderson's *Rushmore*, a movie about a prodigious teen who falls in love with his teacher (the actual quote is 'Well, tell that stupid mick he just made my list of things to do today'), but lyrically the song is a poison pen letter to a former lover. Much of Wentz's contributions to the record concern themselves with an old girlfriend, but none more obviously so than on this opener, where Stump's original lyrics were swapped wholesale for Wentz's. It is one of just two songs on the record where the lyrics were written solely by Wentz; the rest of the songs' lyrics were written by Wentz and Stump in collaboration. In stark contrast to the song's candy-coated, peppy sound, those words are nothing short of venomous, with Wentz baring his fangs most notably on the chorus: 'Let's play this game called "when you catch fire" / I wouldn't piss to put you out'.

'Dead on Arrival' is a flawlessly executed slice of sunny pop punk that careers towards a chorus so irresistible it ought to come with a health warning. The song has a special place in Fall Out Boy lore. Wentz names hearing 'Dead on Arrival' as the moment in which he realised how important the band was to him, after a spell of being ambivalent about the band. Trohman also distinctly remembers Stump playing it to him on an acoustic guitar and realising that in terms of pure song craft it was head and shoulders above the material that had been written up to this point. The lyrics were written primarily by Stump, and though Wentz would come to be known as the lyricist for the band, Patrick proves himself a talented writer, too. When he sings 'the songs you grow to like never stick at first / so I'm writing you a chorus and here is your verse', it's not just a clever metaphor for romance; it's an appeal to the listener, like he's reaching out his hand and welcoming you into the ranks of Fall Out Boy fans. Who could say no?

If 'Tell That Mick' drips with bitterness and 'Dead on Arrival' with energy, then the next track – 'Grand Theft Autumn / Where is Your Boy' – is an open-hearted anthem, full of teenage sincerity. Stump had written it before Fall Out Boy were signed, in response to a concern that the band had heard a few times: 'Dead on Arrival' was great, but was it a stroke of luck? Could Stump follow it up and write more bona fide pop songs? The a cappella introductory chorus alone proves that he can. The intro was once again Sean O'Keefe's idea, and it's fantastic to hear Stump's honeyed tenor without accompaniment, even if Stump was not keen on it at first and had to be convinced to let it stand on the record.

It's hard to imagine Patrick being on the cusp of so much acclaim and yet feeling despondent about his future, but that's exactly what is expressed in 'Saturday'. At the time of writing the song he had a real hang-up about graduating from high school, feeling that he'd accomplished nothing with his life. He kept the song to himself for some time because he was unsure that the rest of the band would take to it, but ultimately he shared it with them and they decided to work on it. The lyrics are a collaboration between Wentz and Stump, who hammered out the lines together on a couch in Smart Studios. The line 'Pete and I attacked the laws of Astoria' was in fact written by Wentz personally, but he wrote himself into the song instead of using 'Pat and I' because Patrick hated to be called Pat. And Pete stamps his influence on the track in another way too: with the hair-raising scream that accompanies the final half-speed chorus, a throwback to his days fronting Arma Angelus.

'Homesick at Space Camp' begins with the line 'landing on a runway in Chicago and I'm grounding all my dreams of ever really seeing California', but this is no literary trick. Stump really was sitting on a plane to Chicago when he wrote it, on his way from visiting family to the band's second session at Smart Studios. The song demonstrates perfectly how Patrick had learned to use his voice as an instrument. Just listen to the way that his vocals are doubled on the words 'sensual' and 'conventional' as he skips between notes; it's like a ray of sunlight streaming across the verse, and it's a world away from the uncontrolled delivery heard on *Fall Out Boy's Evening Out with Your Girlfriend*. Some of the lyrics are less successful here, like the refrain of 'These friends are, new friends are golden' that closes the song. Just like 'God I wish I was tall' from 'Short, Fast and Loud', it suffers from being a little too literal, a little too sincere.

'Sending Postcards From a Plane Crash (Wish You Were Here)' was largely composed piece by piece in the studio rather than by the band in a rehearsal studio, but it's a testament to how comfortable the band were in that environment that it sounds every bit as natural as the other songs on offer here. The line 'My insides are copper and I'd kill to make them gold' almost made its way into an Arma Angelus song but was repurposed to fit this barbed and embittered track that once again sees Wentz taking aim at his ex. *Take This To Your Grave* is a break-up album in the classic tradition, and it's when Wentz gives free reign to his resentment that his blackly comic lyrics make the deepest impression. 'You can thank your lucky stars that everything I wish for will never come true' is a classic Wentzian attack, what he described to Fueled By Ramen as imagining a 'bizarre, horrid situation that could never happen… to take mental revenge.'

'Chicago Is So Two Years Ago' was the source of another huge fight between Wentz and Stump. Stump had been playing the song to himself in the lobby of Smart Studios when O'Keefe overheard it and suggested that he play it to the rest of the band. They decided to work on it, but once again, Wentz was unhappy with the lyrics, and in the changes Stump felt that he was losing the song that he had written. Wentz ended up writing the verses himself and allowing Stump free reign on the choruses, though with certain words as jumping off points. One of the lines nearly got them into some hot water, too. Two months before *Take This To Your Grave* was released, New Jersey's emotive rockers Taking Back Sunday would release the album *Tell All Your Friends*, which contains the song 'You're So Last Summer'. Contained within is the lyric: 'She said, "You're a touch overrated, you're a lush and I hate it"'. 'Chicago Is So Two Years Ago', meanwhile, features the line: 'She took me down and said, "Boys like you are overrated, so save your breath"'. Similar titles and similar lyrics; it was enough for Taking Back Sunday singer Adam Lazzara to bring it up with Wentz when the two bands would later share a bill, though the Fall Out Boy bassist assured Lazzara it was pure coincidence. The song also features guest vocals from Justin Pierre, the singer of Minnesotan band Motion City Soundtrack. As a huge fan of his voice Stump had wanted him on the record, but they were unable to arrange schedules to get him in the studio. However O'Keefe was familiar with him, so he arranged for Pierre to have his vocals recorded off-site and added them to the track in secret as a surprise for the band.

'The Pros and Cons of Breathing' is the second song on the record where Stump and Wentz operate in the manner they would later find the most effective – with Stump writing the music and Wentz taking sole ownership of the words. It's a track with a sharper edge, one that fits in more with the sound of Midwestern emo than of coastal pop punk, and it sees Wentz turn his anger inwards as he considers how he can't move on from his devastated relationship. 'And if I could move I'm sure it would only be to crawl back to you / I must have dragged my guts a block', Stump sings, and it's the most visceral image on the record.

But the album's most agonised moment sits side-by-side with its most joyful. Joe and Patrick had been discussing the idea of writing a fan appreciation song on the record, a moment to shout out to all the people that had supported them so far. The problem was, they joked, there was only one Fall Out Boy fan: Chris Gutierrez. That was the starting point for 'Grenade Jumper', which features the plainspoken chorus, 'Hey Chris, you were our only friend / And I know this is belated, but we love you back'. From here on, Gutierrez would simply be known as 'Hey Chris' to fans, and his status as the first Fall Out Boy aficionado was cemented forever. 'I remember going over [to their apartment] one day and Wentz was like, "Come up, I gotta play something for you,"' Gutierrez remembers. 'So I said, "Alright". We walked in to Patrick's room, because his room was the only one with a CD player. He put it on, and I remember hearing it and thinking it's a pretty good song, sounds about right. Then I heard the chorus, and I thought, "What the fuck?! Are they talking about me right now?" And he said, "Dude, this is your song!"' A grenade jumper, incidentally, is the member of the band or touring entourage who will sleep with a girl so that the rest of the band can stay at her place for that stop of the tour. 'Even now I can recognise if any of my friends do something and acknowledge me like that, it's a great feeling,' Gutierrez continues. 'And regardless of whether it's Fall Out Boy or not, even if it's just some corner pub band, it's still a really cool feeling. I was like, "I hope they record it!"'

'Calm Before the Storm' is the oldest song on the record and the only one that also appears on *Fall Out Boy's Evening Out with Your Girlfriend*, and the version that appears here is very close to its older cousin, apart from altered lyrics and added guitar and drum arrangements. O'Keefe's sparkling production and Stump's carefully layered vocal tracks really bring the song to life, demonstrating how far the band had come since recording the prior version and how important O'Keefe's influence was in developing the band's sound. The song is also notable for its misunderstood lyric 'he's well hung and I'm hanging up', often misheard as 'he's well hung and I'm hanging *on*', a somewhat obscene image that has no place in a wholesome pop-punk song. The lyric was written by Stump and is a personal favourite of Wentz's, who once again brings out his screaming vocals for the song's climax. What you actually hear is some five or six tracks of screaming all happening at the same time; Wentz was particularly delighted with the way O'Keefe mixed them into a wall of sound that adds another texture to the music. It was also O'Keefe's idea for the band to drop out and have Patrick sing the chorus a cappella, a trick that would become something of a signature move for the band.

'Reinventing the Wheel to Run Myself Over' is one of Patrick's titles, and the song was written as a kind of love letter to New Jersey's Lifetime, who had been a major influence on the formation and sound of Fall Out Boy. You can clearly hear the Lifetime influence in the surging opening section, driven by Hurley's precision-engineered drumming, and in the gang chant of 'you have to prove yourself', but catchy melodies are offered up in abundance, too; the song is just over two minutes long, offering snatches of hardcore, emo and pure radio-friendly rock.

The album ends on a darker note with 'The Patron Saint of Liars and Fakes', a song where the guitars cut like a knife and Patrick explores the upper reaches of his range. Then he struggled to hit the notes he does on the chorus here, but over time his range would improve to accommodate them comfortably. Wentz is once again picking through the bones of a failed relationship with a typical combination of self-pity and spite: 'I'm all ears and I'm all scars to hear you tell me "Boys like you, you try too hard",' Stump sings, but then later adds, 'I still know the way to make your make-up run.' It would be easy to dismiss some the lyrics here as typical adolescent angst, but there was already considerable sophistication in the writing. Double entendres and dual meanings abound, and sentences often run on across two or three lines so that you have to pay attention to grasp the sense of what is being communicated. And Wentz and Stump's lyrics are honest – painfully so, sometimes embarrassingly so – but their lack of inhibition in expressing their feelings is what makes the songs so relatable.

Take This To Your Grave is a record that delivers on its promise from beginning to end. From the opening salvo of 'Tell That Mick...' to the elongated fade out of 'The Patron Saint of Liars and Fakes', the bar is kept high; Stump delivers line after line of insistent melody, throwing them at the listener like his pockets are overflowing with hooks, and the memorably acerbic lyrics ensure that the lines dig into your subconscious and stay there. Hurley and Trohman are less obvious but equally vital elements of the record's success. The guitar parts fizz and pop restlessly, whilst the drumming is solid and taut, ensuring the songs have not only a firm foundation on which to rest but also their fair share of power. It tosses together all of the influences that had been important to the band – pop punk, hardcore and emo – and dresses them with a glossy pop sensibility. It was as strong a debut record as the band could have hoped to make, but even they would not have dared to dream at how far it would eventually take them.

CHAPTER TEN

HARDCORE KIDS

Take This To Your Grave was by no means an overnight success for the band, who would find themselves on the road for the best part of two solid years following the release of the album, building a fan base from the ground up in the only way a rock band could in 2003. With that said, the band and Pete Wentz in particular saw the potential in and were early adopters of the Internet, and the blog posts that he posted offered Fall Out Boy's ever-swelling young fan base a look at the inner life of the band, served up with diaristic honesty.

The first leg of the tour was a monster trek across the US that lasted from June until December, though Fall Out Boy did have the privilege of taking their close friends in Spitalfield out as their support. In November the band got a taste of playing to larger crowds whilst supporting Less Than Jake, which also put them on the road with Fueled By Ramen co-owner Vinnie Fiorello – technically their boss. Pete and Andy had dropped out of college to pursue the band full-time, and though momentum was certainly building behind them, shows could be patchy and they had to earn every fan they won. 'I didn't have any expectations going into it, especially when we recorded the Fueled By Ramen record,' Wentz would later reflect to *Soak* magazine. 'We weren't trying to be any band and win over anyone, just wrote and put it out from the perspective [of] us sitting and playing around Chicago.'

Three singles were released from the album in 2003 whilst the band was on the road. 'Dead on Arrival' came first, accompanied by a video montage of the band on tour cut with a live performance. The show was shot at the Arlington Heights VFW hall; Chris Gutierrez was in attendance, and would later list the show as one of his top fifteen of all time on his blog. Watching the video, it's not hard to believe. There's almost no space between the kids in the audience and the band, and both are gleefully making raids into the other's territory. It was a habit that the band had picked up from their hardcore days, where division between performer and audience was discouraged.

The next single, 'Grand Theft Autumn / Where Is Your Boy', would fare even better. Ironically, Wentz and Stump had fought for it to not be included on the record at all, with Patrick in particular feeling that the song he had written had been lost as it was developed in the studio. Even the video nearly didn't happen. On the way to the shoot in New York the band crashed their van in Lamar, Pennsylvania, drifting off the road and into a snow-covered forest. Wentz and Stump were in the so-called 'death seats' at the back of the van, but fortunately everyone escaped unharmed. The van and trailer did not, however, and both had to be scrapped. Joe would later reveal that the van was in such terrible condition that the band got at most $200, but the resulting video was worth it. From the rural-suburban setting to the story of a boy's obsessive fascination with a girl, it perfectly encapsulated both Fall Out Boy and the themes of *Take This To Your Grave*, as well as introducing the dynamics of the band's performance to viewers. Stump is the band's beating heart, belting out the songs with an unmistakable voice but is otherwise restrained whilst Wentz and Trohman put on the show. With support from cable music channels the band found they were getting exposed to an increasingly young and diverse audience, one outside of the typical punk circles.

As of February 2004, they weren't yet a sensation. The band had played a show at Champaign-Urbana in Illinois whilst on tour in support of Mest, and Stump was candid about the unpredictability of the shows. 'I look forward to people giving a rat's ass,' he said to the *Opening Bands* website at the time. 'There's been one or two shows where we've played to like two thousand kids, and maybe ten care, and then we played a show to like one hundred, and everyone went nuts.' That show was also notable for another reason. Pete Wentz was forced to retire the loyal bass that he had used with the band up to this point after accidentally smashing off the headstock. 'I'm sad about that. That bass is a tank,' Patrick lamented. 'It's been around since before the beginning of Fall Out Boy. We've had members not outlast that bass. That thing's been around for so long and it finally couldn't take any more.'

But major milestones were on the horizon. Their shows had started to become more and more hectic; fans were regularly jumping the barriers to get onstage, resulting in the band getting blacklisted from various places, and it wasn't rare for a promoter to ask them to play last rather than in a support slot to prevent the venue emptying out once their set had finished. The buzz resulted in a coveted booking for the summer: the Warped Tour. Established by Kevin Lyman in 1995 in association with *Warp Magazine*, it would outlive its namesake and come to be one of the most influential touring festivals in the United States and the world. By the time the new millennium rolled around, its remit had widened from punk and ska bands to include a whole spectrum of artists, from the radio-friendly to the utterly brutal. And one thing was certain about the Warped Tour: it could represent a whole new level of exposure for a band and quickly send them from the verge of widespread recognition into the stratosphere.

In the case of Fall Out Boy, adulation from crowds had arrived early. Despite manager McLynn claiming that some of the more established bands present were unhappy with a new band like Fall Out Boy getting placed on the bill, the receptions they received justified the booking. One show in Detroit was particularly memorable, when Fall Out Boy were scheduled to play the early slot – the line-up and stage order would change from day to day to keep things fair. 'On that day we were playing a smaller stage that had room for about five hundred kids,' Wentz told *Soak* magazine. 'And since that's a pretty good scene for us not all that far from Chicago, we had over five or six thousand people show up at the stage. We started playing and everyone kept getting closer and the barricade cracked. Then people started coming on the stage and that started to collapse.' Fall Out

Boy would only manage two full songs before the show had to be shut down for safety reasons, though the crowd finished off the set for themselves with a mass a cappella rendition of 'Grand Theft Autumn / Where Is Your Boy'. 'It was a really amazing moment and we went out afterwards to meet everybody and say we were sorry for having to cut it short,' Wentz added.

Mani Mostofi, Wentz and Hurley's old bandmate, was also in attendance at another date on the Warped Tour and remembers the energy of crowd and band alike. 'The stage almost fell over,' he says. 'They were going so crazy, and the fans were going so crazy. I always felt that hardcore kids made the best pop-punk bands, 'cos they always had ten times the energy, a sense of urgency; that's the sort of pedigree that they came up with, and I think that was the key thing about Fall Out Boy's success. [...] Those kids had never seen anything like Fall Out Boy. You throw your guitars around, you don't care how tight you sound, the live show is all about the energy.' A movement was building and it was clear to everyone within earshot – not least the Warped Tour stage crew.

In the same week that a Detroit stage collapsed under the weight of Fall Out Boy's potential, they also appeared on the cover of *Alternative Press* for the first time, and it felt like the baton was being passed from the pop-punk bands that had dominated the late nineties and early two thousands to this new generation. But Patrick was still not entirely comfortable with the idea of being a frontman. He remembers having to take his hat off for the shoot, a hat he had been using for the last couple of years as a coping mechanism to deal with the attention he was getting. And that attention was inescapable. Though *Take This*

To Your Grave had been a slow builder, it would eventually pass the one hundred thousand sales mark, then the two hundred thousand mark before the album cycle was over; by Christmas it was selling two to three thousand copies a week in the States. Not bad for a few Midwestern boys just the other side of teenage-hood. The *Alternative Press* cover is notable for another reason, too. Stump stands to the far right of the shot, half smiling and half grimacing. But at the front of the band, with a smirk on his face and a shock of red streaking through his fringe, is Pete Wentz. He looks like he was born for magazine covers. The cult of Wentz had begun.

All this was too big a noise for Island to ignore, and when thoughts of a follow up to *Take This To Your Grave* rolled around, they exercised their option to take the band on. That meant more money and more resources to support them, but the band were determined to keep doing things on their own terms. 'By the time we got to Island, we got money to record a record, and all that stuff,' Trohman explained to *Modern Guitars* magazine. 'We never really took any tour support or anything like that. We were pretty good at selling our own merch and making our own money on tour and not getting into debt with stuff. That's the worst, getting into debt with a major label.'

CHAPTER ELEVEN

A DIFFERENT ANIMAL

Since 2002, the winds of change had been blowing in popular guitar music. It was the year that a glut of bands with roots in the hardcore and Midwestern emo scenes suddenly made an impression on the mainstream, with Jimmy Eat World, Saves the Day, Taking Back Sunday, The Get Up Kids and Dashboard Confessional all releasing high-profile records that year. But without any obvious stadium-sized bands to market as the forebears to this new sound, they found themselves booked on bills alongside established pop-punk bands like Green Day and Blink-182. Suddenly, it became very difficult for the average passer-by to distinguish between emo, punk rock, metalcore and straight rock 'n' roll, and almost every new band appearing at the time was suddenly getting daubed with the mark of 'emo'. The word had begun its slide into ubiquity and meaninglessness.

However, rather than ride the crest of this wave that was surging towards mainstream acceptance, Fall Out Boy were determined to rise above it. Like most bands, they had started out simply mimicking the bands they loved, but they now had ambitions beyond mere imitation. Why, they reasoned, should they strive to recreate music that already exists, and is already great? Finding themselves caught up in this proliferation of new American guitar bands, they found instinct was leading them to write dramatically different new material, a stylistic change so radical that it was likely to alienate fans. But, eventually, they managed to meet in the middle of the two positions and develop fresh songs that built on the sound that they had established whilst at the same time introducing daring new ideas. 'A lot of bands in the scene are about the competition rather than the music,' Wentz commented to *MTV.com*. 'They're all trying to get famous like Taking Back Sunday or something, and they don't really hold their weight. A lot of that music is very formulaic, and it over-saturates the listener and waters down the bands that are doing it for real. So we chose not to compete and decided to do something different.' It was time for the dreaded sophomore record.

Take This To Your Grave had been made in a few short weeks under time and budget constraints, and with almost two years of straight touring behind them, the band had set their sights on making a record with more complexity and depth. It was an admirable but by no means easy goal; the difficult second album (discounting *Fall Out Boy's Evening Out with Your Girlfriend*) is so called for a reason, as bands often expend many of their ideas on an unfiltered debut and then struggle to find a meaningful way to develop their sound. The first step was to settle on a producer who would take the band to the next level. Enter Neal Avron.

Avron had enjoyed his first taste of radio success after producing Everclear's 1997 album *So Much for the Afterglow* – a record that briefly launched the band into heavy rotation on MTV and worldwide fame – but had cemented himself as the go-to producer for pop punk after his work with New Found Glory. With a crisp and radio-ready sound that was nonetheless driven by gutsy guitars, Avron was an obvious choice to focus Fall Out Boy's ambition into a beam of mainstream-piercing heat. He was first contacted to work with the band through Fall Out Boy's A&R at Island, Rob Stevenson. Avron was not particularly taken with the songs, so he turned the offer down, but Stevenson wouldn't quit, and after a few weeks he came back with a new batch of demos with which to woo Avron. Amongst that new batch were two songs that completely changed Avron's mind: one called 'Sugar, We're Goin Down' and another called 'Dance, Dance'. The potential of the songs was undeniable. Suddenly, he was keen to meet the band.

Avron first met with Fall Out Boy on 29 July 2004, when they were headlining a show in Denver with Bayside and Armor for Sleep in support. Avron was immediately impressed with what he saw. There was no denying the energy of the crowd or the showmanship of the band, but it was Patrick's talent that truly convinced him that he had to be a part of the band's next chapter. 'Patrick, his voice is very different,' he explained in an interview with *MySpace*. 'I'd done three New Found Glory records and had success with Yellowcard, and Patrick's voice was definitely a different animal. He came from some of the same scenes [as those bands] but his voice gave it a whole other rootsy R&B thing.' After the show Avron and the rest of the band headed across the street to a Thai restaurant, and after a brief spell of meaningless chat, Pete came right out and asked Avron to produce the record. With typical prescience, he had seen the band's future.

Pre-production had to fit around the band's touring schedule, which was intensive throughout 2004. Avron recalls flying out to Chicago to sit in on a week of rehearsals with the band first, but there were none of the trappings of celebrity or success evident in their hometown. Patrick and Pete picked him up in Pete's beat-up car, and took him to the basement of a strange building where they had set up all of their gear. '[This guy there had] this shaved head, looked kind of Russian mob,' Avron said to *MySpace*. 'I don't know how they found that place, but it was definitely weird for that first week.'

The next batch of pre-production took place in the more salubrious environs of LA with another round of intensive rehearsing of the new material. Eventually, the band found themselves with a fifteen-song demo, rough clay to hew into their Island debut. But even now, with all of the hard-earned success that they'd seen from *Take This To Your Grave*, Wentz was still prepared for the possibility that it could all end at any minute, a sense only heightened by the fact that they were now little fish in the big piranha-filled pond of the major label. 'What's weird about it now is there are expectations and jobs on the line that come with how well our record does or doesn't do,' he commented to *Soak* magazine. 'Even if the label's disappointed or if people don't like it, it's been a fun ride that's lasted longer than anyone expected.'

The album was recorded in Burbank, California over the

winter of 2004 and into early 2005. The studio, Ocean, is a cavernous space originally built in the 1920s; in a previous life it had been a car dealership, but since then had been refitted by owner Freddie Piro into his dream recording space. The client list reads like a Who's Who of music; everyone from Bruce Springsteen to Motörhead had recorded there, and Avron was already familiar with the studio from his work with Everclear and Yellowcard. Once in the studio, Patrick and Pete found a way to leave behind the tension that had marked the sessions for *Take This To Your Grave*, where they seemed to be tussling for control of the songs. Wentz felt that part of the tension came from a disconnect between himself and Stump as their tastes in music were so different, but after two years of spending practically every day together, he had been able to develop a greater appreciation for Stump's songwriting abilities and the wide range of influences that he was incorporating into the band's pop-punk template. And experimentation was at the forefront of Patrick's mind when it came to putting together the songs for the record. 'I had a very strong sense that if we were ever going to be anything other than *Take This To Your Grave* a hundred times, then we were going to have [...] to set the tone then,' he would later reflect to Scuzz TV. Previously, the band had been constrained by the boundaries of the genre they were operating in; even the falsetto singing part that Patrick had added to 'Saturday' was scary for the band at the time, a step outside the pop-punk norm. But Stump knew that he was only ever going to get to follow-up a grassroots indie hit with a major label record once, to make that jump from a scene to the mainstream, and so this was his chance to establish the band as one willing and able to push the limits. If they could pull it off now, it would prime the audience to expect the unexpected in the future.

Another reason for the more harmonious groove Pete and Patrick had found in their working relationship was the way they now handled the division of labour. Wentz was now taking more or less sole ownership of writing lyrics, whilst Patrick took the lead in composing the songs themselves. Songs could be written in all manner of different ways, but the most common pattern saw Wentz writing as much material as he felt he wanted to, with Stump then coming in to act like an editor, picking through the lines to see which ones worked best and working with Wentz to fit the words to the music.

The actual meaning of the lyrics remained hugely important for Pete, too. This time, they were taking a more introspective turn, leaving behind the bitterness that had marked *Take This To Your Grave*. No one was really interested in his messy break-ups any more, he reasoned, so it was time to delve a little deeper into himself. '*Take This To Your Grave* was very reactionary,' he admitted to *The Independent*. 'It was like this person does this to you. But part of growing up is understanding that if you end up in the same situation over and over again you probably have to examine your own self and wonder whether that's one of the reasons that you have ended up in the same situation repeatedly. This time the lyrics were more about the anxiety and depression that goes along with looking at your own life.'

But that anxiety and depression was taking a heavy toll on Wentz, and during the recording of the album, an incident would occur that greatly adds to our understanding of the resulting record. As he would later describe to *Rolling Stone*, he had been 'isolating himself further and further', and was having trouble sleeping: 'I just wanted my head to shut off, like, I just wanted to completely stop thinking about anything at all,' as he put it. The pressure of making the new album was compounding his fears, as he knew he was on the cusp of something big but was so plagued with self-doubt that he was sure it was going to fail.

Ultimately, Wentz found himself in the parking lot of a Best Buy store, listening to Jeff Buckley's cover of Leonard Cohen's 'Hallelujah' and ingesting the anxiety medication lorazepam. He didn't refer to it as a suicide attempt, although did say to *The Independent* that he didn't really think about whether he 'slept or died.' Shortly after, he called his manager, who was concerned to hear Wentz slurring his words down the phone. He called Pete's mum and dad, who picked him up from the Best Buy and drove him to a nearby hospital. The incident was kept close to the band at the time. Wentz moved back into his childhood home in Wilmette with his parents, while Fall Out Boy were forced to fulfil touring duties in the UK without him. It was a daunting prospect as Wentz was a focal point for the live show, supplying the inter-song talking and a good measure of the onstage energy. All the same, it turned out to be at least something of a positive experience, as the band were forced to step up and do some of the audience interaction themselves for once – which they found that they were able to. Wentz recovered, and would find an outlet for his feelings through the songs being readied for the new album. But he is still unable to listen to Buckley's 'Hallelujah'.

CHAPTER TWELVE

THE FRUIT OF THE CORK TREE

With recording wrapped up, it was announced to the world that the new album would be titled *From Under the Cork Tree.* The title is a reference to a classic children's book called *The Story of Ferdinand*, written by American author Munro Leaf in 1936. The title character is a bull who spends his days relaxing in the field he calls home, sitting under a cork tree and smelling flowers. He has no interest in the glory of being selected to do battle in the bullring in Madrid, but when men arrive one day to select bulls for the occasion, he sits on a bee and stampedes around the field. Seeing his ferocious power and speed, they assume he will be a bloodthirsty combatant, and ship him off to Madrid. But once he is released into the ring, he is overcome by the smell of the flowers in the arena and simply sits down to better enjoy the experience. The humans are deflated, enraged even, and Ferdinand is sent back to his field, where he lives out his days sitting under the cork tree and smelling flowers. Written shortly before the outbreak of the Spanish Civil War, the subtext is clear – whatever honour men think they can gain in war is foolish, and the best in life is reserved for the meek and peace loving. Wentz's mother would read him *The Story of Ferdinand* many times as a child. Using it as inspiration for the title shows just how personal a record this is for him.

Fall Out Boy's nascent fan base got its first taste of the new material on 12 April, when the first single from *From Under the Cork Tree* was released. Entitled 'Sugar We're Goin Down', it had been written by Stump in less than ten minutes and was demoed for Avron to work with, who felt that although the chorus was ready to be recorded (the version you hear on the album is unchanged from the demo), the verse wasn't quite right. He shared his feelings with the band, who were prepared to rework it but it turned out to be no easy feat. Time after time Patrick would come into the studio with a new potential verse part and play it for Avron, and time and again he was rebuffed. However, both had a sense that the song could be something special, so they kept working at it. After five or six attempts, Stump played a part for Avron that piqued his interest. The rest of the band joined in and worked it out together, and suddenly it became clear that they had hit upon the elusive verse part. It was a moment for celebration. But it still needed to be recorded and Avron wanted to ensure that Patrick's voice did justice to the huge chorus, especially since it was so high in Patrick's range. Rather than lay down all the vocals in one day, as would usually be the way, Avron had Stump record one chorus per day. That way, Patrick's voice stayed fresh and he was able to deliver a powerful performance. After finalising the vocals Stump knew what he had. According to *Rolling Stone*, he turned to Andy Hurley and joked, 'Yeah, I just got your kid's college tuition paid for.'

The song wasn't an immediate smash upon its release, but its popularity swelled over the course of a number of weeks. It was accompanied by a remarkable video by director Matt Lenski that no doubt played a huge part in the song's enduring appeal. The video is a surreal re-imagining of a coming-of-age tale, set in an honest-to-goodness American town and with all the trappings of a teen romance apart from one crucial detail: the misfit protagonist has actual antlers growing from his head. Cut with performance footage of the band playing in a wood-panelled lodge-style lounge, we see how he's a pariah in the town and a loner by default until one day a girl gets her kite caught in his antlers. They strike up a romance, much to the chagrin of the girl's huntsman father, who seems to have a good mind to mount our hero's head on a wall. After the typical courtship ritual of a game of bowling, our couple's love seems to be blossoming nicely, which proves all too much for the father. He heads out with bow and arrow to dispatch his would-be stag-in-law, but is run over by a car as he takes aim. With the father lying injured and bootless on the ground, our hero discovers the secret source of the man's hatred: he has a pair of hooves in place of feet. The evocative semi-rural setting and the story itself, at turns hilarious, weird and genuinely affecting, were quite unlike anything else on MTV at the time, and the video is packed with small details that reward repeated viewings. It also offered many viewers their first glimpse of Fall Out Boy as performers, and the band give a no-holds-barred display for cameras, with Pete and Joe throwing themselves over the set while Andy pummels the drums and Stump sings straight down the barrel of the lens. But for all its strengths, the video almost didn't get released.

Director Matt Lenski is the son of an avant-garde filmmaker and so inherited his interest in films from his father, though a brief stint working at MTV had undoubtedly helped his ambitions along. (He would later direct the 2006 video for Band of Horses' *The Funeral* in collaboration with his father.) Prior to the release of the record, Lenski was approached by Jessica Jenkins, the video commissioner, to see if he was interested in making a video for the song. 'She was incredibly bright and responsible for making so many great videos happen,' he explains. 'I had never heard of [Fall Out Boy] and I also didn't really think much of the song, but I had also never done a music video and was quite determined to make one.' The idea for the video had been formed from two distinct sources. The first was the upstate New York town of Margaretville, where the video was ultimately shot. 'I was recovering from a broken heart and my family had a house in Margaretville,' Lenski says. 'I was taken by it. Maybe I was fascinated by the countryside because I was raised in New York City. Who knows? But the locations – the cemetery, the bowling alley, the shed where antler boy tries to clip his horns – they had to be discovered, not fabricated.' The second influence was select paintings from the seventies and eighties by NY artist Judy Rifka. 'She had a series of animal boys she was drawing in the early eighties. One was called Antler Boy. This character resonated with me. [...] Both of those elements had been stewing in my brain for a while. Fall Out Boy just happened along at the right time.'

Wentz recalls that the treatment stood out simply because

it was so strange compared to everything else they'd received. 'We got a zillion treatments where the boy and the girl were in the backyard or whatever,' he told Scuzz TV. 'Then we got this one about a deer boy or whatever and we were like, "Yeah, this one seems right because it's so weird."' The shoot took place over three days on location in Margaretville. The female lead was an Italian found during the casting, but the male lead was a friend of Lenski's called Donald Cumming. In 2006 Cumming would form and front New York City band The Virgins, who released a self-titled debut on Atlantic and a follow-up in 2013, made numerous TV appearances and opened for everyone from Iggy Pop to Sonic Youth. Since then The Virgins have split and Cumming has embarked on a solo career, releasing a debut album called *Out Calls Only*. Other aspects of casting were a family affair, as Lenski relates: 'The little kid who gives [Antler Boy] the finger is my little brother Conrad Lenski, who's now a grown man.'

On set, the band found an unusual way of ingratiating themselves with their new director. 'They were cool,' Lenski says. 'We started playing "nut smack" on set on day one. A dangerous game to get started that early. [There were] a lot of aching balls by the end.' While obviously happy to literally put their balls on the line, the band were keen to keep control over certain aspects of the shoot. 'I remember we brought up all of these clothes and then they just wanted to wear what they showed up in,' Lenski remembers. 'I always thought that felt authentic.'

However, according to Lenski, the band did not like the video once it was completed, and had to be convinced that it was the right move for them. 'Well, they hated the music video,' he says.

'Which was surprising because literally everyone else thought it was genius. [Commissioner] Jessica Jenkins is the one who pushed it through (again, she has vision). But I guess they came around once they realised they might have been mistaken.' The video did not make it through completely as Lenski wanted it. His original cut featured a 'much more graphic' car impact scene of the hunter getting struck, but he was made to change it.

It would take some eleven weeks after its initial release for 'Sugar We're Goin Down' to break into the Billboard Top 10, and then Fall Out Boy were suddenly everywhere. It's not hard to see why the song caught the imagination of the listening public on such a big scale. Avron's production holds the heaviness of the guitars and Stump's sparkling vocal in constant tension, and when the verse arrives, it feels like his voice is breaking through cloud cover and illuminating the whole song. The chorus is an incredibly catchy moment, but it's weird, too; Stump half slurs the words as they tumble over one another, making it hard to discern on the first few listens exactly what it is he's saying. This was doubtlessly pop music, but it sounded like nothing else that was on the radio at the time. And the song is full of little details that escape your attention at first but conspire to make it such a satisfying listen, like the lush harmonies that carry the pre-chorus or the gentle pianistic melody that arrives in the second verse and sits under the vocal line. This is the work of a great songwriter (or, in this case, two) allied with a great producer. If development was what Fall Out Boy were after, then 'Sugar We're Goin Down' offers it in spades, and even the lyrics seem to signal the dawn of a new era. 'I'm just a notch in your bedpost but you're just a line in a song', goes the pre-chorus, a barb directed at one of Wentz's old girlfriends that dismisses the hurt that he had picked through for lyrical content on *Take This To Your Grave*.

When 'Sugar We're Goin Down' broke onto radio and started dominating the coverage on MTV, the band had taken a day off from duties on the 2005 Warped Tour to visit a local waterpark. When they returned to Warped it was clear from the ever-swelling crowd sizes that the band were breaking through on a big scale. One morning Wentz recalls stepping off the bus to brush his teeth and discovering, for the first time, a queue of kids waiting to catch a glimpse of one of the members of the band. Wentz would later reveal that the band had to fight to get 'Sugar' as the first single, and one wonders if the band would ever have taken off in the way they did if another song had been selected. 'That chorus was a throw away,' he told *Spin*. 'Our label told us the chorus was too wordy and the guitars were too heavy and that the radio wasn't going to play it. I felt so good when that song broke. If that song hadn't been written and recorded and released at the exact time that it was [...] I'd be working at a Barnes & Noble.'

From Under the Cork Tree was released on 3 May 2005, and if *Take This To Your Grave* was a near-perfect modern pop-punk record, then its successor kicks the genre into entirely new territory. And you didn't even need to listen to the record to get a sense that the band were coming into their own; even a glance at the back of the record sleeve would clue you in – they were flouting the pop convention of short, punchy song titles in favour of long and wordy ones. 'I think a lot of that comes from not taking ourselves too seriously,' Wentz told MTV. 'On the last record, we name-checked [the movie] *Rushmore*, and there were people who came up to me later and said, "Oh, yeah, I saw this movie and there was a Fall Out Boy line in it." And it's like, "No, you heard this song and there's a *Rushmore* line in it." I just think it's cool to make a nod to something I like that might make other people check it out.'

The album's first track, though, has a title that can't be completely decoded without inside info. 'Our Lawyer Made Us Change the Name of This Song So We Wouldn't Get Sued' literally tells you the story – or at least part of it – in its name. The original title was, according to Wentz, 'My Name is David Ruffin and These Are The Temptations', after the troubled singer of the Motown legends who recorded 'My Girl'. Ruffin was undoubtedly a genius, lauded by fellow artists for the depth of feeling in his voice, but he spent various stints in jail for drug and other offences and ultimately succumbed to a drug overdose in 1991. 'It was kind of supposed to be our nod at a bio piece on The Temptations and David Ruffin and where the separation lies between being a superstar and a megalomaniac,' Wentz explained to MTV, but the label's lawyers warned them off using that title, and were hence immortalised themselves.

It isn't the sound of a phone line going dead that opens the record but the sound of cameras flashing, as if the band already knew that they'd be doing big things with *From Under the Cork Tree*. But 'Our Lawyer…' is shot through with cynicism about the fickle fame that can come with success in the rock scene. With its half-time chant, the final chorus makes an anthem out of superficiality; 'We're only liars, but we're the best / We're only good for the latest trends', it goes, and it is almost enough to make you believe the band could entirely sidestep the pitfalls of fame.

'Of All the Gin Joints in All the World' paraphrases one of the most famous quotes from the movie *Casablanca*, and concerns one of cinema's most iconic love affairs. Accordingly, the song sees Fall Out Boy at their most wide-eyed and lovestruck to date, a perfect accompaniment to the staccato guitar lines and neon melodies. Wentz can't help a little self-flagellation ('You only hold me up like this / 'cos you don't know who I really am'), but when Stump leaps up in his register to sing, 'And oh, the way your make-up stains my pillowcase / Like I'll never be the same', we learn that Fall Out Boy isn't all in-jokes and pop-culture references – they can write love songs too.

The first two tracks make for a very strong opening, but it isn't until track three that we hear the song that couldn't sit comfortably on *Take This To Your Grave*. Wentz first heard Stump toying with the swaggering bass line that opens 'Dance, Dance' while the band were still touring that album, and it's a song that somehow incorporates an infectiously danceable groove into a razor-sharp emo-come-rock-come-pop song, without any of the elements jarring. Stump has cited David Bowie's 'Modern Love' as a forerunner to 'Dance, Dance', and there's a fitting thread leading from the Disco Demolition Night in Chicago that signalled the start of the backlash, through Bowie's so-called post-disco album *Let's Dance* (which was co-produced by Chic's Nile Rodgers) and on to Fall Out Boy. It's almost as if Fall Out Boy are righting the wrongs of the past by creating a true dance-rock hybrid born and bred in Chicago.

'Dance, Dance' is without a doubt the finest song that the

band had written up to that point. The label had in fact wanted to release it as the first single off the record, but the band had fought for 'Sugar, We're Goin Down' to come first, perhaps fearing that 'Dance, Dance' was too much of a jump from their older material. It certainly has a confidence and sex appeal that none of their older material had touched on. Smart and sharp though the lyrical observations may be, this is going out music; this is music that smells of hairspray and cologne, that high heels are broken and drinks are spilled to. Its genius is in the incremental ramping up of pressure from the strolling verse part to the frantic pre-chorus and the explosive chorus, which Stump peppers with falsetto with all the ease of a punk rock Bee Gee. Ironically, that chorus was the source of a disagreement between producer Avron and the band. 'One small battle was some stick up my ass about lyrics in "Dance, Dance"', Avron told *MySpace*. '[The lyrics] talk about "falling apart in half-time", and I kept thinking nobody's going to understand what the hell that lyric meant. While probably a lot of people don't understand a lot of Pete's lyrics, I just felt since we thought that was a potential single, I wanted it to be a little more clear. [...] I think Pete did try and come up with another line but we all agreed nothing ever quite sang as well. I kind of ended up giving in on that.'

Another song, another film reference: 'Nobody Puts Baby in the Corner' has a similarly wholesome, all-American feel to *Dirty Dancing*, the film from which it draws its name. The song pivots between the sugar-sweet harmonies of the verse and the rapid-fire delivery of the chorus, where the double entendres and contrasting lines come thick and fast, both typical features of Wentz's lyrics. And if he was shooting for sex-symbol status, the lines, 'Keep quiet, nothing comes as easy as you / Can I lay in your bed all day?' were certainly encouraging would-be admirers to imagine him between the sheets. The jangling guitar tones and melancholic chorus of 'I've Got a Dark Alley and a Bad Idea That Says You Should Shut Your Mouth (Summer Song)' foreground Stump's influences for the first time on the record, and with the inclusion of the synth strings that float under the Beatles-esque chorus progressions, it's the closest the band come to a ballad on the album. However, in offering more of a classic sound it falls by the wayside compared to the boisterousness of the rest of the tracks.

Pete had never been shy about explicitly referencing details of his private life in his lyrics, but even by his standards '7 Minutes in Heaven (Atavan Halen)' takes on an incredibly personal topic: his overdose on Ativan (lorazepam) whilst recording *From Under the Cork Tree*. But it's typical of Wentz that he spikes all of this with humour, tackling the subject in a song brimming with flashy guitar work and diamond-tipped hooks. The verses are propelled by Hurley's bubbling drum work and we even get something close to a guitar solo from Trohman, which makes the Van Halen reference in the title all the more satisfying. In the grand history of songs that reference potentially self-destructive episodes, '7 Minutes in Heaven (Atavan Halen)' is surely one of the most upbeat, though Wentz doesn't shy from acknowledging his self-destructive behaviour; 'I'm not going home alone because I don't do too well on my own,' he has Stump singing. Next comes 'Sophomore Slump or Comeback of the Year'. A fantastic showcase for Stump's songwriting skill, it's a mid-tempo tune with eminently hummable melodies that belie its sophistication. It's also got more than a hint of Weezer about it, in both its laid-back delivery and the self-referential lyrics.

'Champagne for My Real Friends, Real Pain for My Sham Friends' opens with a cyclical guitar riff that cuts through the abundance of peppy melodies with its more moody tone, but the song quickly switches gears into a buoyant verse with a satisfyingly unusual chord progression. 'Champagne for my real friends, real pain for my sham friends' has been used as a toast for many decades, but given Fall Out Boy's obsession with movies, it seems probable they got it from *25th Hour*, Spike Lee's 2002 film about a man's last day of freedom before he goes to prison. It seems to see Wentz taking aim at the superficiality of relationships within the scene, with lines like 'we're friends just because we move units'; whilst Fall Out Boy, by contrast, 'only do it for the scars and stories, not the fame'.

And if Wentz was finding himself struggling with sham friends then he seemingly wasn't finding respite from his relationship woes, either. 'I Slept With Someone in Fall Out Boy and All I Got Was This Stupid Song Written About Me' marks a return to the embittered tone of the *Take This To Your Grave* material, with Wentz once again railing against disloyal lovers. Like *Take This To Your Grave* it also features some aggressive vocals in the last third, a feature that had been entirely absent on *From Under the Cork Tree* up until this point as the band shed the more obvious features of their hardcore background. Additional vocals were provided by ex-Shai Hulud vocalist Chad Gilbert, and his bandmates in New Found Glory, who weren't listed on the liner notes – much to their disappointment. 'I had brought in Chad Gilbert from New Found Glory to sing on one of the songs,' Avron told *MySpace*. 'I want to set the record straight on this, because on that same song the vocals in the back are sung by New Found Glory who did not get credited on that record. Cyrus [Bolooki, New Found Glory's drummer] never let me forget that.'

The long arm of the law intervened to interfere with song titles on the record not once but twice, with the second victim being the song now called 'A Little Less Sixteen Candles, A Little More "Touch Me"' – the title was originally intended to be 'A Little Less Molly Ringwald, a Little More Samantha Fox'. Molly Ringwald plays Sam in the 1984 movie *Sixteen Candles*, a John Hughes comedy about the travails of a virginal teen girl. Samantha Fox is a British former glamour model turned pop star whose biggest hit 'Touch Me (I Want Your Body)' is famous for its line 'like a tramp in the night, I was begging for you'. The eighties were a less sophisticated time. The implication of the title is simple, but in the lyrical world of Pete Wentz, sex comes packaged with a lot of complex emotions. If it is truly a song about fornication, then the opening lines of 'I confess, I messed up / Dropping "I'm sorry" like you're still around' suggest that sex is very much tied up with guilt; and the refrain of 'I don't blame you for being you / But you can't blame me for hating it' that pins down the chorus suggests plenty of bitterness in the mix to boot. But once again, the tune itself is as sweet as fairground candyfloss, with syrupy melodies that flow in abundance and stick in the mind. That is the essence of the brilliance of *From Under the Cork Tree*. Stump writes unforgettable pop songs, precision engineered for the exact purpose of being unforgettable. The guitar playing and particularly Hurley's drumming show a high calibre of musicianship, but it isn't the riffs or the beats that stay with you – it's Patrick's voice and melodies. Wentz's lyrics are emotionally muddled, a volatile mix of funny and self-pitying and spiteful and insightful, and they're full of literary tricks that defy easy interpretation. When you add the two things together you have the essence of Fall Out Boy: elegantly simple songs about ugly and complicated emotions.

The album's weakest moment is probably 'Get Busy Living or Get Busy Dying (Do Your Part to Save the Scene and Stop Going to Shows)', a song only somewhat redeemed by its outrageously long title. With its militaristic snare work and funereal chord progression it sees the band attempting to experiment with different textures, but it lacks the immediate impact of the other songs on offer here and therefore feels somewhat underpowered. It is most interesting for Pete's spoken word section that acts as an interlude between the final two tracks. When recording, Pete knew that he wanted to add a spoken word interlude but had not yet had the chance to write it, so it wasn't added until the album was being mixed. As Avron didn't have a vocal booth in his mix room, and Pete was too self-conscious to do it right there with Avron watching, Neal instead set him up in the mix room's toilet. It was there, huddled on the can with mic in hand, that Pete recorded this section, and the echoey quality of his voice is down to the marble surrounds of where it was recorded. The story would become a favourite of Avron's, who would surely share it with every other band who came to mix in his studio.

Just as *Take This To Your Grave* ended on a darker note, so too does *From Under the Cork Tree* with the moody 'XO', a song that features possibly Wentz's most poetic lines on the album: 'To the "love", I left my conscience pressed / Between the pages of the Bible in the drawer'. The song has more of an alternative-rock feel, perhaps suggesting that Stump had picked up a trick or two from former tour mates Taking Back Sunday, and much like 'The Patron Saint of Liars and Fakes' it leaves a lasting impression by ending the album on one of its most downcast moments.

What made and makes *From Under the Cork Tree* such a huge success, both artistically and commercially, is that the moment the band released the fullest articulation of who they were was also the moment that the mainstream public became aware of their existence. With the added catalyst of a hit single with a great video, Fall Out Boy's fate was cast. In 2005 pop punk was still big business – Green Day were in the midst of their biggest success after the release of *American Idiot*, and Blink-182 had only just taken a hiatus – but a young generation of potential fans were eager for something new, for a band to call their own. *From Under the Cork Tree* would sell close to 70,000 copies in its first week of release and give the band their first top-ten album on the Billboard 100, but its longevity was even more remarkable than its debut. The album just didn't seem to stop selling. The critics weren't unanimous in their praise, however; *Rolling Stone* said that the album contained 'a peculiar mix of in-jokes [...] and romantic dramas that post-adolescents are unlikely to care about', whilst praising the songwriting and humour. But *Alternative Press* probably summed up the album's successes best in acknowledging that there was something special about it that defies easy explanation. 'Over the past two years, the rise of Fall Out Boy has been exponential,' wrote Leslie Simon. 'Maybe it was the band's deep-seeded and cred-worthy roots in the Chicago hardcore scene, or maybe it's their ability to write concise, three-minute pop-punk romps drenched with the perfect balance of wit and self-deprecation. We'll probably never know.'

CHAPTER THIRTEEN

BUILDING AN EMPIRE

Fall Out Boy were making serious headway, but behind the scenes, Wentz was also starting to build an empire quite unlike anything that had been done in the genre before. In fact, it looked like he was modelling himself on a hip-hop mogul, building a personal brand through his own music and then using that as a channel to bring other offerings to the public eye. It's almost become a cliché to say that Wentz is the businessman of Fall Out Boy, but his drive and curiosity needed an outlet beyond making music. 'Pete's not in La-La Land wanting to be some famous dude,' Fueled By Ramen boss John Janick said to *Billboard*. 'He wants to be involved with artists, and he understands where people went wrong and right. I want bands that are level-headed and understand how things work.' Janick and Wentz had become close ever since he signed Fall Out Boy, spending hours talking together on the phone, and Janick had recognised Wentz's potential as an arbiter of new music. The result of those conversations was Wentz's own imprint on Fueled By Ramen, which he christened Decaydance Records (now DCD2 Records).

The first band signed to the label would end up being its biggest, though their origins couldn't have looked less like Fall Out Boy's. They had formed in the suburbs of Las Vegas and honed their sound in private, polishing songs and recording them in rehearsal spaces without ever stepping on stage due to the lack of a sympathetic music scene. But they had curiously hit on some of the same distinguishing features as Fall Out Boy. They wrote songs that combined alternative rock and punk with an undeniably poppy edge; they had wordy and highly literate lyrics; and they had a singer with a dexterous and distinctive voice. They called themselves Panic! at the Disco, a moniker that seemed a fair representation of their sound, and had just a few songs recorded as a demo when they first heard that Wentz was starting up his own label in association with Janick. On a whim they sent him a link to a website containing their demos and promptly forgot about it – after all, what famous musicians actually read their messages and listen to demos that fans send in? Well, apparently Wentz does, as a few days later he replied to the band telling them that he wanted to sit in through a rehearsal. In late 2004, as Fall Out Boy were recording *From Under the Cork Tree*, he took a drive to Las Vegas to meet the band in person, and shortly after signed the band as the first official Decaydance artist. The band's singer, Brendon Urie, would even end up on *From Under the Cork Tree*, providing additional vocals for 'Seven Minutes in Heaven (Atavan Halen)'. 'I didn't intend on doing a record label,' Wentz explained to *AbsolutePunk*. 'It was not something that interested me. [...] I heard Panic! and my immediate reaction was jealousy. I was like, these guys are writing songs I wish we had written. I think that it's far more important as an A&R to chase songwriters not songs, because anyone can write a catchy song once. I want to find someone with a voice.'

Other signings would soon follow, such as Gym Class Heroes, an alternative hip-hop band who seemed more at home amongst punk bands than other rap acts and who had been making waves on the Warped Tour ('too hip hop for rock, too rock for hip hop', as Wentz put it). Another was The Academy Is..., a fellow Chicagoan act who had come up in the same scene as Fall Out Boy. Later Wentz would also add a clothing line called Clandestine Industries and a website, *FriendsorEnemies.com*, to his list of business projects. He might have been a teen heartthrob clad in eyeliner and skinny jeans, but his money-making acumen most resembled someone like Jay Z, who has made millions as a label boss, the co-creator of a fashion label and recently, the owner of online music subscription service Tidal. *FriendsorEnemies.com* has since shut down, so it would perhaps be a bit of a stretch to call Wentz a tech entrepreneur, but there's no question that he was one of the first mainstream music figures to fully harness and understand the power of the Internet in promoting a personal brand.

2005's Warped Tour was the first engagement of the new album cycle and the band returned as top billing rather than troublesome young upstarts threatening to upend stages. The band co-headlined with My Chemical Romance, who had shot to prominence in 2004 with the release of *Three Cheers for Sweet*

Revenge, drawing on the same pop-punk tradition as Fall Out Boy but injecting it with a dose of heavy-metal riffing and gothic morbidity. It was a tour that cemented the two bands as the vanguard of a new musical movement, a sense that was only heightened when Stump shared the stage with My Chemical Romance to sit in as drummer on 'Thank You For the Venom'. Patrick was extremely nervous about the appearance as he hadn't properly played drums in around five years, so he sat backstage and played the track over and over, to the point that even My Chemical Romance singer Gerard Way had to tell him to calm down.

The Fall Out Boy machine rumbled on through the year, steadily picking up more fans, more accolades and more press. The promotion for the record had kicked off with an appearance on *Late Night with Conan O'Brien* for a performance of 'Sugar, We're Goin Down'. The band were under strict instructions not to break anything, and knew that their spontaneous, high-energy live show was not best conveyed in front of cameras in a TV studio. Other than the instructions regarding breakage the main topic of conversation was the tightness of Wentz's pants, which necessitated him performing without underwear. Apparently the risk of his manhood falling out on live TV was too much to bear for their publicist, who went into a panic backstage prior to the show.

At the MTV Video Music Awards that year the band won the MTV2 Award for 'Sugar, We're Goin Down', beating competition from My Chemical Romance and taking to the stage in a nationally broadcast show. This was definitely not 'scene' fame any more. They had well and truly infiltrated the mainstream.

'Usually if you are going to win an award they come by and make sure you are all in your seats,' Pete told *AbsolutePunk*. 'No one did that so we were pretty sure we were gonna lose, so Joe got wasted – that was pretty funny. It was intimidating because no one in the room knew who we were, but we were really proud of our fans for voting for us.' Naturally, it was Wentz that handled the speech-giving too, giving thanks whilst giving a shout-out to My Chemical Romance, who he felt should have won. In fact, My Chemical Romance had often been pitched as the rivals to Fall Out Boy over the summer of 2005, but the two bands were on good terms.

The follow-up to 'Sugar, We're Goin Down' was going to be vital in maintaining the momentum that the band had built up since the release of the album, and fortunately they had the perfect single tucked right up their sleeves. The band were glad they'd stuck with their guns and released 'Sugar' rather than 'Dance, Dance' first, representing as it did more of a soft introduction to the new material. 'Dance, Dance', with its shimmying bass line and almost-whispered verse, represented an entirely different approach for Fall Out Boy. But with the runaway success of their first single 'Sugar', they had radio in the palm of their hands.

As strong as Fall Out Boy's singles were, and would continue to be, their superb run of music videos was a huge part of their rise to prominence too. The clip for 'Dance, Dance' was directed by Alan Ferguson, the first in a long collaboration that would define the band's aesthetic. 'Dance, Dance' condenses the band's fascination with eighties movies into one original clip that seems to call to mind all of them without obviously parodying any – with the exception of *Revenge of the Nerds*, which was the inspiration for Wentz's climactic dance. It works because the band play the oversexed rock-star roles so well in the performance element, with Wentz licking the neck of his guitar and Stump making heart shapes for the camera, but they also throw themselves into their 'nerd' roles for the narrative aspect of the video without self-consciousness. Patrick shows some real acting talent as a desperately awkward guy who gets caught up in the heat of the moment and ends up flailing around the crowd wildly, and Joe plays the sleazy would-be womaniser to a tee, recalling Mike Damone from *Fast Times at Ridgemont High*.

And if the band were consciously trying to further Wentz's status as a sex symbol amongst teens, then the sight of him tenderly pinning a brooch to his date's prom dress was probably the fastest way of doing it. 'Dance, Dance'. would go on to be Fall Out Boy's second consecutive entry into the Top 10 of the Billboard Hot 100, entering at No.9, and would also see the band fulfilling Chris Gutierrez's prediction and making it to *TRL*. In fact, Wentz would even receive a plaque on the band's behalf to mark the song leaving the chart after fifty consecutive days. To date, 'Dance, Dance' has sold well in excess of two million copies.

The autumn of 2005 brought with it another high-profile headline slot, this time with Fall Out Boy heading up the Nintendo Fusion tour. Also on the bill was Motion City Soundtrack, the singer of whom had guested on *Take This To Your Grave*, and Wentz's brightest hope for Decaydance, Panic! at the Disco. Their debut album *A Fever You Can't Sweat Out* was released the day before the start of the tour, along with debut single 'The Only Difference Between Martyrdom and Suicide is Press Coverage'. They'd obviously picked up on Fall

Out Boy's penchant for wordy, sardonic song titles, and for a band who had literally graduated from high school just a few months before, it was a short sharp shove into the limelight; the sense that Fall Out Boy and their cohorts were on their way to dominating the rock scene was inescapable. All they needed to convince everyone that they were one of the biggest new bands in the world was a Grammy nomination, and sure enough, at the end of 2005 the word came through: Fall Out Boy had been nominated for best new artist at the 48th Annual Grammy Awards. They had spent the best part of three years constantly touring, writing and recording, and now they had reached the tipping point and were about to tumble into superstardom. 'No matter what we sold or whatever, it's the first time your parents don't think you are a garage band anymore,' Wentz remarked to *AbsolutePunk*.

The ceremony was held in February 2006, and saw the band ultimately lose out to John Legend. Even though they had convinced themselves they weren't going to win, nor played any of the pre-award shows to lobby for a win, losing out was still a bittersweet experience. 'No matter what, one second before the envelope is opened you go "What if" and then it didn't happen and you only feel disappointment,' Wentz explained. 'You can't win everything, but somewhere in your head you're like "When they announced our band we got a bigger applause" and you start freaking out and thinking about how you were ripped off. [...] John Legend put out a great record, our hats are off to him, but no one wants to feel like the "second best new artist".'

Stump had a similarly mixed experience, but for entirely different reasons. Hometown hero Kanye West had been nominated in the category of Best Album for *Late Registration*, but he lost out to U2's *How to Dismantle an Atomic Bomb*. It was too much for Stump to bear: he got back in his rented limo, hightailed it back to the hotel, and skipped the after-parties to sit in his room eating a Subway sandwich. Wentz had a slightly more positive experience at the Universal bash when his mum insisted that he introduce her to Sting. Wentz didn't want to, but Sting turned out to be the perfect gentleman, and even gave Wentz a little pep talk on how to handle the disappointment.

The intensive touring schedule continued right through into January 2006, when the band headed over to Europe for a headline run with Gym Class Heroes in support, and at the end of February Panic! at the Disco's profile exploded with the success of their second single, 'I Write Sins Not Tragedies', which pushed them right to the forefront of the modern rock movement. Suddenly, what the general public had dubbed 'emo', represented by the trifecta of Panic!, My Chemical Romance and Fall Out Boy, was everywhere. But the band, and Pete Wentz in particular, was about to have a very difficult week.

It started on 1 March when a post was published online by Chris Gutierrez. Gutierrez maintained a blog called 'Ask Hey Chris' which he used, amongst other things, to document Fall Out Boy's rise to fame and field questions from Fall Out Boy fans. Just a couple of months prior to the post a video had been uploaded to YouTube showing the band playing an acoustic version of 'Grenade Jumper'; the camera keeps turning to Gutierrez in the crowd, who's smiling, flipping off the camera and taking photos (ex-Racetraitor singer Mani Mostofi is also in the clip, singing the song's middle eight). But clearly something catastrophic had occurred in the friendship since then. With a first line of 'an open letter to Pete Wentz', the post accused Wentz of various indiscretions relating to Gutierrez's ex-girlfriend. 'You hug me and tell me you love me then you tell lies to my girlfriend behind my back to lure her away from me?' it read. 'You tell her I cheat on her and then you tell me to come stay on the bus? You are a spineless fucking sham.' It pulled no punches in attacking Wentz's public persona either, decrying the 'shitty glammed up poser image you present to the masses to consume' and calling him 'nothing more than a shitty opportunist business man with even shittier fashion sense'.

Within hours the post had spread like wildfire across the Internet, lighting up chat rooms and fan forums. Wentz issued and then removed his own statement in response, and these days, Gutierrez is diplomatic about the bust-up. 'I'm sure it's happened to you, to anyone that would be listening to this conversation – everybody has had fallouts with their friends,' he says. 'Everyone has had a situation where they got really pissed off at a friend 'cos they thought they were doing something wrong and disrespectful. This one just happened to be a little bit more visible, and that's the only difference. The only way that I knew how to punch back was to do this. For better or for worse, that's the route that I took, 'cos I knew he wouldn't confront me, and I knew that he had been doing some inappropriate shit. [. . .] Was it immature and was it childish? Well yeah, of course it was. But at the same time my fucking feelings were hurt. That dude was my best friend in the world.' Wentz was quick to respond, with a post uploaded to the falloutboyrock journal. 'My first instinct is to blow it off – but then I consider how anytime anything is written on the internet people believe its true – no matter what, no matter the biases or subjectivity of the sources,' he wrote. Nonetheless, he opted to take what he called the 'higher road', devoting much of the statement to expressing his commitment to the Fall Out Boy fanbase and telling Chris to call if he wanted to talk.

Since the rancor Gutierrez launched his own publishing house, DeadxStop Publishing Company, through which he has published many of his own books as well as the works of others (including, recently, a memoir by Fall Out Boy roadie Brian Diaz). Gutierrez regularly gives speaking appearances in the US and beyond, and it was on such a trip that he and Wentz reconnected for the last time. 'We hung out in Scotland – I was speaking and he was playing in Glasgow,' Gutierrez explains. 'I went up to the show and we hung out for a little bit. It was cool and it was great to see him. And we had texted and emailed over the years, but I think that was probably the last time I saw him. I haven't spoken to him in almost a year now, even through email. [...] I bear him no ill will, we're just not friends. And I don't mean that in a mean way, but a matter-of-fact way. [...] It was an important part of my life, and it's something that I view as a mostly positive thing.'

Back in 2006, things were to get worse before they got better for Wentz. On 8 March, his phone suddenly started blowing up with people asking why his penis was all over the Internet. At first he didn't believe it, but shortly after his manager called to let him know that, yeah, he should probably look into the situation. Sure enough, a collection of images originating from Pete's mobile had been leaked on the Internet, selfies taken in a bathroom mirror with his penis in his hand, and they were everywhere. By the next day, his label called to inform him that the pictures were rivalling the war in Iraq as most-searched item on *Yahoo.com*. At that point, he stopped taking calls and completely withdrew, apart from to call his manager and tell him that he didn't want to be in the band any more. Stump had to talk him back into the fold, and it was only with the support of his bandmates and his family that he was able to move on from the situation, with his mum emailing to tell him that he should be more careful but that he was handling the situation well. On the surface, Wentz has indeed handled the situation well, largely laughing it off, but Stump's account of the incident reveals the extent of the damage that it did: 'It nearly broke the band up he was so devastated,' he told *AbsolutePunk*. 'He had to claw his way back up from massive depression to even make fun of it.'

The public's fascination with celebrity sex tapes had reached fever pitch in 2004 when a tape featuring Paris Hilton had gone public. For a few years, the tabloids and glossy mags seemed to absolutely relish the leak of a new clip or set of photos, disapprovingly wagging the finger at both the victim for making the images and the general public for wanting to see them whilst splashing the news on front pages. But since the mass leak of celebrity images in 2014, along with the rise in prominence of so-called 'revenge porn', it has been acknowledged by public opinion and the law alike that stealing and leaking private material like this can have a devastating impact on an individual's life. 'I think that any time you go into someone else's private area, and you take something from that, it's theft,' Wentz would later comment to *The Guardian*. 'I don't know how you define it as far as what kind of crime it is, but it seems like there should be certain human decency that we share. You have to understand that celebrities are still human beings. You still have to treat people with the barest human decency.' The source of the leak has never been identified.

CHAPTER FOURTEEN

A LITTLE BUMP AND GRIND

Fall Out Boy wrapped up the promotion for *From Under the Cork Tree* with the release of 'A Little Less Sixteen Candles, a Little More "Touch Me"', released in June 2006 and accompanied by another high-concept Alan Ferguson video. Inspired in part by the Thai martial arts film *The Protector*, with a healthy dose of *The Lost Boys* thrown in for good measure, the clip casts the band as a group of vampire hunters, with Wentz an actual vampire who's resisting his urge to kill in order to take revenge on those that turned him. Wentz was smart enough to recognise an opportunity for promotion when he saw one, so the video features pretty much the entire stable of Decaydance acts (William Beckett of The Academy Is… puts in the best turn of the lot as the video's fey, trilby-sporting antagonist).

From March to mid-May the band were on a trek visiting nearly every corner of the US on the so-called Black Clouds and Underdogs Tour, but by the time the video for 'A Little Less

Sixteen Candles…' was doing the rounds they were already writing for the new record. Radio had come to them on *From Under the Cork Tree* and they had made a real impact on the sound of modern rock, but now they were faced with a dilemma. Would they embrace their newfound status as bona fide radio rock stars, or would they shy away from it? Wentz admitted to *Billboard* that the first instinct was the latter. 'Your natural inclination as a band or an artist is to write yourself out of this situation,' he said. 'I would compare it to someone like Brad Pitt. He's such a leading man and so good looking, but at times he takes on roles that specifically go against [expectations]. We did that at first, but then we decided to embrace it.' Stump had also experienced something of an epiphany leading up to writing the new album, when he was sitting in the Staples Centre in LA waiting to find out if his band would win the Best New Artist Grammy. Despite all of the success that they had achieved, a part of him still felt like the band was something he was going to do until he had to go and get an education, or find a real job. He still thought of himself as a drummer that was only singing in Fall Out Boy because it gave him enough leverage to be able to write the songs. It was whilst Alicia Keys and Stevie Wonder were onstage presenting an award, with Public Enemy's Chuck D sitting behind him and his lifetime hero Elvis Costello sitting just across the aisle, that Stump realised how far he had come and what auspicious company he was in. 'I remember sitting there thinking, I've got to really work at this,' he told Scuzz. '[…] This is the world of people who actually consider this a craft and take this seriously and I need to have more pride in the band as a thing.'

If *From Under the Cork Tree* had been Stump not taking things too seriously, then the next album was sure to be something special. After the success of that record the band once again decided to work with Neal Avron, who had helped steer them to a completely natural-sounding combination of their guitar-driven punk roots and Stump's versatile, expressive vocal style. Once again Avron came to Chicago to work with the band for a couple of weeks before the whole camp relocated to Los Angeles to refine things even more, both rehearsing as a band and writing. There, Avron had produced some recordings to use as a reference when in the studio. Finally, the band arrived at The Pass in Los Angeles to begin tracking.

The engineer on the sessions was Erich Talaba. Talaba had first found his way into recording after a one-time bandmate brought a four-track recorder into rehearsal. 'I realised that I had more fun doing that in my garage with my band than I did on stage,' he said. 'Mainly because I had a fear of the spotlight. You know, lots of hot lights and people looking at you, that's not my thing.' After studying at the Berklee College of Music in Boston, Massachusetts, Talaba went on to work at a studio called Sunset Sound, where his path first crossed with that of Neal Avron. 'Neal had done a lot of records there and he actually came up through there as well, and I happened to fill in for the assistant that was out sick on the Yellowcard record [*Lights and Sounds*]. I think that Neal was impressed, because the next record he asked to work with me as his assistant. We started working together and now when he has productions I engineer for him. It's been ten years now.'

Talaba describes Avron's process as highly methodical,

ensuring that the production is moving along in good time and in an organised manner so as to leave room for creative experimentation. 'It's very methodical so that you stay on course, but it also leaves room to take the chances creatively. He makes sure the songs are there – he's a really strong proponent of pre-production. And then when he gets into the studio we're focused on getting great sounds, on making sure that we capture the vibe of the song or the performance of the singer, which is crucial, and seeing what makes a song unique and how we can bring it out a little more. He's very good at what he does because he's always looking ahead, and it leaves room for us to say what's missing, what could we try, [what] might be interesting.'

Talaba was well aware of Fall Out Boy through the noise that *From Under the Cork Tree* had made and Avron's involvement with it, though that album predated their working together. The first time that he and the band met was on the first day of tracking, when the band arrived to start recording drums, and Talaba was struck by how easy the band were to get along with. 'Patrick is an extremely nice, humble guy, very talented. Joe is really funny. Andy is very focused – when he's playing, he's in the moment, and I'm sure you've seen it when he's playing shows. His approach when he's playing shows is very much the same as when he's playing in the studio, just hammering on the drums and making them sound awesome. Pete is great – he's got a more outgoing nature as I guess the social icon of the band, and he's very approachable and very friendly.'

It was also clear to Talaba that the band were conscious of wanting to make a record that would play well on radio and find a wide audience. 'I know at times Pete would throw out the idea,

"Would this fit on radio? Where would it fit?" They were definitely very conscious, I think, of making sure they had something that could go to radio, whether it was one or two songs, and that was the mentality for Neal too. I'm sure the label was vocal with Neal about having some sort of radio single, and that was in the back of the mind for Neal and the band, so we had to make sure we got them that. I think it's one thing saying, "We're sticking to our guns and doing what we wanna do", but what made them special in how they embraced the radio outpouring is that they wanted to make sure that they did something that was true to them but also appealed to other people on a broader scale.'

Tracking started on day one with Hurley's parts, and the secret to capturing a powerful drum sound is simply to use great-sounding drums, as Avron told *Sound on Sound*. 'I use a drum tech, and we had a bunch of great-sounding kits, including Andy Hurley's own set,' he said. 'We went through every song and decided which kick to use, and which toms, and which snare, and which hi-hat, and so on.' From there, the focus was simply on capturing the performance in the most natural way possible, making sure that the instrument was sounding good and the mics were placed correctly to get a great take, rather than having to rely on studio trickery to correct mistakes further down the line. After drums, the next stop was the rhythm and bass guitars, with a great range of both amplifiers and guitars to choose from. 'I think maybe we used one or two amps from their touring set-ups, but a lot of it we bought in,' Talaba remembers. 'We had a lot of different amps just to have the options. I think we used Joe or Patrick's Uberschall, which is a Bognor [amplifier], and we used some of Neal's own amps.

We used a lot of the band's guitars, too; Patrick had a lot of vintage guitars that he brought in.'

Finding a great guitar tone was a big part of the process for Avron, Stump and Trohman, cycling through different combinations of guitars, amplifier heads and cabinets to get the right sound for each of the songs. 'I always love getting guitar tones, because for rock records that is the thing, aside from drums,' says Talaba. 'Nothing against the bass player, but unless it's a featured bass song, that's there to enhance the sound of the guitars in terms of the heaviness. You're getting a lot of the vibe from the guitars. I love turning around and seeing seven or eight amps and ten guitars and thinking, "Where do I start?" We would tend to talk about it, say, "This is the type of guitar track we're doing, so maybe we need a [Gibson] Les Paul and a heavier amp like a Marshall, or maybe we use a Vox 'cos we have another heavier guitar track on there."'

Avron was keen to get recording Patrick's vocals as soon as possible, at the earliest point that Stump had enough music to perform along to. Beginning to get vocals laid down in good time allowed Stump to get a sense of what was working and what wasn't, and if a great take just so happened to be captured, then all the better. Once vocals were laid down, additional guitars or synths could be worked out to put the finishing touches to the track. Patrick and Joe did not have set responsibilities – sometimes Patrick would take rhythm guitar duties and Joe would add lead lines in later, or vice versa.

Wentz and Patrick's collaborative approach to lyrics and vocals appeared to work very well in the studio, according to Talaba. 'When they're in the studio Patrick will get Pete's lyrics and he'll either have a melody and work the lyrics to it, or he'll work a new melody into the lyrics,' he explains. 'Pete gives him a lot of lyrics, and Patrick sifts through stuff and picks moments. If Pete hears something and says, "This doesn't make sense" or has a suggestion, they'll rework it. It's definitely a collaborative effort and it comes from them trusting one another. Pete knows that Patrick's gonna sing a great melody, and Patrick knows that Pete's gonna give him some great lyrical content to work from. It's just a matter of making sure they're both happy and the lyrics get across the point of what was originally recorded.'

Lyrically, Wentz also felt like he was reaching a new level of maturity in his writing. 'I feel like our first record was like, "Oh heartbreak, you did this to me, I wanna watch you burn alive,"' he told MTV. 'And then the next one was kind of like, "I'm going crazy, I don't know what's happening right now, change my medication." And this one's kind of like, "Medication's alright, the girl's alright."' Wentz was even offering something for more intimate moments on the record: as he put it, 'There's a couple love songs on there. Ain't nothing wrong with a little bump and grind.'

Avron was not the only producer who worked on the album. In a surprising report from November 2005, Wentz told MTV that he was hoping to enlist Kenneth 'Babyface' Edmonds to work on the new Fall Out Boy record, a statement which initially perplexed those who heard it. Babyface had scored a string of high-profile hits throughout the eighties and nineties as the songwriter and producer behind high-profile pop groups. His lush multi-layered arrangements and smooth vocal production had gifted success to everyone from Boyz II Men ('End of the

Road' and 'I'll Make Love to You') and Whitney Houston ('I'm Your Baby Tonight') to Madonna ('Take a Bow'). But he wasn't exactly known for working with rock bands. Pete and Patrick had watched the 2001 remake of *Josie and the Pussycats*, a live-action version of a seventies cartoon about an all-girl rock band who are first absorbed by and then fight against the evils of the pre-packaged pop music industry. The songs that the band perform in the film were produced by Babyface, and the combination of boisterous guitars and pop vocal harmonies had convinced Fall Out Boy that Babyface had something to offer to rock music. And the experience of recording with Babyface turned out to be a revelation for unexpected reasons: he favoured late starts and long nights, an arrangement which suited the night owls in the band.

Overall, Talaba's memories of the session were of its ease. He struggles to recall any particular sticking points, and praises the professionalism and capabilities of the band. 'They're all incredibly talented,' he says. 'Andy nailed the drums, it was very smooth and seamless, and Patrick is an incredible talent – he comes up with some great ideas and because he's so strong with a few different instruments, it allows us to get through a lot of stuff and work on different sounds. And when Joe comes in to do his guitar stuff, it gives him time to explore and trial out different ideas, or Joe would go home and work on different ideas so we could work on them or modify them. So they all do their homework.'

Talaba stops short of saying that he knew the band had a hit on their hands – is it ever possible to predict what will or won't catch the public's attention at a given time? – but he closed up the recording process feeling that they had a strong album in the can. 'I thought there were some great songs on there that I still really love, and I thought they had a really strong record,' he says. 'I personally was extremely proud to work on it and work with those guys. Their standards were so high, you just had to make sure you maintained that.'

CHAPTER FIFTEEN

FROM HERE TO INFINITY

As the autumn of 2006 rolled around the band put the finishing touches to the new record, and gave fans their first taste of it by leaking one of their own tracks to *AbsolutePunk*. Island confirmed the track would feature on the record whilst denying any knowledge of the leak, and the track, entitled 'Carpal Tunnel of Love', became a minor hit for the band when finally made available on iTunes – despite not being an official single release. When it comes to the game of promotion, Fall Out Boy were turning into Grand Masters. The new album had been announced as *Infinity On High*, and anticipation was at fever pitch.

'The Carpal Tunnel of Love' was a comforting taste of the Fall Out Boy that fans had come to know and love, pivoting between the tension of a highly-strung verse and an undeniably pretty chorus, with Stump's commanding vocal leading from the front. But the first official single from the album was about to test fan loyalty. 'This Ain't a Scene, It's an Arms Race' had a suitable head scratcher of a title, but it slithers in on a serpentine guitar line and a processed drum beat, with Stump flexing his vocal abilities shamelessly – embellishing phrases, layering falsetto harmonies and diving down into the depths of his range before pouncing back up. It's funky and sexed up, a million miles from the heartbroken confessions of *Take This To Your Grave*, even with the big rock chorus that rides a wave of distorted guitars while Hurley delivers his typically pounding, metronomic backing. It certainly represented something of a challenge to the audience; this was Fall Out Boy growing and developing, and they would have to rise to the occasion. But it was selected as a first single because it had the right message. It's a song that criticises, as Stump explained to Al D TV, 'fast food music', music that you can digest easily and purge in a day. But it cleverly borrows the tropes of disposable pop whilst parodying it, like the gang-chanted final breakdown, accompanied by oh-so-organic handclaps inspired by Justin Timberlake's 'Señorita'.

If listeners weren't getting the message from the words alone, then the music video offered the perfect accompaniment. Once again directed by Alan Ferguson, it's one of the best rock videos of the twenty-first century, skewering the artifice of the fame and glamour-obsessed music industry. It opens where the 'Dance, Dance' video closes, but we see just outside the frame of the video the cameras and lights mocking up this cute suburban love story for our enjoyment. We bought the lie of the Fall Out Boys next door, and Pete is exiting in a Lamborghini he purchased with the proceeds of the sale. Next we see them in the studio with a 'hip-hop super producer', but they aren't welcome and are duly 'kicked out of the hood' with nothing but bloody noses to show for it. Elsewhere there's plenty of retreading of music video cliché, from raucous hotel after-parties to funeral fantasies, the latter of which is attended by the cast of Fall Out Boy's old videos. Pete even finds the chutzpah to make light of his own exposé on the Internet, telling *Billboard*: 'If I don't address these things and have fun with them, then I don't know the point of being in this band.' However, the whole overblown affair is shown to be nothing more than the daydream of a sleeping Wentz, years before Fall Out Boy blew up, who awakes and accompanies his band to play a spirited gig in a decidedly unglamorous community hall-type venue. The message is pretty clear. All the trappings of fame and global success are little more than gaudy distractions from the music, and whatever life you thought Fall out Boy were living, they were still just four boys in a band. That it manages to say so whilst producing a highly entertaining clip is a credit to Ferguson.

If 'This Ain't a Scene, It's an Arms Race' was a gamble, then it was one that paid off in spectacular fashion. It sold well in excess of a hundred thousand copies in the first week of its release in the US alone, debuted at No.2 on the Billboard 100 and made *Infinity On High*, arguably the most anticipated album release in the world. Scheduled for release in February 2007, the band got a jump on performing the new material on a headline tour that began in January. Some of the bands that Fall Out Boy had modelled themselves on were this time out on the road in support of them, like pop-punk pioneers New Found Glory and the newly reformed Lifetime, who had been a gateway band for Wentz's discovery of more melodic punk rock, as well as a major influence for Stump.

There might have been a sense of a baton being passed between New Found Glory and Fall Out Boy, but Wentz was insightful when asked about having to have such an important band in their own development play beneath them. 'That band has written a lot of hits, if you ask me,' he said to *Billboard*, 'but when you kick the door in, people sometimes trample over you. New Found Glory kicked the door in for us.' As for Lifetime, since getting back together in 2005 for some marquee shows at Hellfest (which ended up being cancelled), the band had signed on to Wentz's own Decaydance label to release new material. The result was the album *Lifetime*, released on 6 February 2007 and warmly received as a fitting return to action for the band. Decaydance was not just setting the agenda for the modern incarnation of emo, it was giving a platform to its forefathers, too.

Infinity On High was also released on 6 February, and it couldn't have been a more different proposition. That much was clear from the opening moments, when Jay Z's voice emerges out of the speakers as the band's own personal master of ceremonies, dedicating the album to all of the fans who had stuck by the band through the hard times. The opening song is called 'Thriller', for the love of God – they were naming songs after the most successful album of all time, and any coyness that the band had ever had about their own potential had clearly fallen by the wayside. Wentz had first met Jay Z at the Nobu restaurant as Fall Out Boy were in the process of promoting *From Under the Cork Tree*, and Stump had later been invited to head into Jay Z's studio to work with him on a track for the album *Kingdom Come*. He arrived to find some of hip-hop's most celebrated beat makers and producers in attendance, like Timbaland and Swizz Beatz, as well as the undisputed queen of modern pop, Beyoncé. Fairly understandably, Stump froze up, and the incident would inspire the 'kicked out of the hood' scene of the 'Arms Race' video. 'It's so important to begin strong, and I don't think you can start much stronger than this,' Wentz said to MTV about the collaboration. '[...] We called him up and thought we were gonna talk to his assistant. Then he answers the phone, like, "Yo, this is Hov," and we were like, "Um ..." It just happened like that. And it was pretty crazy.' There's nothing remotely hip-hop about the riff that rips through the song after Jay Z's announcement, however. It's a chugging, hardcore-inspired riff that was in fact borrowed in part from an old Racetraitor riff. 'They had a part like that,' Trohman would later explain to *Ultimate Guitar*. 'Patrick told Andy that we should use that, so he did kind of a bastardised version of it. You could kind of say that Andy wrote the part originally, in this weird way.'

Despite the bombastic intro, the song is classic Fall Out Boy fare and a safe but effective choice of opener that serves to gently ease in the album, though there are a couple of tongue-in-cheek real-world references to keep listeners on their toes. The line 'Make us poster boys for your scene / But we are not making an acceptance speech' lets on that the band, or Wentz at least, wasn't yet completely over not winning that Grammy. Similarly, 'every dot com's refreshing for a journal update' acknowledges that the band had become a favourite of bloggers and online gossipmongers everywhere, not least because Wentz was always ready and willing to provide a witty sound bite on scandals big and small.

One particularly ridiculous beef had flared up between Fall Out Boy and Brandon Flowers, singer of Las Vegas indie rockers The Killers, in 2006. It all started when Flowers made a remark to the *NME* about Fall Out Boy's shared A&R man, Rob Stevenson. Stevenson had previously signed The Bravery, about whom Flowers had spoken of less than flatteringly. He then remarked of Stevenson: 'Now he's just signed Fall Out Boy, which means more of his attention will go to them that should have gone to The Killers.' Wentz issued a couple of responses through *FueledbyRamen.com*, some veiled and some not so veiled, before charitably remarking to MTV that 'I think both Brandon and I are alike because we both use too much hair product and run our mouths way more than our bands like.' 'Thriller' seems to be his last word on the spat, and there's no obvious shade directed at Flowers therein, though an earlier title was reported to have been 'You Can't Spell "Star" Without "A&R"'.

'"The Take Over, the Break's Over"' shimmies in on a riff that begs the foot to tap, and it's the first clear signal of the band's new and more radio-ready direction. The riff was directly influenced by David Bowie and more specifically the song 'Rebel Rebel', which is driven by a simple, powerful two-bar glittering glam-rock stomp of a riff. Lyrically, it's another song that addresses the pressures of life in the public eye, something that Wentz had clearly been wrangling with over the previous two years, but the real star of this show is Stump's open-hearted middle eight: 'We do it in the dark with smiles on our faces,' he sings triumphantly, and it feels like an acknowledgement that life occurs behind the curtain, not in front of the camera lens. The end of the middle eight goes against type for the band and features a guitar solo, contributed by not one but two players – New Found Glory's Chad Gilbert, in his second appearance on a Fall Out Boy album, and (now-ex) Panic! at The Disco's Ryan Ross.

After 'This Ain't a Scene' comes the first result of the album's collaboration with Babyface, entitled 'I'm Like a Lawyer With the Way I'm Always Trying to Get You Off (Me & You)', and it's a true highlight, the most plainly beautiful song that the band had ever written. The verse is anchored by a stomping groove whilst a delicate, funk-inflected guitar line dances around the beat as Stump sings of a troubled relationship with Wentz's typical mix of humour and self-reproach. But as the song accelerates into the chorus, it's as if the clouds of cynicism part: 'Me and you, setting in a honeymoon / If I woke up next to you'; they feel like words sung without dual meaning or darker undertones. They're just a simple, lovelorn account of waking up next to someone you love and feeling grateful for it, and in combination with Stump's down-home melody, it works wonderfully. Fall Out Boy had proven time and again that they were capable of writing catchy, sharp-tongued pop-punk hits, but they'd never really ventured into writing something genuinely sweet and simple. Here, they pull it off, and then some.

'Hum Hallelujah' feels, by contrast, like a more flyaway account of teenage romance, and Stump has never sounded as much like a heartthrob as when he sings 'I thought I loved you / it was just how you looked in the light'. But there's more being said here. The song not only borrows the title of the song playing when Wentz overdosed in a Best Buy parking lot, but actually incorporates a part of its melody in the breakdown. It seems to be inviting us to think about that episode, especially as it's littered with references to pills, car parks and death. It's as if Wentz is actually speaking to the depressive part of his nature and acknowledging that there's a certain lure in romantic sadness. He's previously admitted a fascination with music's tragic heroes, like Cobain, Curtis et al. But if it is a love song written by a man and addressed to his demons, then you can't escape the fact that if you 'sing the blues' you 'swallow them too' – and that can be very dangerous.

It feels as if the downbeat heart of 'Hum Hallelujah' bleeds into the next track, 'Golden', which makes its way into the album by way of some plaintive piano chords. There are no riffs, no bouncy-muted chord progressions or booming drumming – it's just a piano and Stump's voice, and it is so simple and short as to almost feel like a song fragment. It's a mark of the band's confidence, and Stump's skills a songwriter, that they can strip a song so bare and still make it one of the most striking moments on a record, and even if *Infinity On High* is their bid for radio-rock superstardom, then they are by no means holding back some of their darker, more introspective tendencies.

The second collaboration with Babyface is 'Thnks fr th Mmrs', a title that uses the abbreviated language of text speak as a double entendre – this is a break-up, but it's only worth a text message. The opening blast of horns accompanied by a swell of shimmering strings sounds more like a Hollywood soundtrack than a Fall Out Boy song, but the vocal arrangement has Babyface written all over it, with Stump's voice layered into a cooing chorus that darts between octaves. When the song was demoed it sounded very little like the highly detailed recording that appears here, something which Wentz attributes almost entirely to Babyface's input; it's the kind of song which has immediate thrills but also rewards repeated listens, with each play revealing a new flourish. What's most remarkable about 'Thnks fr th Mmrs' is that for all of the arrangement, for all the vocal harmonies and strings and brass and the mandolin that appears in the breakdown, it never feels like the band are overreaching. It's proof that they could expand the horizons of their sound, incorporate new textures and different shades of feeling, and still write highly effective songs with a catchy chorus that convey a story in under four minutes. 'Thnks fr th Mmrs' is the first glimpse of the band Fall Out Boy would become, and it's thrilling.

'Don't You Know Who I Think I Am?' is every bit the Fall Out Boy of *From Under the Cork Tree*, right down to its tightly-bound in-joke of a title, but 'The (After) Life of the Party' once again sees the band heading into unfamiliar territory. Opening with staccato synthesised strings and a harmonised guitar part, it seems to float in on a cloud of loved-up serenity rather than the break-up anguish that the songs usually peddled, and the chorus of 'Cut it loose / Watch you work the room' practically aches with yearning. With all of these un-ironic romantic references creeping into the album, you could be forgiven for assuming that Wentz was falling in love.

Infinity On High's closing tracks shift tone somewhat, backgrounding the band's more on-the-nose pop-punk tendencies and foregrounding other influences that are most often attributed to Patrick Stump – R&B, new wave and soft rock. 'Bang the Doldrums', coming after previously released 'The Carpal Tunnel of Love', comes in on a bouncing riff but moves from an off-kilter verse into a harmonically shifting chorus that shows off Stump's abilities as a technical songwriter. On the one hand we're given big, easily digestibly hooks, like the refrain of 'whoah-oh-ohs' that accompany the main riff, but on the other we're given a baroque chorus that refuses to settle definitively in one key. The way the harmonic ground shifts under our feet mirrors the wordplay too: 'best friends, ex-friends to the end, better off as lovers and not the other way round'. This is clever songwriting, matching form and content but still delivering on those big melodic payoffs when it matters.

'Fame < Infamy', by contrast, sounds as if Stump had been taking a leaf from Wentz's protégés Panic! at the Disco. Making a bid for dominance over the dance floor, the chorus is driven by a fidgety off-beat groove that's the perfect tempo to get punk kids moving. Wentz delivers some cracking lyrics here too, particularly the repeated insistence of 'I'm alright in bed but I'm better with a pen'. This is the essence of his mid-period writing, mixing self-deprecation and boastfulness, sex and wit, simultaneously self-obsessed and self-aware.

Lyrically *Infinity On High* is an inward-looking album, inviting us into Wentz's psyche as he picks apart Fall Out Boy's success and the effect it's had on him. But he had not stopped taking an interest in the real-world issues that had been the driving force for many bands in the hardcore scene. 'You're Crashing But You're No Wave' was initially titled 'Law and Order' and is inspired in part by the story of Fred Hampton Jr. Hampton Jr. is a civil rights activist, a Chicagoan and the son of a Black Panther member who was convicted of arson in the wake of the 1992 LA Riots. Hampton had also been the president of the International People's Democratic Uhuru Movement, which had been a significant influence on the ideology of Racetraitor. For Mani Mostofi, songs like this show that even as Wentz was becoming a fixture of celebrity culture, he had not become blind to important issues.

'Pete was always a guy that was absorbing all that stuff,' he says. 'Racetraitor were working on things like the imprisonment of Mumia Abu-Jamal, those were the issues for us. This is down in the dirt, radical politics, but Pete still includes that messaging in the things that they do. Even though ninety per cent of the songs are about what's going on in Pete's brain on a very personal level, whether it's girls or dealing with fame or whatever, he still finds these moments to bring it up. And their genre in particular, these bubble gum, mascara-wearing bands, none of them are thinking about that shit. None of them. It's not part of their thing. But Pete comes from a place where that stuff's important, and it carries through. I think that's really honourable.'

But it's the album's final song that is perhaps its most surprising. 'I've Got All This Ringing in My Ears and None on My Fingers' stomps along on a piano-rock groove while some triumphant brass spits out an ascending melody fit for a *Rocky* training montage. Stump barks and snarls his way through the verses before setting controls for the heart of the sun on the soaring chorus, and then a cartoonish guitar melody brings in the second verse. This is pure David Bowie-T. Rex glam, but born in the cornfields of heartland America, and it sounds for all the world like Stump finding his voice as a writer. It was a glimpse into the future of Fall Out Boy.

The album did well critically, with reviewers noting how the band could not only pack an album with undeniable hooks and finely tuned pop hits, but also experiment with other styles and still come off sounding like Fall Out Boy. *Entertainment Weekly* declared that 'lo and behold, it turns out these pasty emo boys are a pretty great blue-eyed soul band'; and *Spin* said that the band had 'grown so confident with success that the members are willing to give in to their every musical whim'. But it was *Rolling Stone* who accurately summed up what had been, and remained, their most defining characteristic, the thing which invited both obsessive fandom and obsessive hate. It was the magical friction between Stump's sweet-as-apple-pie voice and Wentz's bitter lyrical observations. 'Singer-guitarist Patrick Stump's gee-whiz earnest voice strains with the strip-mall soul of classic Eighties car-radio voices like John Waite or Night Ranger's Jack Blades,' wrote reviewer Rob Sheffield. 'But that voice wouldn't mean a thing without bassist-lyricist Pete Wentz's tortured egomaniac confessions.'

In fact, it was getting harder to distinguish between Fall Out Boy's fans and those that were simply voyeurs, getting their kicks by peeping at Wentz's private life, something which his tendency to overshare but under-explain in his lyrics was encouraging. Though his words were being sung by another man, everyone knew that Wentz was the band's lyricist, and in littering the songs with references to romantic entanglements and complicated sex, he only stoked the frenzied appetite of the press to know who he was dating and where they were hanging out. In true rock-star style, he'd been linked in the past with Hollywood starlets like Michelle Trachtenberg and Lindsay Lohan, and a *Rolling Stone* article published just after the release of the album would devote a good deal of its word count to discussing his relationship with a twenty-year-old hairdresser from Chicago called Jeanae. Whether he desired it or not – and you get the impression it was a combination of both – he was a fixture of gossip magazines, tabloids and scandalous blog posts, and all of this conspired to make *Infinity On High* the year's most high-profile new album. The album flew off shelves upon its release, going straight to No.1 on the Billboard 200 and selling over a quarter of a million copies in the US in its first week. The album was also the major breakthrough for the band overseas, and to date has been registered platinum in the USA, Canada, the United Kingdom, Australia, Ireland and other countries.

In that moment, in 2007, Fall Out Boy were the biggest band in the world. But the media's gaze wasn't really fixed on Fall Out Boy: it was glaring at Pete Wentz.

CHAPTER SIXTEEN

SEVEN CONTINENTS

Patrick Stump liked the fact that Wentz drew attention away from him. He had no desire to be a 'rock star' anyway; as he'd said countless times before, he was only singing in the band because Wentz encouraged him into it, and it gave him a pass to write songs. He seemed to be dealing with the fame with remarkable level-headedness. 'You wake up every morning, brush your teeth, look in the mirror and you are still the same person,' he told *The Aquarian Weekly*. 'There is no amount of attention from people that can change that. Secondly, you don't see it. You are out there playing shows and you're removed from seeing it in front of you. When we played to one hundred people, it's the same experience, day-to-day, as it is playing to ten thousand people.'

Stump is the band's creative labourer; he was the one meticulously constructing the songs, and he prized the idea of music as a craft that could be honed through study and application. His grandfather, who had worked on cars, had been a major influence on his approach to making music. Stump watched the way he would carefully repair and maintain the vehicles and noticed that he didn't seem interested in the money he would make from selling them. The final sale wasn't the reward. The work itself was the reward, and making sure that everything was done right was worthwhile in and of itself. It was a work ethic that Stump had adopted and prized over any of the obvious measures of success, like album sales and gold discs. So, in his own quiet way, Stump had set about honing the craft of making music away from Fall Out Boy. He'd previously produced Gym Class Heroes' album *As Cruel as School Children*, which featured the worldwide hit 'Cupid's Chokehold', on which he also features as a vocalist. Whilst *Infinity On High* was being made Stump was also producing a record for The Hush Sound, another Chicago band who had been signed to Decaydance. ('With The Hush Sound, I've always wanted to work with a band that had a girl in it because I feel like this scene is a giant boys' club,' Wentz explained to *AbsolutePunk* on signing the band. '[Lead singer] Greta was perfect. On top of that, they didn't sound like any other band around to me.') Later in 2007 he would return to the studio to produce *¡Viva la Cobra!*, the second studio album by dance-rock band Cobra Starship, and also produce a track for Lupe Fiasco, a Chicagoan rapper.

At the same time Fall Out Boy were making all of the right moves to make good on the hype they'd received. They launched *Infinity On High* by playing three shows in one day; they started at NY's TRL studios in front of a pack of screaming fans, continued at Chicago's House of Blues with a show that included a guest appearance from William Beckett of The Academy Is…, and wrapped up on the rooftop of downtown LA's Pacific Stock Exchange. The promotional cycle suffered a minor setback when the band's headline slot on the Honda Civic Tour, due to start in early April, had to be postponed due to 'health issues'; the rumour mill naturally fired up, forcing Wentz to state that, no, the band wasn't about to break up, and no, none of the band had been admitted to rehab. He was also quick to add that while bloggers and Internet commentators everywhere might assume every hiccup was directly linked to him, this one in fact was not. The band had already toured the US once in 2007, and had just got back from a stint in Australia, the Far East and Europe. Exhaustion was taking its toll. But the Wentz-related chatter was fixated on something else: his new love interest.

Wentz had first mentioned Ashlee Simpson to the press a full year before *Infinity On High* was released – in 2006, admitting to *Rolling Stone* that he had a crush on her. Ashlee is the sister of Jessica Simpson, who had become a reality TV star in the mid 2000s through an MTV show called *Newlyweds: Nick and Jessica*. The show portrayed the marriage of Jessica and Nick Lachey, both of whom were pop stars, and also launched Ashlee, who would ultimately star in her own MTV show, into the spotlight. A pop career followed and her 2004 debut album reached No.1 on the Billboard 200. After the *Rolling Stone* piece ran, Wentz and Simpson would run into one another at a party and feel drawn together, even though both were in relationships at the time. Pete and Ashlee stayed in regular contact all the same, and since 2006 photos of the pair hanging out in LA, where Wentz was now based, were cropping up online and in magazines. But Wentz was adamant, at least at first, that the two were just friends. It wasn't until later that he would admit they had started dating in 2006, explaining to *Chicago* magazine: 'There was a definite six months where it was like, "Are we, are we not?" because we were friends beforehand.' In fact, Wentz would later reveal much more about the circumstances surrounding the pair hooking up, under pressure from shock jock/interrogator extraordinaire Howard Stern. The details included, but were not limited to, how Wentz used to masturbate over Ashlee's cover shoot for *Blender* magazine, and that the pair's first night together in the Soho Grand was 'the single greatest sexual encounter' of Wentz's life. Back in the innocent days of 2006, photos of the pair together were enough to get tongues wagging, and the Pete Wentz media circus rumbled on.

Wentz was using his celebrity to highlight important causes as well, though. Before heading out on the Honda Civic Tour he slept on the streets of southern California, along with 67,000 other people across the US, for Invisible Children. The charity was highlighting the refugee crisis in Uganda, which had displaced legions of young people fleeing violence in the north of the country. At the time Wentz was further expanding his empire with the opening of a bar and nightclub in New York called Angels & Kings, but he still committed to taking a trip out to Uganda to help raise awareness of Africa's longest running war. 'People went and slept out in a little cardboard city,' he told MTV. 'You could only bring one pack of crackers and a bottle of water. [...] I don't feel like we got anywhere near what it's actually like, but it was an attempt at empathy. So we got the shots [necessary to travel to] Africa, and we're going to go to Uganda in July.'

If the period from *Take This To Your Grave* to *Infinity On High* can be classed as the first incarnation of Fall Out Boy's career, the following months would be its high watermark. On the Honda Civic Tour they played to the largest crowds of their career to date, and with Decaydance acts The Academy Is… and Cobra Starship in support, there was no question that they were calling the shots when it came to the scene's direction and sound. The tour included three consecutive sold-out nights at the Charter One Pavilion in Chicago (now the FirstMerit Bank Pavilion), an outdoor amphitheatre with a capacity of, at the time, close to ten thousand. It was a lap of victory for the band, only slightly marred when Wentz reportedly got into an altercation with a heckler at an acoustic club show after the main gig on 27 June.

The run was bookended by the release of two singles, and the first came with another doozy of a promo from Alan Ferguson. Fall Out Boy had always known how to take the piss out of themselves, but even by their standards, the video for 'Thnks fr th Mmrs' is out there; it features such surreal images as Stump struggling to gain the upper hand over an orang-utan in a game of chess and Wentz being fitted for a pair of designer jeans by a chimp, as the band film a music video staffed entirely by a crew of primates. Wentz even nearly – very nearly – steals a kiss off Kim Kardashian before the fedora-wearing director (dubbed 'Alan Furryson') takes over and demonstrates how to do it monkey-style. The single reached No.11 on the Billboard Hot 100 and the video was a huge success for the band, in near constant rotation on satellite music channels in the weeks after its release. And by the time the boys were coming off the tour they had also released the '"The Take Over, The Breaks Over"' video too. We'd seen videos taking place in Pete's mind before, but the one for '"The Take Over..."' is enacted in the mind of his real-life dog Hemingway, who takes the opportunity to stand up for the band against the detractors pelting them with vegetables and accusing them of selling out – man's best friend indeed. The single was a more modest success than its predecessor, but nonetheless ensured the band were a constant presence on the radio.

Whilst on the Honda Civic Tour they had made preparations to put on the biggest show they'd ever taken on the road. This was no sweaty basement gig; this was going to be a full-blown rock show, complete with all the bells and whistles a modern-day arena act could be expected to bring along. The challenges of putting on such a big entertainment had not passed the band by, but Wentz was determined to make an impression. 'I'm usually not very OCD about a lot of things that go on with our band, but with mapping out this show, I was,' he told MTV. 'I think there's a lot of directions we could've gone in and we decided to go in the direction of the biggest "rock" show we could do.' Stump, on the other hand, was practically anticipating a certain level of calamity. 'There's so many things going on with this show and so much could go wrong – it is a Fall Out Boy show, after all,' he said. 'But if even two of these things go right on any night, it'll be a really entertaining show.'

The biggest rock show they could do turned out to be quite a lavish affair. The band recorded the Phoenix leg of the run for a CD and DVD release, and it shows just how far the band had come from their early days jumping in vans to play club shows and school halls across the country. After an animated intro that saw the band portrayed as targets in a shooting gallery – with Wentz, mocked up in devilish horns, the main target – the musicians were literally shot out of the floor like vampires popping up for a nightly feed. And things pretty much continued in that same raucous, ridiculous tone. Giant 'FOB' letters flash red over the stage while Wentz and Trohman whirl, wriggle and head-bang their way through the set below. Trohman stomps along the stage with his mouth open in ecstatic appreciation of his licks, his loose curls bouncing back and forth in time. (His signature 360-degree jumping spin had even earned its own name amongst fans: the Trohmania.) Wentz cuts a somewhat more distant figure with his hood up as if to deflect attention, but he nonetheless carries the segues between songs with his easygoing chatter. Stump and Hurley, meanwhile, hold down the fort musically. Stump's voice is every bit as flexible and characterful live as on record, but clad head to toe in black and with his hat pulled low over his eyes, he seems happy to be the musical rather than visual anchor.

There are flames spitting out into the vast black space above the stage, a full-blown drum solo, a section where Wentz and Trohman appear in the midst of the audience to play a song, and a strange moment where Wentz inexplicably gets changed onstage, though the deafening screams of girls in the crowd may be all the explanation that's required. It's fast, furious and undeniably fun, but there was something of a sense that they were caught between the band they used to be and something else. They hadn't yet fully embraced the lavish pomp of a full-blown pop sound, and in customary finale 'Saturday', when

Wentz screams his vocals down the mic from his knees whilst reaching out to grab the crowd, it felt like the band hadn't fully managed to jump the gap from homegrown punk heroes to arena rock conquerors. But there would be a time for that.

Confidence was not in short supply, however, and the set also included a cover of Michael Jackson's 'Beat It'. Stump had started messing around with the main riff in rehearsal one day, and it had snowballed into a full-band cover that eventually started sneaking its way into sets. The band decided to record it in a studio and put it out with the DVD for a little bit of added value, but much to their surprise, it took off on iTunes after its release. Before they knew it, it was all over radio and they were recording an accompanying video, though Wentz made sure to tell MTV that he would rather have been at home eating honeydew melon than recording yet another promo. While the video is a loving homage to Jackson that borders on parody, with Stump looking oddly comfortable crotch thrusting in leather pants, the cover itself has no trouble making the Michael Jackson classic the band's own. The original famously featured a guitar solo from Van Halen virtuoso Eddie, whose playing was reportedly so good it caused a monitor to spontaneously combust in the studio, so Fall Out Boy needed a contemporary player to give them a red-hot lead for their version. There wasn't exactly a wealth of gifted young guitarists who were also bona fide stars to choose from, but Wentz eventually managed to get John Mayer to lay down the solo, who took a grand total of five minutes to record the part after agreeing to do it over email.

In the summer of 2007 the band left the US and played headline shows at dates all over the world, including Japan,

Russia and Mexico, before a headline run of European festivals from Pukkelpop in Belgium to Reading and Leeds. Trohman was particularly keen on the European dates as they were often sharing a bill with Dinosaur Jr., and he got to watch J Mascis every night. Pete, meanwhile, cemented Decaydance's reputation as tastemakers for the scene with a Decaydance mini-festival, held at L'Olympia in Paris and at the Hammersmith in London on consecutive nights. Fall Out Boy headed up a bill that also included Cobra Starship, Panic! at the Disco, The Academy Is..., Gym Class Heroes and Plain White T's. As if to signal just how big of an impression the movement had made on the mainstream, the UK's *Sun* tabloid was even in attendance to try and interpret the Decaydance phenomenon for its readers. 'To outsiders, this scene may seem unfathomable if not exactly an arms race,' it offered. 'But the popularity of emo, Decaydance – or whatever label you want to give it – is clearly going from strength to strength.'

June 2007 was also the month of Wentz's twenty-eighth birthday, an occasion that was cause for extra celebration for all the wrong reasons. For the previous year of his life he had been, as he explained to *The Guardian*, '...toxic, just completely over-medicated: I was stoked to make it past twenty-seven,' he said. 'Everyone was really worried. My management company were panicked, because I was out of the office, and "pharmaceutically engaged".' His manager called him up on his twenty-eighth birthday and congratulated him on reaching the milestone, presumably for surviving the so-called 'twenty-seven club', twenty-seven being the tragically young age at which many famous musicians have died. In a 2015 interview with Howard

Stern, Wentz would elaborate further about his use of prescription medications. 'I think I have a strange brain chemistry and I think we are the pill generation, we are so prescribed,' he said. 'I would play drugstore cowboy, [think] I'm gonna dabble with a little bit of this, a little bit of that, and that's when it gets all wacky. It was mostly anxiety, like hardcore anxiety.'

The year ended with an American tour with Gym Class Heroes, Plain White T's and Cute Is What We Aim For, named the 'Young Wild Things Tour' in reference to Maurice Sendak's legendary children's books *Where the Wild Things Are*, and included set design inspired by the book. Wentz was a longtime fan of the book, and for him it encapsulated a lot of the coming-of-age themes that Fall Out Boy also addressed in their songs. Whilst on the trek the band released their final promotional single from *Infinity On High*, 'I'm Like a Lawyer...' which featured a beautiful video chronicling the trip to Uganda that the band had made in July. The video was released in association with Invisible Children and features a narrative about a boy taken from his home and forced to become a child soldier before escaping and returning to his village. It's easy to think of Fall Out Boy as a band obsessed with tongue-in-cheek references to themselves and their legacy, which is in part what makes the sad but beautiful video for 'I'm Like a Lawyer...' so disarming.

2008 started quietly for the band, but that doesn't mean they were sitting on their hands. In fact they were planning an audacious tour that would see them take their place in *The Guinness Book of World Records*. The plan was to play a gig in the gymnasium of a research facility in Antarctica, thereby becoming the only band to play on all seven continents in the span of nine months. They had already played Africa, Europe, Asia, Australia and North America in 2007; they were scheduled to play in Chile in March, thereby ticking off South America too. But a conversation between manager Bob McLynn and Wentz brought up the idea of making it seven for seven. Fortunately, Chile was also in possession of a research facility on the Fildes Peninsula of King George Island in Antarctica called Base Presidente Eduardo Frei Montalva, so following the show in Santiago they made arrangements to hop on a flight and play there too. And as is appropriate given the globe-hopping nature of the feat, the show would also be attended by scientists from nearby Russian, Chinese and Czech facilities, though the audience would still be about ten thousand people shy of the number Fall Out Boy had grown accustomed to playing to.

But some ambitions are too extravagant for even Pete Wentz to realise. Weather on the island had worsened considerably since the band arrived in Chile, and as each day ticked by it became less and less likely that they would be able to get flight clearance to land. A round-table was held to discuss other possibilities to get the attempt moving again. Could they charter a boat for the two-day sail? Could they simply play an acoustic set on a boat from within the boundary of the Antarctic Circle? Could the flight crew be convinced to fly in poor conditions? To make matters worse, the hysteria for Fall Out Boy's presence in the city had reached Beatlemania-like proportions, and the band were all but being held hostage in their hotel by a four hundred strong mob of fans camped outside.

Finally, on the final night they were able to stay in order to jump on the south-bound flight, the news came through. The weather was not clearing up, and the world record attempt was off. That meant no entry into *The Guinness Book of World Records*, no selfies with a penguin (something Wentz had been particularly excited about), and three days locked inside a Chilean hotel for no particular benefit. Naturally, the band were disappointed. Stump lamented that Guinness would probably never return their calls again, but reasoned that the fiasco had still ensured some hard-won publicity for Greenpeace, with whom the trip was organised, and the issue of global warming. Andy promised that the band would be back to try and top the attempt. But Wentz was most frustrated of all. 'It's an utter fucking disappointment,' Wentz told the MTV reporter who had accompanied them on the trip. 'We had this idea, and then to not be able to fulfil it is just disappointing, especially when you put it out there. [...] It's the worst feeling I've felt in Fall Out Boy, [we were,] like, two hours away from being able to do it. [...] There's no spin for it; we got two hours away from Antarctica and we can't go.'

In retrospect, it was something of a curious statement. Of course the excursion had been a time-consuming proposition and no doubt swallowed a big chunk of money, too. But was it really the worst feeling Wentz had ever had in Fall Out Boy? Worse than the fateful night he found himself locked in his car, with too much Ativan in his system and Jeff Buckley singing him to sleep? As it would later transpire, the three days trapped in the Chile were memorable for Wentz for an entirely different reason. Whilst there he had received a call from Ashlee informing him that they were going to have a baby. It was all too much for Pete, with the stress of the Antarctic expedition, the howling gang of fans at the window, and now, the woman he loved pregnant with his child thousands of miles away on another continent. He would later tell Amp Rock TV that he was overwhelmed with anxiety whilst at the hotel, and became convinced that the band were not going to make it back to the States. 'It got real dark,' he said. 'I just had this feeling in the pit of my stomach, that this was the last one. We weren't gonna come back. It was a weird one.'

Of course Wentz and his bandmates did manage to make their way to the US to fulfil their remaining tour dates before taking a break in May for Wentz to attend another very important date: he and Ashlee Simpson were to be married. Speculation had been rife since February when Ashlee was spotted sporting a diamond engagement ring, but an official statement was not made until April, released through *FriendsorEnemies.tumblr.com*. They tied the knot at Simpson's parents' home in Los Angeles in an Alice in Wonderland-themed ceremony in front of one-hundred-and-fifty close friends and family members. Wentz's dog Hemingway, the star of the '"The Take Over, the Break's Over"' video, was ring bearer, and the ceremony was officiated by Ashlee's dad Joe. Joe Simpson had something of a bull-in-a-china shop image in the public eye, partly because of his overbearing antics as depicted in Jessica and Ashlee's MTV shows, and partly because of his status as both a Baptist minister and an agent for his daughters, but he and Wentz were on good terms. In fact, the only reference Joe had made to Wentz's wild child reputation was to impart a bit of paternal wisdom regarding image protection: 'We saw a bit too much of you on the Internet last year,' he told Wentz at their first meeting.

Infinity On High had earned Fall Out Boy a seat at the top table of pop music. They were bona fide stars, recognised everywhere they went, with Top 10 hits on the radio and platinum plaques on the wall. And more than ever they had an icon in Pete Wentz, a handsome artist-come-marketeer with a broad smile and a beautiful wife from a famous family. But as Fall Out Boy were about to learn, it could be lonely at the top.

CHAPTER SEVENTEEN

A DREAM RECORD

Infinity On High had pushed the pop-punk template that the band had set down on *Take This To Your Grave* as far as it would go and then hinted at ambitions beyond, but early demos on the follow-up were proving to be more wide-ranging than ever. At Wentz's wedding the band had started to discuss plans for a new album, and in early interviews Trohman was mentioning everyone from Iggy Pop to The Smiths, and the Madchester scene by way of R&B with a little bit of folksy lyricism thrown in.

The band did not set aside a block of time to write a new record as such, as they had been working on new riffs, melodies and ideas for songs pretty much since the last album dropped. In fact, by the time studios were being booked, the band had close to fifty songs in various states of completion to choose from. But this time pre-production was going to be done in a slightly different way. The band would once again be working with Neal Avron, but whereas before they had hired a rehearsal space in Chicago or LA to work through the new material, this time it was going to be done in Neal's home. It's a testament to how close Neal and the band had become, and it proved a more relaxed environment to work on the new songs. He had a pool and a trampoline sunk into the ground and a young child who Wentz could test songs on. It sounded like a joke when Wentz had first mentioned it, but Avron would later tell *USA Today* that the album had 'lots of great riffs with lyrical hooks my five-year-old could sing, which is a good sign', so perhaps Avron's child really had been used for early market research.

By the time the band had deemed themselves ready to record they opted to head back to The Pass Studio in LA, which is unsurprising – *Infinity On High* had been such a huge hit, there was no need to fix what wasn't broken. And this time round Avron was going to be solely in charge of production, as Trohman told *Guitar World*: 'We're real happy with what Babyface did for us, and I think it was cool for us, as a rock band, to work with someone known for R&B. But Neal is like our fifth member. He understands us inside and out. We have a shorthand with him, and it makes the whole record-making process very easy. [...] Neal pushes us. He gets in our face and tells us when a song isn't working or if we're not coming up with the goods. He has really great ideas and opinions and helps us make sense of what we're trying to do.' Andy Hurley seconded Trohman's sentiments, likening Avron's role with the band to that of George Martin with The Beatles or Nigel Godrich with Radiohead.

Erich Talaba was again on hand to work with Avron once the band had set up camp at The Pass, and one thing that he immediately noticed was that there were paparazzi waiting outside as he and the band arrived: 'At that time there were paparazzi hanging around the studio sometimes. The studio had a big gate that would slide behind the cars as you drove in, so they couldn't get in. He was with Ashlee, so [the interest] was even more heightened, and it was very interesting to see that side of it.' However, he quickly saw that the distraction of flashbulbs outside was not a problem for Wentz once he was at work inside the studio. 'Once everybody's in there the focus is one hundred per cent on the record or the songs or whatever we're working on,' Talaba explained. 'We talk about it for five minutes and then we move on. I think for [Fall Out Boy], hanging on that or talking about that isn't a priority in their lives. At least that's what I got. Everybody involved, we're not concerned with that outside noise – we came here to do a project and we need to get it done. Maybe at lunch you take a breather and have some laughs, then you get back to it. I mean you're paying for time to be in a facility, you wanna maximise your dollar.' Talaba's sentiments were matched by Stump, who was keen to point out that because Wentz was always being photographed on the streets, coffee in hand and on his way to this engagement or that, it was easy to forget that he actually had a job: on stage performing, or in a studio working.

Andy once again laid down his drum parts first, and true to form, he got the job done with a minimum of fuss and in a remarkably quick time. Stump attributes the pace at which he works to Hurley's background in metal and hardcore. He had come up in the scene playing complex beats and technically demanding fills at light-speed, so when it came to writing parts for Fall Out Boy, his rhythmic brain was able to work in real time.

He'd do a take and write as he played, bending and shifting parts as he interpreted the songs, adding a stroke here or subtracting a fill there. After a few takes, which were always done in complete run-throughs rather than in sections, the band would talk about which beats and fills they liked best and decide on the final version of the drums to a given song. From there, Hurley would play the song the exact same way every time, without fail. Even at this stage of their creative partnership fellow drummer Stump still found himself impressed by Hurley's abilities. All of the drums were recorded to tape, as would have been the case for decades prior to the digital revolution in music recording; the process was less flexible and more expensive, but Avron felt that the audio quality was noticeably superior for drums. Within five days, all of Hurley's drum parts were completed, a remarkably short amount of time for a record of this magnitude.

Wentz had shifted his focus as a writer, and Stump felt his bandmate had been producing some of his best material ever for the new songs. Whereas in the past Wentz had ransacked the inner workings of his mind for lyrics, more than ever he was writing from the perspective of a character, be that a completely fictional construct or someone he knew in his life. The key for Stump was to reflect this wider emotional palette with a wider musical one, too, and Talaba noticed that there was a greater emphasis on experimentation in the sessions. 'I think on that album there was definitely more chances being taken,' he says. 'I know that they really wanted to try a lot of different things. I think it was more of their artist record, trying to explore more stuff. [...] I know Patrick was into a lot of funk, he loved Prince and stuff like that, and you can hear that for sure. Pete would come in with ideas for stuff that was really heavy on eighties synth pop and you would hear some of that, too.'

And whereas in the past the songs had been heavily prepped and polished in pre-production, this time there was more space allowed for material to develop in the studio. 'I want to say that about seventy-five per cent of the record was done and ready to go going in, but there were a few things that we did do that weren't involved in pre-production,' Talaba explains. 'There was a newer song idea that morphed into something and we took it from there, some songs that took a left turn and became a different song from what was intended. It was a conscious choice to make, to try different things and work with their influences.'

Stump would later reveal to *Rolling Stone* that he had literally had a dream of what the new album should sound like, which he then attempted to realise in the studio. While Talaba does not say that Stump was dominating the recording process, he was in the studio for pretty much the entire process of making the album. 'I know that when we were in the process he was heavily into it,' he says. 'He was there every day. [...] I don't know if that was [Stump] taking ownership or him saying this is gonna be the "Patrick Stump and Fall Out Boy" type of record, but he was in there every day, putting in the work. The other guys would pop in for their parts – it wasn't like a collective group in the studio, all hanging out and making decisions. It was more like, Pete came in, and he and Patrick would discuss a lot of things and go over a lot of stuff. I can't speak to pre-prod; I don't know how much it was [Patrick] as opposed to everybody else, but in the studio I spent most of the time with Patrick.'

In the same *Rolling Stone* interview where Patrick spoke of his dream, he also revealed that the sessions had seen himself and Wentz arguing far more than they had on their last two releases. 'Making this record has been painful,' he said. 'Pete and I fought more than we have in a long time. I threw something across the room over a major-to-minor progression.' Nonetheless, Stump and Wentz were still drawing from the well of their collaboration, with Wentz producing large amounts of material for Stump to shape and cast into songs. Talaba observed Stump often laying down so-called 'scratch' melodies, either on vocals or guitar, where wordless musical ideas would be added to a track to get a feel for how they would fit before he attempted to assign words to them. He would even sit at the back of the studio and sing ideas straight into his laptop if Avron was busy working on something else.

Just as the band were allowing more diverse influences to work their way into the sound, so too they were utilising more unusual equipment and techniques, as Talaba relates: 'We were playing piano and we wanted to be able to have a natural piano performance and have another sound behind it – but using the same performance. [...] We didn't want to use a MIDI piano because we wanted the sound of the real piano. So there's this device that I had used many years ago with someone else, and I told Neal about it. It's like an electronic bar that you put down on the back of the piano, and it senses where you're playing and translates it into MIDI notes for you.' MIDI is short for musical instrument digital interface, and allows musical data to be saved and processed through any number of digital applications, and can thereby be translated into almost any sound you can think of from a single performance. 'It was a very tricky process because

Patrick would be playing and it wouldn't track a certain note or something like that,' Talaba continues. 'It got a little difficult, but we got through it and it allowed us to put that performance to the other sounds that we were looking for and blend that into the piano.'

In the quest to broaden the palette of sound on the record, the band also enlisted a whole host of guests to appear on the record. Some were musical, like the string arrangements which were recorded in New York and sent down to The Pass, or the brass parts, which were arranged by Jerry Hey, a legendary session musician who had appeared on Michael Jackson's *Thriller* amongst a variety of other timeless albums. Other figures were enlisted for their vocal talents, such as the usual suspects from the Decaydance stable – Gabe Saporta, William Beckett, Travis McCoy and Brendon Urie. But the band also managed to pull off some seriously impressive guest features from artists a little further out of reach than Wentz's own label. The jewel in the crown was Elvis Costello, Stump's personal icon and a huge influence on his decision to become a musician. Costello's name had been top of the list of possible collaborators, so when the band realised that they had a mutual contact, they sent him a song to listen to and asked him to consider appearing. Initially it seemed like it might not happen as Costello was suffering from a lung ailment that inhibited his ability to sing. But he managed to record his part remotely and send it to the band for inclusion.

The same process was used to get the first lady of punk on the record – Blondie's Debbie Harry. But the most unlikely guest spot on the record was without a doubt the creaky, inimitable voice of New Orleans rapper Lil Wayne. While Fall Out Boy were in the studio their fellow Chicagoan Kanye West had released *808s & Heartbreak*. True to his reputation as a trendsetter for hip-hop, West had completely upended expectations by packing the album with his singing, heavily processed through auto-tune to create a synthetic, otherworldly effect. It made an immediate impact on the genre and popular music at large, and Fall Out Boy started discussing the possibility of getting an MC to sing on the record. In the new millennium it had become par for the course to have a rapper do a guest verse on a pop track, and it had even been attempted on rock songs with varying degrees of success, but having a rapper sing on a rock song was practically unheard of. The band asked Lil Wayne because, as Stump told *Chicago Tribune*'s *RedEye*, he 'isn't exclusively into rhyming, he also likes musicality and melody' – and his 'hilariously distinctive voice' was bound to make listeners sit up and take notice.

As the band were prepping what was shaping up to be the most ambitious album of their lives, life also shifted in a new direction for Pete Wentz. On 20 November Ashlee gave birth to her first child, Bronx Mowgli, and Pete was present at the birth to welcome his son into the world (in fact, Simpson had to calm him as she went into labour, as he thought he was having a heart attack). The band were right behind Pete, determined to help him balance his responsibilities as a father with his career. 'I know Pete is a consummate workaholic, so he'll still try to do everything while being an awesome dad and probably bringing Bronx out whenever he can,' Hurley said to *NME*. 'I don't think he can do that now because he's still too little but I don't think he wants it to change too drastically. It's a balancing act when it's your first baby. There'll be some time for us to get used to it, but either way it's awesome.' The name Mowgli was derived from the couple's shared love of Kipling's *The Jungle Book*, but they kept the origin of their son's first name to themselves. Wentz might have got used to life in the public eye, but he was still determined to keep some things to himself and his family.

CHAPTER EIGHTEEN

SHARED MADNESS

An ambitious promotional campaign kicked into gear in August 2008, before the album was ready. That month Decaydance's website was supposedly 'hacked' by an anonymous collective called 'Citizens for Our Betterment', and numerous references were made to 4 November of that year – the same day as the US presidential election, a showdown between Barack Obama for the Democrats and John McCain for the Republicans. Ashlee Simpson was photographed holding a pamphlet for Citizens for Our Betterment, inciting more chatter that the online missives were a lead-in for an announcement about Fall Out Boy's next record. Sure enough, a mixtape entitled 'Welcome to the New Administration' was eventually released online, featuring various rarities and demos from Decaydance acts as well as the official announcement – from rapper Ludacris, no less – that Fall Out Boy's new album, *Folie à Deux*, would be released on 4 November. *Folie à Deux* is a psychiatric term for a syndrome whose symptoms are passed between two people. Stump later defined it to *USA Today* as 'the materialistic dance between any two parties obsessed with each other, whether it's teenage girls and handbag makers, politicians and lobbyists, or tabloids and stars.' It seemed all the more appropriate given the media's escalating obsession with Fall Out Boy, and in particular, their charismatic bass-player-come-icon.

This intriguing trail of breadcrumbs, and the fact that the release date coincided with one of the most important presidential elections in living memory, was a clear sign that *Folie à Deux* was to be Fall Out Boy's 'political' record. But the high-concept viral campaign was beset with problems from the start. The band was clearly encouraging fans to do some detective work to obtain information about the upcoming release, but one particularly entrepreneurial band spotted the potential for sabotage. Copeland, an indie rock act from Florida, had for a few months been tossing around the idea for their own viral campaign, whereby they would hijack another band's promotion to steer attention towards themselves. Fall Out Boy's campaign was singled out as a likely candidate, so the band launched their own website – *CitizensFourOurBetterment.com* – and further confused an already complex campaign by directing Fall Out Boy fans to their own site.

'There was nothing malicious about it,' singer Aaron Marsh told MTV. 'We just saw an opportunity to reel in way more people. [...] And when I think about how it might affect Fall Out Boy, all I can say is that Pete's a clever bloke, and he probably would've done the same thing had he thought of it. I mean, think about it: the two campaigns are very similar – theirs is supposed to look like an ominous organisation that's mucking around. The way [the two campaigns] crossed didn't hurt anyone.' To their credit, Fall Out Boy responded to the hijack with good humour. It had always been their intention that people pick up on the campaign and run with it; it had simply taken a rather unexpected turn. All the same, the prevailing response from fans seemed to be one of confusion.

The first single from the album, 'I Don't Care', was released on 3 September, and was a rollicking glam-rock stomper with a T. Rex-alike riff and a chorus as big as anything they'd ever done. Lyrically, it was a perfect fit with the campaign's themes of political power and media manipulation, pivoting around the main refrain of 'I don't care what you think as long as it's about me', and came accompanied by a video that saw the band performing at their very own ominous rally. But the impact of the album's promotion was reduced even further when the release date for the record was postponed from 4 November until 16 December. They put out a statement explaining that while the album was still bound up with themes of social and political commentary, they had begun to feel that releasing it on election day was a gimmick, and only served to distract from a historically important day. It was a noble decision, but it's hard to argue that the whole Citizens for Our Betterment Campaign wasn't now totally derailed.

The album's second single came out on 3 December, and whatever missteps had led up to it, there was no doubting that the band were still writing fantastic songs. 'America's Suitehearts' rides in on a wall of tremolo-picked guitars and off-beat accents before ushering in a funk-flavoured verse; Stump delivers a vocal melody that showcases his love of blue-eyed soul whilst dancing all over the track before unleashing one giant hook of a chorus, perfectly pitched for a mass singalong. The song had been hanging around since before the release of *Infinity On High*, but the band had only managed to get it working in the way they wanted for the release of *Folie*. Creatively, it seemed, they were firing on all cylinders.

Folie à Deux begins in understated fashion, with Stump singing over a sparkling organ line before opening track 'Disloyal Order of Water Buffaloes' kicks in in earnest. Named after the fictional fraternity that Fred Flintstone and Barney Rubble belonged to (with 'disloyal' in place of 'loyal'), the booming power chords bolstered by piano sound for all the world like Bruce Springsteen repackaged for the emo generation. But where Springsteen's cause was the ennui of America's blue-collar everyman, Wentz's is the madness of a generation hooked on cheap thrills and the lure of fame. 'Boycott love / Detox just to retox' Patrick sings in the chorus, before challenging the notion that fame and fortune is a panacea for heartache: 'Perfect boys with their perfect lives / Nobody wants to hear you sing about tragedy'.

After a track so open-hearted, the cynicism of second song 'I Don't Care' makes for a marked shift in tone. Despite the political themes of the video, the song was actually written for and about the YouTube generation, and Stump wanted to reflect the venomous satire of the lyrics with the music. 'So you have this blues riff,' he explained to *AbsolutePunk*, 'and the blues is such an honest, organic thing, but it's totally buried underneath these synthesisers and all this overproduced drum stuff, it sounds like Gary Glitter but like, Gary Glitter meets [early twentieth century blues singer and guitarist] Big Bill Broonzy, and that was kind of mocking that whole commerciality thing.' Whatever you wanted to say about the band you couldn't argue that they weren't challenging themselves and their audience, though the riff did raise a few eyebrows for its similarity to Norman Greenbaum's 'Spirit in the Sky'. Trohman reasonably pointed out that the swagger of the riff could be compared to any number of artists, from John Lee Hooker right through to ZZ Top. Whatever the lineage, it's hard not to tap your foot when you hear it, though its inclusion on the album was anything but a dead cert. Stump had written the song but quickly gone off it, whilst Wentz was very keen on the song and pushing for its inclusion. The disagreement ended up flaring into an argument between the two, but Wentz eventually convinced Stump that the song was better than he realised and that he shouldn't give up on it. Patrick eventually came around to his way of thinking.

Songs that analysed narcissism and self-medication were de rigueur for Wentz, but his newfound status as a father had obviously had an effect on his perspective as a writer. 'She's My Winona' was written before Bronx Mowgli was born but is Wentz's attempt to imagine what being a father would be like, the title a reference to Winona Ryder in the film *Reality Bites*, a personal favourite of his. Sweetness and sincerity had been creeping into Fall Out Boy's world view in increasing doses, but even by that measure 'She's My Winona' is a heartwarming ditty. 'Hell or glory, I don't want anything in between / Then came a baby boy with long eyelashes, and daddy said "you gotta show the world the thunder"' goes the chorus, and it's as profound a statement on the life-changing power of parenthood as you could ever wish to hear in a pop song, even if it was written by a father-to-be. Add in Stump's Weezer-esque vocal hooks and the insistent, driving rhythms and you have one of the best songs that the band had ever put out. It still has a special place in Wentz's heart: he named it one of his top ten favourite Fall Out Boy tracks, although admitted that he wasn't spot on in his predictions about being a dad. 'When I look back on it, it's interesting,' he told *teamrock.com*. 'Some of the stuff I got really right, but there are other things about having a child that I couldn't possibly have known.'

After 'America's Suitehearts' comes 'Headfirst Slide Into Cooperstown on a Bad Bet', a song originally titled 'Husband', which once again showcases Stump's new appreciation for strutting blues riffs. The lyrics are an example of Wentz's new tack of writing from the perspective of a character, in this case a night-time prowler and serial seducer; 'When he walks into the room the walls lean in to listen,' we're told, and there was never a better line to make the case that Wentz is a storyteller in a rock-star's garb. But what makes the song so clever is the way in which the tone shifts to reveal the insecurity and self-loathing that the character hides behind his confidence, both lyrically and musically. The drums drop out, the buzzsaw riffing dies away, and a melancholy piano line creeps into the song like an uninvited guest, before the veil is dropped again. By the time the brass is introduced it feels like our protagonist is doubling down on his masculine fortitude, but we have already been shown the weakness underneath. Stump explained to MTV that the song was about an adulterer relishing the chase of a new seduction whilst knowing that his own partner is faithful, and having to lie to himself to keep the deception going. 'People ask all the time, "Oh, Pete got married, how does that affect the record?"' he said. 'I think, if anything, he just wanted to point out how lightly people are taking their marriages.' This is virtuosic character songwriting, worthy of Randy Newman.

'The (Shipped) Gold Standard' pulls off a similar trick in switching between an emotionally vulnerable chorus and a more complex verse, with Wentz seemingly squaring the challenges of being in love with the challenges of being famous. 'Sometimes I wanna quit this all and become an accountant now / But I'm no good at math and besides the dollar is down' he offers, with typical humour, before the declaration of love that can't be announced: 'I wanna scream I love you from the top of my lungs / But I'm afraid that someone else'll hear me'. The swells of strings that accompany the chorus give it an appropriate emotional heft, and the song takes a brief but bold turn into neon funk in the middle eight, complete with falsetto backing vocals and frantic handclaps.

The album's next two tracks are two of its most starkly ambitious, and represent the highpoint of both *Folie à Deux* and the culmination of its stunning first half. '(Coffee's For Closers)' references the film *Glengarry Glen Ross* in its title, a story about a pack of desperate real-estate salesmen who are thrown into turmoil after being informed that all but the top two performers will lose their jobs in the coming days. The song takes some of the pitch-black cynicism that the movie is famous for and inserts it into one of the band's biggest productions to date, complete with full string parts that shimmer over the driving rhythms and Patrick's superb vocal performance. The track was initially called 'Never Believe' and featured what at the time Stump felt was one of his favourite Fall Out Boy lyrics ever: the chorus of 'Change will come, but I will never believe in anything again'. It's a reference to the passion and earnestness of the nineties and how that morphed into the self-interest and vacuousness of the new millennium. 'I think people stopped believing in the goodwill of man and that you can change the world or do any good,' Stump said to MTV. 'So everything became internalised. The past decade has been totally about "me". It's totally about "Oh, I'm sad. I want this. I know somebody who knows this person. Me me me me me," so that's what that song is about.' The composition may be a critique of modern-day airheadedness, but there's nothing unsophisticated in its delivery; just take the coda, for example, an elegant instrumental string passage that makes a strong case for Stump's potential as a composer.

It is 'What a Catch, Donnie' that is the album's central moment, the pivot around which the rest of the songs on *Folie à Deux* move. It is a tailor-made lighter-in-the-air moment, one built specifically for a grand finale in an arena packed to the rafters, like the closing number of a rock opera about the life of Fall Out Boy that takes in all of their biggest hits before the curtain falls. But at the same time it's an introspective ballad in the classic sense, a song that seems to address Pete's inner turmoil in a very personal way. It glides along gracefully on a piano line accompanied by delicate string parts and guitar lines but switches key for its emotionally climactic chorus. 'I've got troubled thoughts and the self-esteem to match, what a catch', it goes, and the words drip with the sarcasm of those dogged by depressive thoughts. The 'Donnie' of the title refers to Donny

Hathaway, a soul legend born in Chicago who produced a string of hit duets with Roberta Flack ('Miss Flack said "I still want you back"') before being found dead on a sidewalk in January 1979. He'd most likely taken his own life after jumping from the window of his hotel room, and the reference to Hathaway's brilliantly creative partner makes it hard not to read parallels between their relationship and the musical chemistry – and occasional friction - of Stump and Wentz.

'What a Catch, Donnie' is the track for which Fall Out Boy managed to recruit Elvis Costello, who sings a reprise of the chorus from 'Headfirst Slide into Cooperstown On a Bad Bet'. Following his appearance we also get Gabe Saporta singing 'Grand Theft Autumn / Where is Your Boy'; Travis McCoy singing 'Sugar We're Goin Down'; Panic! singer Brendon Urie singing 'Dance, Dance'; Crush Management employee and Berklee College of Music graduate Doug Neumann singing 'This Ain't a Scene, It's an Arms Race'; Alex DeLeon of Decaydance act The Cab singing 'Thnks fr th Mmrs'; and William Beckett singing 'Growing Up'. From the artist that first inspired Stump to play music to the contemporaries that turned Fall Out Boy's success into a movement, all are represented here, and the sense of the band reflecting on what they'd achieved is overwhelming. 'More than anything, they serve the purpose of a character in a musical, where this character's voice makes the most sense,' Wentz explained to *TIME* magazine. 'I mean, what if Darth Vader had spoken in that regular dude's voice? You needed James Earl Jones. Certain lines need to be conveyed in certain ways.'

Twenty-seven, as previously mentioned, is a number that has attained infamy in rock circles for being the age at which some of music's most tragic figures have passed away; the so-called '27 Club' includes Kurt Cobain, Amy Winehouse, Jimi Hendrix, Janis Joplin, Jim Morrison and many others, and has become a shorthand for the lives of excess associated with rock 'n' roll. Sure enough, '27' the song has plenty of allusions to the 'live fast, die young' mentality. 'I want it so bad I'd shoot the sunshine into my veins' we hear in the first verse; and while we understand that Wentz covets fame, the 'milligrams in my head / Burning tobacco in my wind' seems to suggest that he's not able to resist dangerous indulgences. Whereas up to this point the arrangements on *Folie à Deux* had been some of the most complex that Fall Out Boy had ever put down on tape, '27' is a straight ahead rock song, one that even features the relative rarity of a guitar solo to hammer home the message of rock-life excess.

'Tiffany Blews' puts Stump's love of Prince on proud display with its strutting rhythms, laser-beam synths and brazenly sexy vocals, but transitions into an emotionally charged rock chorus. It's an impressive feat that Stump is able to combine two completely distinct sections into one song, but it does make for a somewhat disjointed listen, made all the more bizarre with the appearance of a heavily processed Lil Wayne singing over layers of Stump's wordless harmonies. It feels more like an experiment than a great song in its own right, but it's by no means an out-and-out failure, and on an album with so many experimental tendencies it's amazing that it took until track ten to hear a misfire.

'w.a.m.s.' was written in collaboration with The Neptunes, the production alter ego of Pharrell Williams and Chad Hugo, the men behind a heap of glossy hip-hop pop hits for everyone from Jay Z to Justin Timberlake. Stump had already made inroads into hip-hop as a producer and Wentz had made no bones about his admiration for rappers who could marry artistic integrity with business nous, but this was the band's first attempt at a real synthesis of modern pop with the Fall Out Boy sound. The title is an acronym for 'waitress/actress/model/singer', a reference to the would-be stars that flock to Hollywood to make their names and find themselves waiting tables whilst waiting for a break. With the funk-influenced dirty bass of the verse and the melodic rock pre-chorus and chorus, there's not a huge amount in the song that bears The Neptunes' hallmarks until you get to the song's instrumental middle section. A lush curtain of vocal melodies drops over the track while retro-futuristic jazz licks and space-age synths streak back and forth. It's an exhilarating break, but before we know it we're back into the driving chorus which ultimately fades out, leaving an a cappella blues melody accompanied only by the sound of the rain. It feels like another ambitious but only partly successful experiment for the band, with The Neptunes' production wizardry not entirely consolidated into Fall Out Boy's rock template.

Brendon Urie makes his second appearance on the album on '20 Dollar Nose Bleed', where his soulful tones are the perfect accompaniment to Stump's. Both have character, flexibility and range to spare, and it makes for a memorable sparring between two of modern rock's most distinctive voices. Jerry Hey's brass arrangements give the track a sunny feel, but lyrically Wentz is once again in dark territory, and the contrast between the breezy Motown-inspired music and the soul-searching of the words is striking. 'Call me Mr Benzedrine', goes the biggest hook in the chorus; Benzedrine is a drug often used to treat ADHD, which Wentz had been diagnosed with as a child. Wentz's new status as a family man had obviously not dulled his ability to draw from dark places, and in the monologue that ends the song, he seems to disclose some serious anxieties. 'And the charts are boring, and the kids are snoring, and my ego's in a sling,' he says, a nervous anticipation of what might be around the corner.

The album finishes on 'West Coast Smoker', a high-octane funk-rock hybrid that manages to squeeze a guitar solo, a choral breakdown, some anguished screaming and a Debbie Harry feature into less than three minutes. It sounds as if it's come roaring out of the eighties on a hog, equipped with the snarl and swagger of *Appetite for Destruction*-era Guns N' Roses – not exactly what we'd come to expect of Fall Out Boy, but an attention-grabbing final track all the same. Even in a track as brash as this, you can still find the band's fine attention to detail at work in the songwriting. After Stump sings 'Knock once for the father, twice for the son, three times for the holy ghost', Hurley delivers three snare hits, acting out the words and simultaneously referencing one of Stump's favourite Ray Charles songs. 'That's actually something that someone could listen to the album a hundred times and never hear unless they were looking for it, like one of those Beach Boys *Pet Sounds* things,' Hurley said to *Drum!* magazine. 'Unless you listen to the album with headphones you don't hear these little subtle things that I've thrown in there.'

Fall Out Boy had first started to expand the boundary lines of their sound on *Infinity On High*, but *Folie à Deux* takes them into completely new territory, introducing a much broader range of genres, more guests, bigger arrangements and more sophisticated songwriting. It's a new phase in the band's development, and stands quite apart from what they'd done before. The pop-punk template that had so defined them in their early years is still detectable, but they no longer sound like a pop-punk band; they sound more diffuse, more ambitious and more consciously 'grown up'. Whether that was what people wanted from Fall Out Boy remained to be seen, but reviewers had plenty of good things to say. *NME* acknowledged that the band had outgrown the confines of their scene, calling it a 'staggering achievement' and saying: '*Folie à Deux* obliterates the other major diss proffered by emo purists, that they're nothing more than a boyband [...] because it transcends the genre. It's a big, stupid guitar-pop album, as much in thrall to Jim Steinman rock operas as it is to The Neptunes, and held together by what had always made Fall Out Boy sound like Fall Out Boy.' *Alternative Press* also praised the band for their determination to experiment: 'There aren't any other groups who have achieved such widespread mainstream success but still tinker with their sound this much,' they wrote, and while lamenting that the album's second half 'woefully lacks standouts', they said that 'the album's standouts are *so* good that they will undoubtedly become standards for the band's live shows for years to come'. The *Los Angeles Times*, however, summarised how some felt the album's ambition had spilled over into excess. While acknowledging that it offered 'A little something for everyone, all of it played to the max', they felt that the album's roster of high-profile names 'barely surface above the album's aesthetic gluttony'.

Fall Out Boy had never been a band who craved critical approval, nor did their habit of pulling their sound this way and that suggest they were particularly concerned about fulfilling fan expectations – they were a band who had always done what they wanted to do, and found huge success off the back of it. But the outstanding run of form was about to come to an end.

CHAPTER NINETEEN

SWAN SONG

The day before *Folie à Deux* was released Fall Out Boy were due to play a free show in New York's Washington Square Park. In the same spot where Bob Dylan and his fellow freewheeling ideas men of the counterculture used to hang out, Fall Out Boy would begin the next chapter of their legacy. But they had not obtained the correct permit and moments before the band were due to take to the stage the NYPD shut down the show. The band led the assembled throng of fans, who had heard of the show through Wentz's blog, in an a cappella rendition of 'Grand Theft Autumn / Where Is Your Boy', but it was not much of a consolation prize. 'I'm kind of bummed by all that, to be honest,' Stump told MTV. 'That was going to be awesome. Those cops back there – and I have no problem with the cops, trust me – but those cops were like the Grinch. They just took all the presents.' If ever there was a bad omen for the start of a tour, then that was it, and sales for the album were not matching up to what the band had come to expect. Whereas *Infinity On High* debuted at number one, *Folie à Deux* had only made it to No.8 on the Billboard 200, with 149,000 sales in the first week – around 80,000 shy of its predecessor.

There were plenty of high-profile engagements to push the album, from an appearance on *Jimmy Kimmel Live!* to the Super Bowl Bash event in Tampa, Florida, where the band appeared on the same bill as Rihanna. They even got to play for the newly inaugurated President of the United States himself, Barack Obama, on 20 January 2009. With tongue firmly in cheek, Wentz dedicated 'Thnks fr th Mmrs' to George Bush, and all got the chance to meet Obama after the show. It was a big moment for Wentz, who had been involved in campaigning for Obama in the run-up to the election.

The band began a world tour in February 2009. Dubbed Believers Never Die Part Deux, and named for a tour that the band had undertaken in 2004, it began in Japan before heading to Singapore, the Philippines, Australia and New Zealand. At this stage, at least, they seemed to be happy with the way the tour was going. Patrick felt that the Japan leg was one of the best few shows he had ever done, with the band playing and sounding better than ever. After that they flew to Europe and then, in April, back to the States for a two-month stint across all of North America. It was a big production onstage, with the band going heavy on themes of political oppression and corporate greed; they would take to the stage wearing black dress suits and with their eyes heavily made up, tearing into 'Disloyal Order of Water Buffaloes' accompanied by two ominous figures dressed in riot gear. Wentz would then welcome audiences to the 'corporate retreat', promising to teach them the secrets to getting rich before the band reappeared as Fall Out Boy.

But a month into the American leg of the tour the mood seemed to be turning in the Fall Out Boy camp. Wentz told *The Aquarian Weekly* that he thought the tour was 'cursed'. Between bands and crew there had been two trips to the hospital, a bout of food poisoning that ran through the bus, a broken ankle and a show cancelled due to lightning – and Wentz joked that they needed a shaman to come and lift the hex that had been placed over the tour.

However, it wasn't just illness that was against the band; their own fans, famous for their passion, were less than impressed with the new material in the set. The band were playing more than twenty songs a night, and only six or seven of them were from *Folie à Deux*, but the disinterest was palpable. At the same time, a comment Wentz made on Twitter got some Fall Out Boy fans very hot under the collar. Responding to a question enquiring if another Fall Out Boy record would be released in 2010, Wentz responded by saying 'this may be our swansong'. He later explained that what he was referring to was the single 'What a Catch, Donnie', which he felt would be an appropriate way to go out should the band not make another record; no new songs were written at that time because the band had no immediate plans to head into the studio, but that did not mean they would be splitting up. They would stop doing the band when they no longer enjoyed it. The internet rumour mill did not seem entirely satisfied with the statement, and perhaps they had good reason.

Following Believers Never Die Part Deux, the band headed

on tour with a newly reformed Blink-182, who were hitting the road for the first time in over five years. It should have felt like a lap of honour for Fall Out Boy. They were the biggest contemporary pop-punk band in the world, if they could even still be called that. Though the newly reformed Blink were the bigger draw, they were riding on the successes of yesteryear. But it didn't turn out as hoped. In fact, it came to represent much that had gone wrong in the touring cycle for the new album. Firstly, Stump found that the two band's fan bases were not as similar as one might have assumed. 'Everyone I talked to in the music industry assumed automatically that that would be the perfect bill, that those audiences would totally enjoy both bands,' Stump told the *Chicagoist* website. 'And it was absolutely disparate. Blink-182 and us got along great, but those were not the same audiences. It pointed out to me how foolhardy a lot of those assumptions can be.'

And once again, it was not just Blink's fans who were unimpressed with Fall Out Boy. Whilst playing in Chicago, a show that should have represented a hometown triumph, Stump noticed a group of twenty or so people right in front of the stage who were obviously dedicated fans of theirs. They knew every word to every old song that they played and would sing along at the top of their lungs, but as soon as the band played something from *Folie*, their attitude changed. They would get visibly angry. At one point, Pete declared that they would be playing a new song and Stump looked out to see one of the group staring straight back, giving him the finger. It was the culmination of a series of disappointments in the response to the album, and Stump was no longer able to shrug it off. 'The first time there's that kid, I'm like, "Yeah, OK, whatever. I get it,"' he told *DIY Magazine*. 'The second time there's that kid, you're like, "Wanna know what? We're happy. The four of us, we meant this and we're proud of it." But, by the hundredth time, I just take it home. I don't know how to shut it off. I want everyone to be happy, I want everyone to feel good, I don't really want bad things to happen. I'm a wuss like that. The look on that guy's face is just so haunting.'

The band's star had been in the ascendancy for five consecutive years, appearing in the sky with the release of *Take This To Your Grave* and suddenly burning bright with the release of *From Under the Cork Tree* in 2005. Their singles had been all over the radio, their tour bus had been all over the world, and their music videos were ubiquitous on MTV and beyond. Seldom a month would go by without Fall Out Boy's faces appearing on the covers of *Alternative Press*, *Rolling Stone* or *Kerrang!*, and to add a particularly volatile fuel to the fire of media attention, Pete had been a firm favourite of the gossip rags ever since his engagement and marriage to Ashlee Simpson in May 2008. With the benefit of hindsight, the time was ripe for a backlash.

With typical acuity of vision, Pete was under no illusions that his celebrity was probably a contributing factor to the frosty climate that the band found themselves in. 'Especially in America [...] people really want to build you up to tear you down, to build you up again, and we were building at a time when people were like, "No, we're tearing you down now"', Wentz said in an interview with Scuzz TV in 2013. 'And whatever my persona in the media was, and our band's persona in the media, wasn't helpful for the record. [...] We were reviewed, we were thought of and talked about based on who we were and not what the record was.' There were certainly other elements at play too, as Wentz noted in that same interview. 'The album came out a strange big turn for the music industry, the Internet was raging in a whole new way... and I think our band had suffered a series of successes then backlashes.' In an era of YouTube stars and free mixtapes, a big budget rock release like *Folie à Deux* was starting to look a little old fashioned, even with its zeitgeist-riding viral marketing campaign.

Patrick Stump has called *Folie à Deux* his *Pinkerton* in reference to the sophomore Weezer album that was famously disavowed by its creator, Rivers Cuomo. (After the success of Weezer's debut *The Blue Album*, *Pinkerton* was released to critical chagrin and disappointing sales, and Cuomo was nothing short of ashamed of the record's hugely personal content.) 'I put a lot of my personality into that record, and it wasn't that it didn't sell,' Stump explained to Scuzz TV. 'I don't really care about that, and it did sell [...] The thing that was really rough and was a tough thing to swallow was the people that hated it, and they really hated it.' But the irony is that the music press were not really the ones that turned on the band; *Folie à Deux* was relatively warmly received across the board. It was Fall Out Boy's own fans that rejected it the most vehemently.

The truth is that Fall Out Boy only stood to lose with the release of their fourth album, regardless of whether it was *Folie à Deux* or something entirely different. Each time a band reassembles their sound and heads into new creative territory they stand to both lose and gain fans. It happened in the jump between the relatively straightforward pop-punk stylings of *Take This To Your Grave* and the slick, decidedly modern *From Under the Cork*

Tree. But the number of new fans gained, so vastly outnumbered the tally of 'I prefer the old stuff' dilettantes that the album can only be regarded as a huge success. *Infinity On High* is the clear spiritual successor to *From Under the Cork Tree*, created using the same methods, and it furthered the band in their march to global superstardom. But after five years making their way to the top, the band had accumulated practically every fan they were ever going to in their current guise. If you were predisposed to liking Fall Out Boy, chances are you already had their albums on your iPod. They only ever stood to lose fans on *Folie à Deux*, with the possible exception of them making another *Infinity On High*, in which case the press would have certainly dismissed them as out of ideas and on the shortest path to mediocrity. It's unfortunate, as *Folie à Deux* is probably their best record.

Stump's comparison of *Folie à Deux* to *Pinkerton* is a telling one. Despite Cuomo famously calling the *Pinkerton* record a mistake, it found an audience, one that built slowly but eventually came to recognise its stark emotional content and unfussy production. It even prompted Cuomo himself to reappraise the album, telling online music magazine *Pitchfork* in 2008 that '*Pinkerton*'s great. It's super-deep, brave and authentic. Listening to it, I can tell that I was really going for it when I wrote and recorded a lot of those songs.' Perhaps Stump will one day come to say the same about *Folie à Deux*.

But regardless of the way *Folie* will come to be regarded, the negativity was having seriously damaging effects on the members of Fall Out Boy, with some of them more unhappy than others. Joe seemed to be one of the most worn out. 'It felt like an out-of-body experience,' he would later tell *Rolling*

Stone. 'Some of us were miserable onstage. Some of us were just drunk. The fans were just trudging through the new songs. They didn't want to hear them.' Patrick, similarly, had become more and more convinced that if Fall Out Boy was to have a future, then they needed to take a break. He sat the band down and told them that if they continued the way they were going, they would ultimately end up hating one another and the band and their demise would be inevitable. He compared it to being on a gyroscope: the demands of the schedule – the touring, the promotion, the interviews and the shows – kept the band together, because there were always commitments that they needed to fulfil. But five years of near constant grind had taken its toll. Cracks had started to appear in the members' friendships and they were not communicating like they used to. At certain points they were only speaking through managers.

The band played its last date of the Blink-182 tour on 4 October 2009. At the end of Fall Out Boy's set, Mark Hoppus came on stage and shaved Pete Wentz's head. It might have looked like a rebirth to some in the crowd, but to Hurley, it looked like the end. He wasn't ready to take a break from the band; he'd come more or less straight out of high school and spent pretty much his entire adult life touring and making music with Fall Out Boy. He found himself in tears before the band took to the stage, wondering if this would be the last show that Fall Out Boy ever played together.

It was also Andy that first let slip to the outside world that Fall Out Boy would be taking a bow and leaving the stage for a while. Over a month after the end of the Blink-182 tour he published, and then deleted, a tweet stating that the band were on a hiatus. The response from supporters was naturally one of panic – hiatuses have a way of turning into break-ups in music – but Pete was quick to do damage control. He didn't want to call it a hiatus because of the baggage that word carries; nor did he want to call it a break, because it sounded a little too much like 'break-up'. Fall Out Boy were merely decompressing, he said. It did little to calm the jitters of the band's fans.

CHAPTER TWENTY

THE BLESSED AND THE DAMNED

For a couple of months all was quiet in the Fall Out Boy camp, but in January 2010, it emerged that Patrick Stump was working on solo material. His website was relaunched with a quote from Anaïs Nin – 'And the time came when the risk it took to stay closed in a bud became more painful than the risk it took to bloom' – and while he denied it was the beginning of some extravagant viral marketing campaign, it was easy to read a dissatisfaction with Fall Out Boy into the words.

Back in 2007, Sasha Frere-Jones had written a feature on Fall Out Boy for *The New Yorker*. 'If success confounds him and makes the band implode,' he wrote, 'Stump could easily survive by writing big, hopeful hooks for whichever team [...] wants him.' In 2010, it was starting to read something like a premonition, except Stump was now writing for his own team. A video was uploaded to his YouTube channel showing him putting a track together, piece by piece, with everything from the drums to the white hot funk of the bass line to the sunny horns played by him. It was a clear message. Stump had talents and tastes that were not expressed in Fall Out Boy, and now was his time to show them off. The desire to write lyrics had also been a big driving force in deciding to start producing music solo. 'Pretty much all three major label records, I didn't write a word,' he said to *Chicagoist*. 'I'm very into the sound of things and I do write constantly, which is another driving force behind this new record. I've been writing lyrics for ten years with no outlet, which has been really frustrating.' But this venture came with its own risks. Fall Out Boy had always written and played within the framework of pop punk, even as they later expanded the definitions of what that could mean, but now Stump was having to figure out a sound from scratch, deciding where he wanted to take the music and working hard to carve out a niche for himself. What's more, Stump knew that his new material was not going to automatically appeal to Fall Out Boy fans just because he happened to be the singer in that band. His intention was to put his love of blue-eyed soul, pop, funk and new wave front and centre, and while those elements had often found their way into Fall Out Boy's sound, this time they were going to be undiluted by heavier influences. Far from automatically inheriting a fan base from his other band, he would have to work even harder to justify this new material's existence. His manager even had some words of warning for him, cautioning that being a solo artist would feel completely different to being the singer in a band. If he were received warmly, it would be a feeling sweeter than anything he'd experienced with Fall Out Boy. But should he be judged harshly, it would be all the more difficult to bear.

He played his first show as Patrick Stump at the South by Southwest Festival in Austin, Texas in March, appearing at the Dirty Dog Bar on a bill headlined by Hole. This was a solo appearance in the truest sense of the term. He appeared on stage completely alone, playing everything himself, as the video he had released to YouTube had hinted at. Armed with guitars, a keyboard, a drum kit and a variety of samplers, he showcased a forward-looking take on R&B, building tracks from a bed of sampled beats and then layering funk-infused guitars and his nimble vocals on top. And to make it feel like even more of a break from what had come before, Stump had also lost one hell of a lot of weight, and took to the stage looking like a whole new man. It was a statement of intent, and displayed just how single-minded Stump was prepared to be in bringing his own unique vision to the public. The one-man-band theme was going to carry through to his record, with Stump playing every instrument, writing every stitch of music and producing the album himself. If anyone had ever doubted his influence on Fall Out Boy, they were about to see just what he was capable of, though he joked that the true intent of venturing out under his own steam was to have an excuse to play drums again. Stump had plans to have his album out in the summer of that year, though he also told MTV that a number of traumatic events in his personal life, including the death of a family member and of a friend, had given him cause to exercise the cathartic writing impulse again, which was slowing down preparations for the recording sessions.

Though Stump had barely taken a few steps out into the wilderness of a solo career, he was still dogged with queries about the future of Fall Out Boy. Just prior to his first appearance in Austin, Wentz had responded to some questions from fans on Twitter about the future of the band with an ambiguous response, which was quickly interpreted as confirmation that they had split up. In response he released a post on his blog, but that too failed to offer any more certainty on the situation; he genuinely didn't know, he said, if the band would ever play together again. Stump, in turn, was asked about Wentz's comments by *Spin* magazine and told them: 'I'm not in Fall Out Boy right now.' Once again, everyone assumed that meant he had quit. Actually, he later corrected, he just meant he didn't know what the future of Fall Out Boy was either, and he was focused on his solo material. The whole situation was as clear as mud and equally as messy, which only made fans more nervous and more determined to get answers.

Meanwhile, Joe Trohman was not sitting idle. While he was a big presence on stage, in Fall Out Boy he had always seemed to take something of a back seat. With Stump and Wentz handling the majority of the songwriting duties, they tended to have the most to say to the press – or, at least, the press had the most to say to them. But an intriguing news story had broken in 2007 that illustrated, just briefly, how much Trohman had to offer creatively. In August Fall Out Boy were in Belgium to play the Pukkelpop festival and were staying at a hotel along with a variety of other bands set to play the fest. Two of those bands were Liars, a Brooklyn-based dance-punk act with a predilection for sonic exploration, and Architecture in Helsinki, an Australian indie rock band. The pair of bands had got to talking, and Architecture in Helsinki told Liars how they had been surfing the shared iTunes libraries of the other laptops connected to the hotel's Wi-Fi, only to happen upon a treasure trove of incredible hard rock and heavy metal riffs. With a bit more investigation they discovered that the recordings were ideas that Trohman had laid down on his computer, and Liars took to their MySpace to publicise (with no small degree of surprise, given that Liars and Fall Out Boy are at opposite ends of the alternative music scale) what a killer bank of material Trohman was sitting on. At first Trohman was panicked to discover that others had been snooping around his private bank of music, and disclosed that he had very little confidence in his own abilities, but after reading the positive things that Liars had to say in their online post he was flattered. At the same time, he had no plans for a side project, given how hectic Fall Out Boy's tour schedule was in 2007.

All Trohman needed was the outlet to perform his own material and the time to do it, and an unlikely meeting soon provided the first. Scott Ian is the guitar player for Anthrax, one of the so-called 'Big Four' of thrash and a legend in his own right for his three decades of commitment to metal. He is also, like Wentz, a non-vocalist who writes lyrics in his principal band. On a list of people least likely to be interested in forming a band with Trohman, you might put a grizzled middle-aged veteran like Ian somewhere near the top, but you'd be wrong. For a start, Trohman was no fair-weather metal fan, and for the entire time he had been in Fall Out Boy he had been indulging his love for all things heavy. Similarly, Ian is a famously gregarious character who wasn't about to let the invisible fences of genre stop him hanging out and playing with musicians he liked.

The pair first met through the guitar manufacturer Washburn, who had endorsed both artists. The A&R man for Washburn had repeatedly told Trohman and Ian that the pair should get together, even specifically telling Ian not to let the fact that Trohman was in Fall Out Boy discourage him from meeting the young guitarist. He needn't have worried: Ian didn't know anything about Fall Out Boy, other than that they were named after a character from *The Simpsons* and that Pete Wentz was their singer.

A dinner was eventually arranged where Trohman and Ian could meet. There was some trepidation on Joe's part. He was a fan of Anthrax and had often stood by the maxim 'never meet your heroes', but he decided that the opportunity to hang with Scott Ian was too good to pass up. The pair met over dinner and once Trohman had explained that Wentz was actually the bass player, not the singer, the two ended up bonding over their mutual love of Black Sabbath, Thin Lizzy, Led Zeppelin and all of the other classic rock acts that had set the template for heavy guitar-based music from the sixties to the eighties. But the origins of the pair's musical collaboration came a couple of nights later, when Joe was in LA waiting to fly out to Japan to play some shows. He gave Ian a ring to ask if he felt like swinging by the hotel, sharing a drink and trading a few riffs. The meeting went well, and from then on whenever the pair could meet to work on ideas, they would do so. Ian ended up spending a fair amount of time in Chicago whilst working on an album with Anthrax, which was ultimately never released – their then-singer Dan Nelson parted ways with the band in early 2009, derailing the record. The longer the pair spent writing, the more they had the sense that their ideas could be spun out into something more substantial.

If this band was to have any hope of making a mark, it was going to need a singer. Fortunately, Trohman hadn't spent the last five years touring practically constantly without making a friend or two – quite the opposite, as Trohman was known as the member of Fall Out Boy most likely to be drinking and fraternising with other bands backstage. One night, Ian and Trohman were driving together listening to Every Time I Die, a metalcore band from Buffalo that had come to prominence in 2005 with their incendiary blend of heavy metal technicality and southern rock swagger. Their singer was Keith Buckley, a man possessed of both a hair-raising roar and a tuneful croon, as well as a hefty dose of star charisma. Early on in Every Time I Die's career he'd been known for the ranting, half-manic delivery of his vocals, but on later material he'd begun to sing more and more. As Ian and Trohman spitballed about possible vocalists, Ian declared that Buckley's singing voice would be a perfect fit for the kind of hard rock-influenced tunes they were developing. There and then, Trohman got out his phone and texted Buckley, and a couple of minutes later, Buckley was in.

Recruiting a drummer was going to be an easier task, and Trohman was adamant from the start that Andy Hurley would be the man to sit behind the skins. 'I'm very close with him, and there's no problems between us,' Trohman explained to *Ultimate Guitar*, perhaps unwittingly alluding to tensions that may or may not have been present amongst other members of Fall Out Boy. 'He's also a huge Anthrax fan, an old-school metalhead, and he's played in Slayer thrash-type metal bands before ever doing

Fall Out Boy – that's where he comes from.' Another guitarist was drafted in, in the form of Rob Caggiano, a fellow member of Anthrax, taking the total number of axemen up to a most unorthodox three. Caggiano was asked to join the fold after a night of drinking in New York, and when Trohman awoke, he realised he might have just oversubscribed the position in the band – but after a writing session with Caggiano revealed how well they worked together, he was convinced that they had to make the three-guitar set-up work. (The line-up would later be completed by Every Time I Die bassist Josh Newton, but Newton does not appear on any recordings.)

With the core members in place, the band set about recording in various different locations, from Chicago to Buffalo to Brooklyn, focusing on honing a sound that took in the best of classic rock and blues-based riffing, chewed up and spat out in a modern way. They took their name from Ram Jam's cover of Lead Belly's classic track 'Black Betty' (the damn thing gone wild, bam-ba-lam). Thus, The Damned Things were born. As early as 2007, Trohman, Buckley and Ian had been demoing tracks in California with Joe Barresi, a producer who had previously worked with The Melvins and Queens of the Stone Age. From that point the band was building up to make an album, and with Fall Out Boy no longer requiring any of Joe's time, they set about recording their debut in 2010.

The launch of the band in the public eye caused quite a stir. First off, a whole heap of old-school metalheads couldn't believe Caggiano and Ian were in a band with one half of the Hot Topic generation's favourite band, and knowing nothing of Trohman and Hurley's backgrounds, griped that these emo upstarts had no place sharing a stage with thrash legends. On the other end of the musical landscape, Fall Out Boy fans had only just got their heads around the fact that Patrick would be striking out on his own, and now Joe and Andy were in a heavy metal band. 'From all across the board, people were definitely weirded by it and I knew they would be,' Trohman said to *Ultimate Guitar*. 'On paper it looked really fucked up, but I knew once the music got out there it would coalesce and make sense to people.' The Damned Things made their live debut in June, and for all the noise about this most improbable of supergroups, the response to the shows was that of quiet surprise. They had riffs, they had chops, they had songs. This was a real band.

Since the demos had been recorded, they had taken to the decision to keep production in-house, with Caggiano and Trohman sharing duties as producer. The songs were coming together as a true collaboration, and Scott Ian for one seemed extremely enthusiastic about the way the material was shaping up. 'It represents the genres of music that we all come from, but it doesn't sound specifically like any of our bands,' he told rock website *NoiseCreep*. 'For me, I hear a lot of elements of classic rock, I hear a lot of elements of older school heavy metal, but at the same time I hear a lot of modern rock as well. There are definitely influences coming from Rob, Keith and Joe because the three of them were really responsible for most of the melody ideas and the big choruses.' Buckley pushed his singing voice further than ever before, even taking lessons from go-to metal vocal coach Melissa Cross to make sure he put down the best possible performances for the record.

Even though Patrick Stump had been first out of the gate

in unveiling his new project, it was The Damned Things that released their album first. *Ironiclast* came out on 14 December and offered ten slices of chunky, groove-laden hard rock songs, packed with fast-fingered guitar riffing, big rock choruses and bruising drum work from Hurley. Musically it manages to plot points all over the rock map. Opener 'Handbook for the Recently Deceased' trips along on an almost Celtic, Thin Lizzy-esque riff, where 'Bad Blood' draws on a shared love of Sabbath with its doomy walls of ominous guitars washing over the track. 'We've Got a Situation Here' recalls the furious metalcore of Every Time I Die with a hugely melodic pop-punk chorus, and 'Little Darling' combines a desert rock groove with a vocal performance from Buckley that Nikki Sixx would be proud of. The title track, meanwhile, is the most brutal song on offer, showcasing why Scott Ian is considered one of metal's most influential figures and giving Hurley a chance to dust off his double-kick pedal. But while the album sounds quite like a lot of other bands it never sounds exactly like any of them, and it's on that count that the result is such a success.

The press liked it, too; *Rock Sound* gave it nine out of ten and dubbed it 'a near-perfect album'. The *Big Cheese* was more reserved, but still acknowledged 'there are some great Thin Lizzy and Led Zeppelin-influenced rockers here'. And *AbsolutePunk* identified how in bringing together previously distinct elements from each of the member's own skill set, the album brought a breath of fresh air to a tired genre. 'Still scratching your head over how this will sound? Well, it's not that complicated, as *Ironiclast* features a lot of the elements originally heard on records from each member's respective band,' wrote reviewer Drew Beringer.

'Thrash, metal, and pop collide to create a well-balanced rock record. [...] Trohman finally gets to show off his chops, as Fall Out Boy never really gave him the chance to show off his guitar skills. In fact, *Ironiclast* is a chance for each member to do new things. Ian and Caggiano have never been a part of something this poppy, Trohman and Hurley finally get to unleash their heavier side, and, of course, Buckley gets to dive into the vocal style he's only dabbled in on previous ETID records. *Ironiclast* is familiar yet unique.'

Hurley had always been acknowledged as a formidable player, but if Trohman had an itch that he wanted to scratch – to play heavy music, to step out on his own, to prove his worth as a guitarist – then he'd done it all, and in spectacular fashion.

CHAPTER TWENTY-ONE

'MR MOM'

For Stump and Trohman, taking a step away from the giant machine that Fall Out Boy had become had given them the space they needed to grow into something else. But many observers were wondering what Wentz would do. He was practically the nominated spokesperson for the band, and certainly its most famous member. His whole public persona was irrevocably linked to Fall Out Boy. All of the members faced a formidable set of expectations about whatever project they involved themselves in next, but none more so than Wentz.

Musically, Wentz played it smart. 'I didn't want to do anything that was cathartic – I wanted to do something that was escapist,' he told *Billboard*. 'It was more oriented, especially where it ended up, in dance and escaping.' From a young age Wentz had listened to reggae, the influence of his family ties to Jamaica, and a holiday with Ashlee and Bronx to the country had further stoked his interest in dub-based music. Whilst hanging around on the beaches he would hear roots reggae from the seventies and though he was hearing songs that he'd never listened to before, he was struck by their power, by their ability to convey emotion across cultural divides. He decided to combine his desire to make some escapist dance-orientated music with the island sounds that he'd heard, and called his friend Sam Hollander to help him realise his vision. Hollander is a songwriter and pop producer who had been involved in working with a host of artists, but had first moved into Wentz's orbit through Gym Class Heroes when he worked on the *As Cruel as School Children* record. Since then he'd been involved in various collaborations with Decaydance artists, but it was his interest in British electronic music that convinced Wentz he was the man for the job. After a couple of aborted experiments, the pair came up with the track 'Summer Nights', an airy dub-influenced pop track with fluttering electronic beats and a bouncing steel drum melody, and dubbed the new project Black Cards.

They had found the anchor for their sound; all they needed was a singer. Wentz didn't want to work with another male vocalist because he couldn't see anyone stepping into Patrick's shoes, and had decided a female vocalist would work better for the project – preferably a 'quirky British girl', as he told *Rolling Stone*. One day whilst in the studio, they heard a female singing voice emanating through the walls, and suddenly Wentz realised that, British or not, what he was searching for was right next door. The voice belonged to Bebe Rexha, an Albanian-American New Yorker who was at that point a complete unknown in the industry. Immediately the pair clicked, even though they came from completely different scenes. 'We have completely different influences,' he said to *Rolling Stone*. 'If I cite a band from the punk scene, she often has no idea who I'm talking about. Then she'll cite a dance band and I'll have no idea who she's talking about. She's just an awesome, natural talent.' Though working with a different voice, Wentz resumed his old role of writing lyrics for the project.

As both Stump and The Damned Things were working on their debut, things started to pick up pace with Black Cards. Wentz recruited drummer Spencer Peterson, who had briefly been a member of influential emo act Saves the Day, and guitarist Nate Patterson, a founding member of Massachusetts rock act The Receiving End of Sirens. A debut single called 'A Club Called Heaven' was unveiled in September, and sounded a lot like a soulful, American Lily Allen, with its playful ska rhythms and Rexha's rich voice. With a touring unit in place, in October 2011 the band went on a short US and European run, and continued to roll out tracks on social media as they built to an album release. But the scheduled date kept being moved back. First it was intended to be mid-2010, with Wentz remarking that while they had an album's worth of material to put out, they couldn't quite settle on a sound, and were continuously writing new material to see if it would trump what they already had. The summer came and went, and Wentz mooted an early 2012 release date. 'It's taken about nine months to figure out what the dynamic and the sound is,' he told website *Cambio*. 'It's definitely a body of work that's just a weird pop album. It's like everything that I've been into for the past five years mashed up.'

But as January rolled around, there was still no sign of the album, and the whole raison d'être of Black Cards seemed to shift. By this point the band had been pared down to just Rexha, Wentz and Peterson, but became a two-piece with the departure of Rexha. 'A lot of fans have been asking me about my status in Black Cards, so I thought I'd clear the air,' she said in a statement. 'My depart [sic] from Black Cards was a mutual decision between the boys and I. I will support Pete and Spencer 100% in everything that they do. They will always be my homies.'

Now down a front woman, Black Cards morphed into more of a DJ and production duo-type format between Wentz and Peterson, who would ultimately release a mixtape and an EP of dubstep and house-tinged material in 2012. They also appeared together for DJ sets, a format that Wentz found refreshing. 'When we played EDM [electronic dance music] shows, it was a lot of fun, and "Pete Wentz" doesn't have a name in EDM at all, so it was cool and different,' he told *Billboard*. But the truth was that there was much more going on in Wentz's life behind closed doors than what the public saw at the time with Black Cards.

The *Folie à Deux* fiasco, if it can be called that, had left its mark on Wentz. 'I could feel the backlash against the band,' he'd later say to *Rolling Stone*. 'I mean, I was in such a haze of selfishness and pills it was hard to believe I could feel anything. [...] I was high on being Pete Wentz.' But taking a break had challenges of its own, too. At his busiest, he used to wake up and dread opening his inbox and seeing all the messages he had to answer, but soon he found himself not getting any, which was just as difficult. In December 2010 he appeared at the Jingle Ball, an annual concert held in LA where Travie McCoy of Gym Class Heroes was appearing, but he was upset to be there without the band, to not be performing. He drank too much and fell over and hit his head, which required a visit to the emergency room for stitches. His whole identity had been tied up with the band, and if he had been 'high on being Pete Wentz', then this was the comedown.

With no commitments to fulfil he threw himself into parenting and became, as he put it in a 2015 interview with Howard Stern, 'Mr Mom.' Photographers were less interested in pursuing him to take his picture, so he started taking less interest in the way that he looked. He grew a beard and let his grooming slip, which in turn contributed to his low mood, but he was too caught up in the cycle to do anything about it. It was, as he told *Rolling Stone*, a 'really dark, weak period', further exacerbated by the fact that he didn't have any creative outlet to address the way he was feeling.

Then, in 2011, the news broke that Wentz and Ashlee Simpson would be separating, with Simpson filing for divorce and citing 'irreconcilable differences'. It would be some years before Wentz would open up about the split, but he would later reveal to Howard Stern that while he had got married with the intention of it lasting forever, the fact that the couple were so young when they tied the knot, plus the media attention that had dogged them from day one, had contributed to the break-up. 'I think there's an important thing where you know how to fight, because you can fight with somebody and it's not the end of everything,' he said. 'But if you don't know how to have those arguments, then they become nuclear. And we were doing this all in the public eye, which as you know, it doesn't help, because you have people scrutinising everything you do.' In the interview Wentz also stated that the pair have remained friends and share custody of Bronx fifty-fifty, ensuring that despite their unusual lifestyles, he's always in a healthy environment.

The period away from the band also gave Wentz time to think about the way in which his celebrity status had affected Fall Out Boy. Having a handsome face to associate with the band who was always ready with a witty sound bite had been a huge part of their success. Wentz had become a genuine icon of the scene, adored and maligned in equal measure, a shorthand image for everything that the mid-2000s emo movement had come to mean. But Pete Wentz the celebrity had become so big that it was drawing focus away from the rest of the band and the music that they made together.

'I think I have to look at Pete Wentz in capital letters; the version of me that TMZ knows about,' he said to *Spin*. 'That stuff is like a black cloud over the band. When I read a review, ninety per cent of the review is about my lifestyle and the last two sentences are about the record.' In Stump he had a songwriter whose talents could not be overstated, but he had been in Wentz's shadow from the day that he first answered the door in his argyle sweater; it was no surprise he had a desire to pursue his own music. As the band had got bigger their personalities had developed; Stump had come out of his shell, stopped hiding under his trucker cap and learned how to be a performer as well as songwriter, but Wentz felt that he hadn't created enough space for Stump to keep growing. But having Bronx had forced Wentz to rethink his priorities in life, and though this period of change had been painful, it had forced an awakening of sorts. 'I think that having a kid made me understand myself a lot more,' he said to *Rolling Stone*. 'Back then, I didn't respect people's time. I would show up to stuff whenever I felt like it. I was a selfish guy that ended up in a position I didn't even understand.'

Wentz was able to enjoy what The Damned Things and Stump were putting out, though, especially as the styles were all sufficiently distinct that no one was stepping on toes. Patrick had been working on his debut throughout 2010, despite initially hoping something would be out in the middle of that year; as he explained to *Icon vs. Icon*, it had taken a while for him to be able to distill all of his ideas into a clear vision. 'I had to be really restrained,' he said. 'I had to be really focused, you know? Because I'm kinda scatterbrained as far as my taste in music and my interest in music. [...] That extended to the production sound of the music and the instruments and the way they were played and the lyrics and every word choice mattered. [...] I had to be the band all by myself. You know, I mean that more emotionally, intellectually. I play all the instruments, but that was the easy part. The hard part was making the decisions myself.'

A perfect example of that difficulty in committing to decisions came in November, when he put out two versions of his first official release. One was called 'Spotlight (Oh Nostalgia)', and the other, 'Spotlight (New Regrets)', and he accompanied the two arrangements with a post explaining that he couldn't figure out which version he preferred, so it was up to fans to vote for which would ultimately make it onto his album. 'Spotlight (New Regrets)' floats in on some plaintive synths borrowed straight from the wax of the eighties' best new wave records, and mixes them with layered vocal melodies to challenge the best R&B harmony groups out there; it's a sparer, slightly more aloof arrangement than that of 'Spotlight (Oh Nostalgia)', which bounces along on an octave piano bass line, slows the tempo a bit, and makes more of an anthem of the chorus. Both songs were more overtly 'pop' than anything that had been associated with Fall Out Boy before, but there was nothing generic or watered down here. They were a bright and unique expression of Stump's influences carried by his honeyed voice. Plus, much like Wentz, he had a penchant for tongue-in-cheek rhyming couplets that paper over a darker interpretation: 'Depression is a little like happy hour, right / It's always gotta be happening on any given night,' he sings.

It was 'Spotlight (Oh Nostalgia)' that claimed a narrow victory in the poll held on his website, but plans changed when Stump announced the surprise release of an EP in February 2011. Entitled *Truant Wave*, it gave a home to songs Stump didn't feel quite fitted on his record – including 'Spotlight (Oh Nostalgia)' – and was released with absolutely no promotion or warning from him. Two of the songs that appeared had been debuted at his South by Southwest performance. The first, 'Love, Selfish Love', opens with a crystalline key part, which is carefully wedded to a hesitantly funky bass line before the song opens into an unexpectedly melancholic chorus awash with affected guitars, where Stump pleads, 'God bless the sad and selfish, stay helpless.'

'As Long As I Know I'm Getting Paid', on the other hand, brings carnivalesque percussion to choppy funk guitars and Giorgio Moroder-like arpeggiated synths, and sees Stump pulling every rabbit from his hat of vocal tricks – falsetto breaks, breathy accents and distinctly Michael Jackson-style melismas included. 'Cute Girls', meanwhile, is a space-age R&B jam that suggests Stump had really been paying attention when he collaborated with The Neptunes. The EP explores textures, sound and atmospheres that Fall Out Boy hadn't even gone near in their discography, and was partly released to prime listeners for how different his debut album – which had been announced as *Soul Punk* – was going to be. 'I really want *Soul Punk* to have as much of a chance to have it be [*sic*] listened to discerningly,' he told MTV. 'And if I'm going to disappoint people by not [making] *Take This To Your Grave, Part II*, I would rather do that before *Soul Punk*, because that record means something to me.'

Soon after the EP was released Stump started performing live shows with a band made up of the great and good of rock and pop. Bassist Matt Rubano had previously been in Taking Back Sunday, keyboardist/saxophonist Casey Benjamin had performed with Mos Def and Q-Tip, and drummer Skoota Warner was a session musician who made his name with alt-metal outfit Ra. Performing without Fall Out Boy backing him up could have been an unsettling experience, but Stump found that working with hired players came with benefits. 'Performing is totally different, and the thing that's funny is when you're in a band and you come up together, you put up with a lot of behaviour and engage in a lot of behaviour that isn't really professional,' he told *US Weekly* magazine. 'Whenever I think back to some of the things I said or did, I'm like "man, what a jerk! That's a jerk thing to say." But with this, all the guys do this for a living and they want to get called back so it's all easy, it's a very easy work environment when you're working with a "for hire band".'

Stump had been working on *Soul Punk* under entirely his own steam and financed it with his own cash, recording at various facilities in Chicago. It wasn't hard to see why he'd titled the album as he had. It might not have sounded very punk, but it was a true DIY effort. And at the same time, it was allowing Stump to give free reign to his own musical passions. It was soul music in the purest sense of the word, and unsurprisingly, it was a hugely personal endeavour. The album was released on 18 October 2011. The first track, appropriately titled 'Explode', sounds like a positively flammable blend of screeching synths, robotic beats and late-era Michael Jackson vocal stylings, with a chorus hot enough to melt the plastic on your speakers. It was slick and undoubtedly dance-floor-ready, but paranoid and nervy too, a perfect soundtrack to the noirish tale of a bomb-disposal officer's mid-life crisis which formed the lyrics. It was a blazing opening to the record and solid evidence that Stump really had become a master of his craft; it seemed like he could turn his hand to practically any instrument, understand it, get to the heart of what makes it special and then recruit it into a great song.

The album is at its best when it takes Stump's R&B, soul and pop influences and throws them together in a daring way, without reverence or self-consciousness. 'Dance Miserable' benefits from a killer bass line and an outrageously infectious groove, which is punctuated by shards of glistening synths whilst Stump delivers a breathy, seductive vocal performance. In another life it could easily have been a Justin Timberlake single. 'The "I" in Lie', meanwhile, takes the futuristic sound and applies it to balladry, with Stump purring his best Prince impression whilst he sings of the lustful fever of night and the regret of morning. It's disarming to hear this garrulous boy-next-door sing so candidly about sex – 'We could make love tonight, but you're gonna hate yourself in the morning light', he insists – but he pulls off the persona of the anguished lover effortlessly.

As slick as it is, the album takes risks. 'Run Dry (X Heart X Fingers)' clocks in at over eight minutes, kicking off with some big catchy hooks over a slap bass line like a funk-pop tune for the instant-gratification generation, even as Stump sings of its pitfalls: 'Step one: drink, step two: make mistakes, step three: pretend you don't remember'. It's the classic Fall Out Boy tactic of putting serious topics to an upbeat tune, one of the few ways in which this album does recall Fall Out Boy, but at the halfway mark it segues into a deftly delivered Prince-style instrumental breakdown. It isn't just The Purple One's voice Stump can imitate; he can shred like him, too. 'Greed' has an almost ragtime shuffle to it, but lyrically it's a takedown of corporate greed, as Stump implores 'my Gordon Gekkos and my Bernie Madoffs, I want to see you pop your white collars up'.

Elsewhere, 'Allie' offers a clever reimagining of Jay-Z's 'It's a Hard Knock Life', with its title a play on *Annie*, the musical from which Jay-Z sampled his famous chorus. It's got the bombast of a rock opera, and also gives Stump the opportunity to showcase his chops as a drummer and guitarist. He even manages to squeeze some jazzy licks into 'Coast', a song with a big, plainspoken chorus perfectly crafted to get lighters in the air. It's only when Stump flies too close to the burning sun of radio pop that the album slides into mediocrity, such as on 'This City', an all-too-sweet paean to Chicago, and 'Everybody Wants Somebody', a forgettable Motown-esque tune. ('Everybody Wants Somebody' was something of a key to writing the record, as it was the first track Stump penned that distilled what he was trying to achieve into one song, but it's surpassed by others on *Soul Punk*.)

But as a record overall, this is bold, inventive stuff, quite unlike anything he'd done before but executed with panache. Reviewers agreed, but in almost every instance acknowledged the gap Stump would have to leap in finding a new audience for this left-field collection of songs. '"Dance Miserable", the bump of "Spotlight" or the glam synth of "Run Dry" but if a listener can loosen his or her mind there is plenty to admire on this effort,' wrote *Rock Sound*, portentously. 'It's good – really good – but only if you want it to be.'

That October Stump took his new sound and new band on the road in support of Panic! at the Disco, a tour that took until 10 November, and then played a couple of momentous venues: the first at the Metro in Chicago, the venue at which Stump had coveted a headline show before Fall Out Boy formed, and the second at New York's Webster Hall, in the smaller Studio room. And boy, was he putting on a show, dancing furiously in dapper suits cut to fit his now rake-thin frame, even taking to the drums to perform a cover of Phil Collins's 'In the Air Tonight'.

All was not well, however. Despite the positive critical reception, he had found himself the subject of a serious amount of online heckling for his drastic change of direction, a rebrand many saw as a betrayal of his pop-punk roots regardless of the fact those same influences were a crucial part of the Fall Out Boy sound. He was accused of selling out, despite the fact he'd funded the album entirely out of his own pocket and was losing money by heading out on tour to promote it. It was the inanity of the objections that got to him; criticisms of the record or of the new direction were one thing, but to claim he was doing it for the money, or that his ego had swelled to the point he thought he could be the next Michael Jackson were meaningless. And the anger was not just present online. It had spilled over into shows, where he was being heckled from the crowd. He felt, for the first time in his life, like he was being bullied. Perhaps in retrospect it was a mistake going on tour with Panic!, whose fan base was too closely associated with Fall Out Boy's. Or perhaps it would have made no difference. Perhaps the world simply wasn't ready for a Patrick Stump solo album.

CHAPTER TWENTY-TWO

THE RISK IT TOOK TO BLOOM

Outside of music, Fall Out Boy had always presented themselves to the watching world as very human rock stars. The band were accessible to fans through forum posts, diaristic blog entries and social media; they would give candid interviews about their awkwardness in the face of fame; we even got to see the inside of Pete's parents' house. But faced with the growing backlash for *Soul Punk*, Patrick dropped the veil like never before and revealed the true cost of taking creative risks in the public eye.

The episode began on 28 February 2012 with the publication of a piece by Jacob Tender on *underthegunreview.net*. Entitled 'The Cure to Growing Older – A Musical Retrospective', the editorial is a sweet and personal account of Tender's musical coming of age that orbits around Fall Out Boy's *From Under the Cork Tree*. As Tender writes:

> In my youth, I was heavily guarded by my parents in most aspects of life. I was a Boy Scout and church-going boy with straight A's and soccer as an interest. I was a good kid. The kind my mother was proud of. I didn't swear or get into trouble, I had good friends and made responsible decisions. My Internet access was limited by dial-up, AOL child-locks, and previously determined web-browsing time. Middle School was pretty normal for me until something new came along. That thing was Chicago based, pop-punk band Fall Out Boy and they were not allowed. My first illegally burned album was Fall Out Boy's *From Under the Cork Tree* and when I received my copy, I learned a few things.

The piece recounts how he fell in love with the record and in turn pop punk in general, a passion unfettered by his discovery that his mother was not a fan of Fall Out Boy's 'obscure lyrics referring to sex and blasphemy'. 'Luckily, my mom wasn't aware that I had my coveted burned CD, so I continued my listening in secret,' he reveals. 'The songs were even better than before. Why? Well, that's because I wasn't supposed to have them of course. The "forbidden fruit" effect was placed on pop-punk music and thus, my departure from good boy Jake began.'

But 'The Cure to Growing Older' is also an astute examination of the way in which music can come along at a certain time in your life and make an indelible imprint on your consciousness, which time and the march towards maturity cannot scrub away. It is a tribute to nostalgia that celebrates the joy of falling in love with an artist for the first time whilst also acknowledging that these experiences are rarely repeated, and have as much to do with the listener's circumstance as the artist themselves. Tender continues:

> *From Under the Cork Tree* was the first CD I listened to on repeat for days, months even. It was the first album for which I memorised all the lyrics, inflections, and harmonies. Fall Out Boy was the first band I learned all of the members' names for. Patrick Stump was my 'favourite singer' for at least two years. I joined AIM chat rooms and sought out others who listened to FOB. I didn't like those pretentious assholes who didn't like anything after *Take This To Your Grave*. I now recognise that I'm one of those assholes, but I still fume when some of my favourite records are so easily discredited by ignorant semi-listeners.

As the article was published, few would have guessed how strong a response it was to evoke from one particular member of Fall Out Boy. 'I think I was turning nineteen, and I decided that that was the day that I wanted to publish this thing that I'd written,' Tender recalls. 'I was going to college in southern Ohio at the time and my mother brought my sister and my best friend from back home just to spend the day and hang out. So I didn't even look at the piece for the rest of the day to see how it was going or how many hits it was getting or anything like that. And it was after my family left and I went home that a friend of mine, Zack Zarrillo who ran [alternative music blog] *Property of Zack*, sent me a tweet. It just vaguely said, "You're about to lose your shit".'

If anything is likely to make a music writer lose his shit, it's the lead singer of their favourite band penning a response to the piece they'd written, just as Patrick did. Published first on *patrickstump.com* and later reprinted by *Alternative Press*, the post was called 'We Liked You Better Fat: Confessions of a Pariah', and while Stump praises Tender's article in the opening line, it is a jumping-off point for Stump to air his disappointment at the response to *Soul Punk*. It's a funny but undeniably sad piece, remarkable in its honesty and vulnerability, which outlines the level of animosity that had greeted his debut solo effort:

> The reality is that for a certain number of people, all I've ever done, all I ever will do, and all I ever had the capacity to do worth a damn was a record I began recording when I was eighteen years old. That I can live with. That's fine and fair; I have those records in my collection that seem to stand out far above the rest of my favourite artists' catalogues (and especially for artists in whom I only have a passing interest). [...] If I am to be obscure and financially unsuccessful, there's nothing disheartening in that. The thing that's more disheartening is the constant stream of insults I'm enduring in my financially unsuccessful obscurity.

Stump explains how the reception to *Folie à Deux* had given the band their first taste of open hostility from the demographic that was supposedly their fans, and that that coupled with modest sales and some negative reviews had made the band feel like 'rotten vegetable targets in Clandestine hoodies'. Being in Fall Out Boy, he spells out plain as day, stopped being fun. The experience of making *Soul Punk*, by contrast, had been the fulfilment of a lifelong dream, and he'd managed to shed at least sixty pounds at the same time (weight that he says had been hanging around since a 'month-long drinking binge after a bad break-up'). But though there was plenty of positive press reception to *Soul Punk*, as well as astonished admiration of his physical transformation, he was not universally lauded for these achievements. They made him the target of taunts and, worse, out-and-out aggression. 'What I wasn't prepared for was the fervour of the hate from people who were ostensibly my own supporters (or at least supporters of something I had been part of),' he explains. 'The barrage of "We liked you better fat", the threatening letters to my home, the kids that paid for tickets to my solo shows to tell me how much I sucked without Fall Out Boy, that wasn't something I suppose I was or ever will be ready for. That's dedication. That's real palpable anger.'

The sum of all this was an impasse. Stump could never go back to being the same teenager who wrote *Take This To Your Grave*, though he expresses a sincere wish that he could. At the same time, he was unable to escape the legacy that Fall Out Boy had built, casting a shadow so large that his new ambitions, though straining for the sun, would wither and die. The piece ends with little by way of resolution. Stump even states that he is tempted to retire from touring and recording altogether, though he stops short of actually making that announcement. He offers little by way of information about Fall Out Boy's return, apart from enthusiasm for the idea, and points out he'd been getting some work as a producer/songwriter for hire in between acting lessons. He'd even found the time to catch up with episodes of *Downton Abbey* and *The Office*. It's a sobering read. The complaints of rock stars so often fall on deaf ears because the public has little sympathy for a class they consider so elite as to have no real problems. But Stump's piece is so self-effacing, measured and warmly humorous that the pain at the heart of it becomes very relatable.

For Jacob Tender, the experience of entering into the narrative of Patrick's life in such a profound way was bittersweet. 'When I initially got the link and saw the line, "There's this really nice piece at *Underthegunreview.net* by Jacob Tender", I was just like, "The singer of my favourite band who no one's heard from online in three or four months is now singing my praises"," he recalls. 'That was really strange. That was surreal. And I read through the whole thing but I don't think I really absorbed it, and I don't think I did for three or four days. But once I'd had some time away from the high and the exhilaration of all the praise, and the random Facebook requests I was getting from Fall Out Boy fans and stuff like that, I dug into it to see what was actually going on in his mind, and it was really kind of depressing. On the one hand he was saying that this piece that I wrote really affected him in a strong way, but that's not necessarily a positive thing.'

Tender, too, was impressed with how open and honest Stump was, and was struck by the crisis of identity that he wrote about. 'What he spoke about there was the way that a lot of his fans were unhappy that he and the band were changing,' he says. 'And Patrick Stump has never been the guy that wanted to be in the limelight. I think he was always happy to step to one side and let Pete Wentz take the frontman role. But I can see how for him a lot of that change could be difficult, going from being in this very successful pop-punk band that was touring the world, then reeling back and trying some of his own stuff, some pop-driven stuff, that didn't go over quite as well. Then, everyone seemed to be saying, "Oh, we want Fall Out Boy back – we don't want you, we want the band that you were a part of."'

That was a feeling that Tender himself shared, being a fan of the band who wanted to see them get back together, but where he differed from Stump's most outspoken detractors was that he had no issue with the band's desire to evolve and change. 'I was definitely one of the ones that wanted Fall Out Boy back – I wasn't rallying for it, but I definitely wanted the hiatus to end so we could get some new stuff,' he explains. 'There's that line I wrote that he quoted himself, that goes, "I didn't like those pretentious assholes who didn't like anything after *Take This To Your Grave*. I now know that I'm one of those assholes..." I didn't mean that in the way that I think some people reading it took it. What I was saying there was essentially that there are a lot of people that are unhappy that Fall Out Boy or their favourite band change. They go through a creative evolution. And to a certain degree, yeah, of course, I'm gonna wish those times and more songs like the ones that I liked but not for any good reason. It's just nostalgia, and nostalgia hits a lot of people pretty hard and blinds them to the good stuff that's in front of them.'

Though it had brought to mind some sour feelings for Stump, Jacob had written the piece as nothing but praise. 'I had no intention of making people believe that I didn't like the work that he put out after,' Tender explains. 'Objectively, I think that the last record they put out before the hiatus [*Folie à Deux*] was my favourite Fall Out Boy record of all. This one [*From Under the Cork Tree*] just happened to be the one that hit me first and made such a big impact on what it was that I chose to do.'

At the same time, though, it's clear Stump was exorcising some demons that had been haunting him for a while, and that 'A Cure to Growing Older' offered him a way in to start discussing them. 'I [Tender] still feel really conflicted about it... I still feel half bad. He was obviously going through a pretty rough time at that point. Though a lot of the stuff that he wrote in response to my piece wasn't necessarily in response to my piece – really I think my post was just a catalyst and a starting point for him to say probably what he had wanted to say for a couple of months at that time.'

It's somewhat ironic, too, that although it is not mentioned in his article, Tender was and is a big supporter of Stump's solo material. 'I loved *Soul Punk*,' he says. 'I loved that record. I think I'm one of three people I know that actually sought it out on vinyl. Somewhere I have a zip folder where I ripped all the YouTube covers he was doing of Kanye and stuff like that, which I put on a mixtape. Patrick has such a great voice and his sensibilities come from such an interesting place – there are so many awesome influences, from Elvis Costello and his deep roots in blue eyed soul.' And Tender is one the many admirers of the band who recognise how bright a talent this softly spoken, retiring frontman singer and songwriter is. 'I'm not saying that Patrick makes the band. There's obviously a lot of other stuff, like Pete's writing and the musicianship of the other guys. But what makes Fall Out Boy special for me is Patrick Stump's voice. [...] I think he sounds better now than he ever has, and he's really a very fantastic musician.'

'And the time came when the risk it took to stay closed in a bud became more painful than the risk it took to bloom.' Those were the words, first written by Anaïs Nin, that heralded the start of Patrick's solo career. With the publication of 'Confessions of a Pariah', you have to wonder what Patrick's feelings about the quote would have been. Would he still have considered the pain of not pursuing his dream intolerable, or was the fierceness of the world that greeted him more damaging? What we do know is that Patrick later came to regret ever publishing his piece, telling *Rolling Stone* that 'people genuinely thought it was a suicide note. Every part of me wishes I hadn't written that thing.' But Patrick's unvarnished honesty is praiseworthy in an era when so many celebrities and musicians hide behind a smokescreen of infallibility, and this low ebb was not to last forever. The rising tide was soon to take Patrick and his bandmates higher than they'd ever been before.

CHAPTER TWENTY-THREE

ELVIS'S PYJAMAS

By 2012, Fall Out Boy may have been unofficially retired for the previous couple of years, but its members were still in close contact with one another. Joe had married his longtime girlfriend Marie Goble in 2011, and the ceremony had given the band the chance to hang out together as a unit free from the pressures of the band. After going through a rough period in his life, Pete was back in the spotlight again, hosting a reality TV show called *Best Ink*, which pitted tattoo artists against one another, on the Oxygen channel. But he felt that he needed some kind of creative outlet, and after seeing the pain in Patrick's blog post, he got in touch with his old friend and bandmate to see if he wanted to spend a few days with him writing songs together. They met and knocked out a couple of tunes but there was nothing special about them; Wentz wondered if Stump was really there as a favour to a friend, rather than out of a genuine desire to fire up Fall Out Boy again. Stump was still Wentz's best friend – Pete would be best man at Patrick's wedding, when the latter married his partner Elisa Yao in September 2012 – but Wentz was troubled by the thought that he had overshadowed Patrick in the past.

Though this first attempt at reviving the spirit of Fall Out Boy was not particularly promising, Patrick came back to Pete to try again. With three or four songs written that hadn't caught the pair's imagination, Pete posed Stump with a challenge: he had an idea for a song that combined different emotions and moods, and he wanted to see if Stump could put them together in an effective song. 'Pete and I had been throwing around a lot of ideas, and sometimes Pete speaks in really funny kind of riddles,' Stump told *Entertainment Weekly*. 'That's one of the classic things that used to frustrate me, when people would complain about our long song titles that don't make any sense and don't have any relation to the song. I always thought, "You need to talk to Pete Wentz, because when you hang out with him for ten minutes, you realise that's how that guy talks." He threw this puzzle at me, and he wanted me to combine a whole bunch of songs and feelings that were so disparate. As a trained musician, I thought, "Those things literally can't go together".' But he tried anyway, and to his surprise, the result felt like something special. It was called 'Where Did the Party Go', and it felt like a Fall Out Boy song, but one written by the band that they could be, rather than the band they had been. It was a signpost pointing to an unknown future.

Wentz was seriously excited about the track and his passion was infectious. Soon the pair had built up a head of steam and with a few more songs written that felt like they could work with 'Where Did the Party Go', they decided it was time to get in touch with Andy and Joe to discuss the possibility of trying these songs out as a band. Patrick called Andy, who was up for the possibility straightaway.

The hiatus had been very hard on Andy, who would later reveal that the winter after Fall Out Boy went their separate ways he had fallen into a serious depression. He had gone from having a hectic schedule planned out months in advance to having more time on his hands than ever, and six months later, he and his girlfriend broke up. In a shock revelation to Kerrang! Radio he spoke of how he had even contemplated suicide. 'Being in Fall Out Boy for so long, and having a schedule like we did, it kind of institutionalises you,' he said. 'And then you're home, you have nothing and you don't know what you're going to do. It was really hard and I was really depressed. I wanted to kill myself... that first Christmas was the worst. I mean, I own a lot of guns, so it wouldn't be hard.' Since then Hurley had been able to find meaningful diversions to occupy himself. He lived in a shared house with members of the hardcore band Misery Signals, and had been working on putting together a new band called Burning Empires. Together they had also formed Fuck City, a collective of like-minded people who made and distributed music, books and clothes. He'd even had the chance to sit in as drummer for a short tour with the band that had led him to straight-edge veganism – Earth Crisis. But all the same, he was ready to think about a return to Fall Out Boy.

Joe was not as sure. For the first three years of being away from Fall Out Boy he had no interest in rejoining the band. The Damned Things had given him an outlet for his writing that he'd never had before, and though he'd kept in touch with Patrick, Pete and obviously Andy throughout the break, he had reached a place in his life where he was perfectly content without Fall Out Boy. The Damned Things had reached a natural conclusion of sorts when Keith, Scott and Rob had returned to their respective bands to work on new albums, but Joe had launched a new band with Damned Things bass player Josh Newton called With Knives. With Knives had begun as Newton's pet project, a name under which he could make instrumental, noise-rock influenced recordings, and Joe had later come on board; demos were recorded at Trohman's home studio and he had even been laying down vocals for the tracks. He was, to use his own word, 'ambivalent' about Fall Out Boy.

It was new bandmate Josh Newton that had first got him thinking about the possibility of returning, telling him that he should consider going back. But if he was going to do so, things would have to be different. One of his main issues with the band was that it offered him little opportunity to write, so he prepared a list of stipulations to discuss with Patrick. But to his surprise, when the pair eventually spoke – in a phone call that went on for over three hours – Patrick had anticipated all of his grievances. Stump had been in attendance at a Damned Things show at the Roxy, and it had made him realise how much Joe had to offer as a writer that Fall Out Boy had not been utilising. 'At this point, the four of us have grown into a strong enough bunch of dudes that we should probably integrate that, rather than keep this – quote end quote – "Pete and Patrick show" going,' Stump explained to *DIY Magazine*. There were other things about the old Fall Out Boy that needed correcting, too, like the fact they were so burned out from touring all the time that they never got a chance to practise. With reassurances that he would have an equal stake in the band's creative output, Joe agreed to meet up with the rest of Fall Out Boy.

The band met at Patrick's house, where he has his own studio built in the backyard. As they began running through the old material, it seemed like the mojo might have gone. It had been years since the band had played together and they were seriously rusty – 'like the worst Fall Out Boy cover band imaginable,' as Joe put it to *Premier Guitar*. But with a bit of persistence the sharpness started to come back, and soon enough the band was sounding 'better than the last time we'd ever played – back when we were a well-oiled machine'. After all, Joe had spent the break honing his craft like never before, going toe-to-toe with some of the best guitarists in the rock and metal world and holding his own. Patrick and Andy had always been musos, but even Wentz, not typically seen as the musician of the band, had been working on his chops. He hadn't spent as much time playing music as the others during the break and he didn't want to show up and find himself leagues behind, so he'd committed to a regimen of practice, playing to a metronome and working on his technique. For all the time that the band had spent apart pursuing their individual visions, there was no denying the power of these four unique personalities when they met in a room. Stump probably summed it up the best: 'We did all these other solo records to prove that we don't need each other to make music, but we do need each other to make this music,' he told *Entertainment Weekly*. 'I think there's something about these four personalities that is special.'

Tentatively, the band started sketching ideas for a new album, and met at their manager's apartment in New York to talk. One thing they agreed on was that if they were going to do this again, they had to forge forward in the spirit of creativity, coming up with a new sound that was relevant in the current day and age rather than resurrecting the sound they had created on their first go-around. What was it, they wondered, that made Fall Out Boy sound the way they did? If you stripped away genre, would you still be able to identify Fall Out Boy by sound alone? It was agreed, firstly, that the band would refresh their approach by working with a new producer. Neal had been an integral part of creating Fall Out Boy's sound and the records had stood the test of time, but the band did not want to repeat themselves. They did not want to cash in on the legacy of Fall Out Boy; they wanted to write the next chapter in the story.

But things had to be different on a personal level too. Wentz had realised that people who tend to be extremely successful in the professional or artistic sphere of their life can often be more withdrawn or selfish in their private lives, because, as he put it to the *Huffington Post*, 'Whatever it is that drives them to be this great force probably negates other parts of their personality.' But Pete was a father and Joe and Patrick were both husbands, so family had to come first. 'Whatever made our band that larger-than-life thing, hopefully we can find things that make this monster that is Fall Out Boy work but also let us go home and see our families,' Wentz said.

With all four members on the same page, they went about recording a new album in secret. The privacy was central to what the band were trying to achieve. 'Elvis didn't have anyone come to his house and watch him practise his dance moves in his pyjamas,' Wentz explained to *Billboard*. 'There's obviously a reason for that, because it's part of the art.' Wentz imagined how he would feel if one of his favourite bands announced they were getting back together, and realised he wouldn't want to be drip-fed details and scraps of new material. He'd want it all in the moment he found out it was happening: single, album, tour. And that was what Fall Out Boy were going to deliver for fans. The band had opted to work with Butch Walker, someone who they felt could offer them not just a new sound but also help them develop a new dynamic in the studio. Walker is a musician in his own right, having fronted the Atlanta band Marvelous 3, on whose records he also got his first credits as a producer. After the demise of Marvelous 3 he forged forward as a solo artist and built a career behind the desk, often working in the sweet spot between rock, pop and punk with the likes of Avril Lavigne, Pink, and Katy Perry as well as Bowling for Soup, American Hi-Fi and Panic! at the Disco. If anyone could help Fall Out Boy integrate their punk roots with modern pop sensibilities, it was Walker.

In the years that Fall Out Boy had been dormant, the heavier end of guitar music had all but disappeared from the radio, and the band had also decided to move away from thick slabs of distorted guitar chords as the basis of their sound. Stump knew that the guitar sound they and Avron had crafted was a huge part of Fall Out Boy's identity, but he also felt that it had become a crutch – whatever chances he wanted to take with his songwriting, he felt that as long as it had loud guitars, it would be accepted. On *Folie à Deux*, Stump laid down more guitars than ever before, sometimes putting four guitar tracks over one another on a single song. But now the band were ready to take risks, and Butch Walker pushed them in the direction of simpler guitar work.

Patrick also felt that Walker helped the band to overcome some of the tensions that they'd previously come up against whilst recording. 'I kind of had turned into this worn-out [person saying], "I slaved over a hot stove for ten hours!"' Stump explained to the *Chicago Tribune*'s *RedEye* about his demeanour in the studio on previous efforts. 'I turned into that kind of character in the studio on every record and so they weren't fun to make because I always felt like conversely everyone wanted me to be doing everything, but secretly probably no one really did want me to do everything. [...] I think that what was the big difference with this record was that we were able to lose a lot of that. I think again Butch is a huge credit to that because he is a type-A personality, and you do not mess with him.' As soon as Stump started to complain, Walker would step in and take control of the situation. But just as Joe was now getting a look-in on the songwriting, Stump was also getting more say in the lyrics, and would ultimately write about one quarter of the words for the upcoming album.

With the album finished, Fall Out Boy planned their return to the stage. Whether the lights were still on for them remained to be seen.

CHAPTER TWENTY-FOUR

PLUGGING BACK IN

Rumours had begun circulating in January 2013 that the band might be coming back, but as the tenth anniversary of *Take This To Your Grave* was approaching, the most that fans dared to hope for was a reunion tour to play that record in full. An entire new record, made in secret and offering a bold new vision of the band that Fall Out Boy could be, was far from their minds. *Property of Zack*, a blog run by an ex-intern at Crush Management, even leaked on 25 January that they were returning (with the words 'you can stop refreshing for a journal update'). But still fans were sceptical, not least because the band staunchly denied it until the very last moment. But on 4 February the news hardly anyone had let themselves believe came through:

> When we were kids the only thing that got us through most days was music. It's why we started Fall Out Boy in the first place. This isn't a reunion because we never broke up. We

> needed to plug back in and make some music that matters to us.

The announcement came with a shot of the band burning their old records, a re-enactment of the Disco Demolition Night of 1979. They had a new album, cheekily titled *Save Rock and Roll*. They had a new track, 'My Songs Know What You Did in the Dark (Light Em Up)', with an accompanying music video. And they were playing a tiny club show at Subterranean in Chicago that night.

For those expecting to hear that Fall Out Boy were hitting the road to play *Take This To Your Grave* again, 'My Songs Know What You Did in the Dark (Light Em Up)' must have been a shock – the title is pure Fall Out Boy, but the sound is anything but. Opening with a chopped-up sample of a woman's voice and some disembodied handclaps, it soon builds into a sinister electro-rock groove that stalks Patrick's unadulterated R&B vocal line. Instead of exploding into full-bodied pop punk for the chorus as they'd previously have done, the song sticks with a brooding mood and tempo, with just Pete's rumbling bass and a scything guitar part to accompany Patrick's electrifying squeal of 'I'm on fire!' The song had inspired sessions for the new album, providing a sound that the band could get behind and build other songs based upon it, so it's no surprise that they selected it as the first single. It was rock music, but not as we knew it; it was heavily processed pop, without being artificial; and crucially, it was radio-friendly without pandering to the radio.

Over the previous couple of years Wentz had heard the likes of fun. and Gotye whilst driving around LA with Bronx, and it had convinced him that there could still be a place for Fall Out Boy in the big leagues – and he wanted to be in a band that could have a wide reach and a big impact. That was the essence of the title; it was tongue-in-cheek, of course, but there was sincerity there too. 'Rock and roll means more than leather jackets and blues riffs,' he said to the *Huffington Post*. 'We're never going to be a Pitchfork band, we're just not those kind of darlings and we never aspired to be. But I think that we could be a band that's a gateway drug for people.'

Even the music video, starring larger-than-life rapper 2 Chainz, spoke of the band's determination to be a contender in the charts – and the ceremonial record-burning it depicts was filmed on the original site of Comiskey Park, torn down in 1990, where Disco Demolition Night had taken place. (2 Chainz had actually nearly blown the band's cover in the run-up to the return, tweeting a picture of him and Wentz at dinner with the caption 'Fall Out Boy featuring 2 Chainz'. Fortunately, fans thought it was too far-fetched to believe, so no one in the Fall Out Boy camp even had to deny it.)

Before the show on 4 February started, the atmosphere in Subterranean was cagey. Fans weren't quite sure exactly what to expect, and there were some nervous jitters from within the band too. Joe later admitted that he was concerned that he'd get off stage and feel like he'd made a mistake, that he should never have returned to the band at all; it took him a couple more shows to settle in and realise that he was having a good time. Andy, on the other hand, immediately felt that whatever spark of magic the band had held in the past had endured. There were plenty of familiar faces in the crowd, too: Chris Gutierrez attended and wrote powerfully about the experience on his blog. The day after the show in Chicago the band headed to New York for a show at the Webster Hall, where a queue had started forming ten hours before the doors opened. But as excited as the initiated and unwavering were, there was scepticism too. Fall Out Boy were back and sounding as tight as they ever had, and they had a new single that showed they were willing to move their sound past the boorish guitar attack of their older material. But could they really initiate a whole second phase of their career?

Save Rock and Roll was released on 12 April 2013, and right from its opening track it showcases just how far Fall Out Boy were willing to go to reinvent themselves. From the thunderous peal of strings that open the album to the melodious flutter of strings that closes it, we are given a completely reimagined vision of what Fall Out Boy could be, and the transformation is astonishing. 'The Phoenix' couldn't be a more appropriate opening song name, and it rolls in like a dark day on a repeated orchestral refrain inspired by Shostakovich. 'I was listening through one of his symphonies and found one little string moment that I loved,' Stump explained to *Entertainment Weekly*. 'I'm an idiot, because I don't just sample things, I try to write something that is inspired by a thing I like a lot. So I wrote this whole new song around this string part, but come to find out that there's a pretty popular German hip-hop song that actually samples the exact same moment from the Shostakovich symphony.' (The song Stump is referring to is 'Alles Neu' by Peter Fox, though you can also hear the same sample in 'iLL Manors' by Plan B.) 'It's in the middle of eight minutes of music, but we both latched onto this two second bit.' Once Stump had the loop down he shared it with Wentz who sent him some lyrics, and within minutes, the basic structure of the song had been completed. It's a shamelessly melodramatic track set to a dancefloor-ready beat, where strings and distorted guitars weave contrapuntal melodies whilst Stump shows off his falsetto skills.

After 'My Songs Know What You Did In the Dark' comes 'Alone Together', a song that recalls old Fall Out Boy tracks a little more, with Stump delivering the hooky, emotive chorus straightaway before the band comes crashing in. Stump was unsure about the song for a long time, only falling in love with it when he heard the final version, and it's a great showcase of mix engineer Dave Sardy's sparkling mix – all popping synths and gunshot snares. Next comes 'Where Did the Party Go', the song that kick-started Fall Out Boy's rebirth. It opens with a bouncy bass riff that half recalls 'Dance, Dance', but where that song had the nervous energy of a teenage breakdown, this is a look at young love through the wearied eyes of an adult set to a candied pop backing: 'And when she touched him he turned ruby red,' Stump sings, before a funky clipped guitar comes in for the irresistibly catchy pre-chorus. 'We were the kids who screamed "we weren't the same" in sweaty rooms / Now we're doomed to organising walk-in closets like tombs' Stump half sings and half raps, and it almost sounds like he yearns to go back to the days when Fall Out Boy had to fight for every scrap of respect that they earned.

'Just One Yesterday' opens with Stump carving out a bluesy vocal line over an inky piano line before a soaring chorus takes the song into the stratosphere, bolstered by backing vocals from British singer Foxes. Butch Walker was instrumental in seeing the track through to completion, but for all the pop sheen it's great to see that the band hasn't lost some of the acid that marked them out lyrically. 'If I spilled my guts the world would never look at you the same way / And now I'm here to give you all my love so I can watch your face as I take it all away,' sings Foxes in the breakdown, and the sweetness of her voice only partly offsets the spite of the words.

The album's second feature comes on 'The Mighty Fall' in the form of Big Sean, a Michigan rapper who made his name through Kanye West's GOOD Music. The band had bumped into Big Sean at The Grammys and proposed the idea of him appearing on the record, and his contribution was recorded in Berlin when Fall Out Boy were over in Europe. The band had always positioned themselves on the fringes of hip-hop; 50 Cent had appeared on some dates of the 'Believers Never Die Part Deux' tour, Kanye West himself had remixed 'This Ain't a Scene, It's an Arms Race', and Lupe Fiasco had contributed a verse to a single version of Stump's 'This City'. But, discounting Lil Wayne's appearance on 'Tiffany Blews', which was more of a singing performance, this is the first time a rap had appeared on an album track, and it's a signal that the band had fully embraced the popular music zeitgeist.

'Miss Missing You' is a dyed-in-the-wool synth-pop track – yearning, vulnerable and powered by bleeping synth sounds. It has a flavour of *Soul Punk* about it, which is not surprising given that Stump had first started toying with the song in the run-up to that album, but he downed tools on it because it reminded him of Fall Out Boy too much – not a song they had written, but a song they might write in the future. He could imagine the rest of the band playing it, and that was an indication to him that it wasn't right as a solo track. Hearing it finally finished and on a Fall Out Boy record was, as he told *Spotify* in a track-by-track breakdown of *Save Rock and Roll*, a 'personal triumph'.

'Death Valley' bursts into life straightaway with a driving drumbeat and a repeated two-bar guitar riff, but really comes into its own in the verse, where Stump throws a bit of pepper on his usually sweet voice over a strummed acoustic guitar. Spotted with bluesy guitar licks, it bears the clear mark of Joe's guitar work, but things take a completely unexpected turn in the breakdown, which throbs with a dubstep beat as the melodies quiver like a mirage, as if the track is melting in the heat of the sun. 'Death Valley' had started life as a demo that Trohman recorded in the wardbrobe of his wife's parents' house, and then taken to Stump. It was the first time the pair had ever sat down together to compose something from scratch, and they were surprised to discover they worked very well together.

Wentz had spoken of his admiration for fun. in the run-up to the record, and 'Young Volcanoes' is the song that most obviously bears the influence of that band, with its quasi-island vibe and chanted, wordless refrains. It was another song that Patrick wasn't sure about for a long time, but he sensed that the rest of the band, and Walker, liked it; so where previously he would have been content to let it fall away, this time the band kept working on it until it was album ready. Good job, too, because it contains one of the album's most memorable lines: 'We will teach you how to make boys next door out of assholes'.

'It's Courtney, bitch': that's the venomous declaration that opens 'Rat A Tat', and if Britney is the princess of pop then

Courtney Love is punk rock's Bride of Satan, and love her or loathe her, the bratty missives that she spits over the frantic post-punk noise on offer here bring 'Rat A Tat' to life. The band had run into Love various times over their journey through the world of rock 'n' roll, and Wentz felt her inclusion was a strong message to send out to his female fans. 'It's important for girls to understand that they don't need to just be coat hangers for boys, it's not all about being groupies,' he told *Huffington Post.* 'So we thought it would be important to have an iconic female voice on the album, and Courtney screams rock 'n' roll.' 'Rat A Tat' sounds the least like Fall Out Boy than any song on the album, and it was once again birthed from an idea of Joe's; it also features singing from Hurley, another hallmark that shows the band were determined to do things differently this time around. It's a schizophrenic change of pace from 'Young Volcanoes', but you have to admire the way the band grab genres by the scruff of the neck and kick them through the Fall Out Boy filter.

Over their career the band had made a habit of securing scene-stealing cameos, but here they save the best for last with the appearance of Elton John in 'Save Rock and Roll'. It's one of the highlights of the record, a soulful ballad that attests to the power of music and love. Word had reached the boys that Elton was a fan, and though they almost struggled to believe it, they decided to send word out into the ether anyway that they'd be interested in working with him. The album was more or less finished by this point, but when Elton's people came back saying that he'd like to be on the album, they pushed a giant red 'stop' button and Patrick flew out to Atlanta to meet him. Elton is famous for his voracious appetite for music, and Stump was astonished to discover just how much he knew – not just about music from his generation, but the modern day's cutting edge too. 'One of the things that really struck me, and Elton and I talked about this a lot because of the song title, is how not snobbish he is about any music,' Stump said to *Entertainment Weekly*. '[...] Elton has survived in the charts long enough to have seen every manner of genre and style come and go, and cream rises, and the only thing that matters still are good songs.' The words 'I will defend the faith, going down swinging / I will save the songs that we can't stop singing' could so easily have stumbled in parody, but to hear Elton and Patrick sing them together is a standout moment on an album full of them, and close *Save Rock and Roll* in unforgettable fashion.

Save Rock and Roll won the band no small amount of critical praise, and many publications acknowledged it was a career-saving record. *Alternative Press* put it best, praising the band for progressing their sound so much despite the weight of expectation, and their writing: '*Save Rock and Roll* might not actually, well, save rock and roll – but it certainly has brought Fall Out Boy back from the brink.'

Of course, there were many who disliked the record's new direction, given how sharply it diverged from the sound of their previous efforts, but the band were completely nonplussed by the criticism. As Andy put it to *FasterLouder.com*: 'If you're not willing to take a gamble as an artist, and put all of the chips on the table and try something different, like succeed or fail, then why bother?'

Deciding whether *Save Rock and Roll* was a success or failure was about more than good reviews, though, and the general public voted with their wallets. A week after its release the album debuted at No.1 on the Billboard 200, their second career number one in the US, and at No.2 on the UK album chart. It was a revelation. To many, Fall Out Boy had had their day; they were the vanguard of a particular movement at a particular time, but to expect the millions of fans they had once had to follow them on a new path some six years after the release of their biggest album, and with three years of non-activity, was stretching the limits of common sense. But Fall Out Boy had defied all logic and pulled it off anyway.

CHAPTER TWENTY-FIVE

HALLELUJAH

Since the release of *Save Rock and Roll*, Fall Out Boy have turned an unlikely return to the good graces of the music industry into one of the most astonishing comebacks in recent memory. They have attacked this second phase of their career with more energy, ambition and enthusiasm than ever, becoming bona fide pop stars in the process. But the band did not jump straight back into arena shows. They spent the spring and summer on the Save Rock and Roll Tour, playing mid-sized theatres like Philadelphia's Electric Factory and The Wiltern in LA. It felt like a thank you to the fans for waiting as long as they had, and by the time an arena tour came around in the autumn, Fall Out Boy were all over the radio once again.

It seemed that this time around everything the band did was on a bigger scale than last time; Panic! at the Disco, who had also been working on a new record with Butch Walker, were in support and Urie would come out to accompany Stump on

'20 Dollar Nosebleed', and mid-set, the band would decamp to the middle of the audience for two acoustic numbers before returning to the stage as Hurley ripped through a thunderous drum solo. New material was taking up a big chunk of the set, with eight of *Save Rock and Roll*'s numbers getting an airing – but the more things change, the more they stay the same, and it was 'Saturday' that the band chose to close the set every night.

Music videos had been a huge part of the band's identity, but this was Fall Out Boy version 2.0, and so the promos for the album went a step further than ever before. Inspired by Daft Punk's *Interstella 5555: The 5tory of the 5ecret 5tar 5ystem*, a film based on the French duo's 2001 album *Discovery*, the band revealed that the 2 Chainz-starring video for 'My Songs Know What You Did in the Dark (Light Em Up)' was in fact one section of a narrative that would be released, bit by bit, with a music video for every track from *Save Rock and Roll*. The final film was entitled *The Young Blood Chronicles*, and tells the story of Fall Out Boy's kidnap by a cult of music-hating 'vixens' who subsequently brainwash Patrick into hunting down the other members of the band. Mashing together the schlocky aesthetic of exploitation films and B-movie horror with the traditional pop video, it's gory, overblown and outrageously fun stuff. Where else could you expect to see Patrick getting his hand sliced off, the band taking communion with plectrums in place of wafers, Pete Wentz showing off his falconry skills, and Elton John's pristine white suit getting splattered with blood?

But not everything that the band were doing in this second phase was bigger scale just for the sake of it. In July of 2013 Wentz posted a picture to his Instagram page of the band hanging out in the studio with Ryan Adams, a Jacksonville singer and guitar player known for his mutual appreciation of country and western, folk and raw-edged punk rock noise. The band had been put in touch with Adams through Butch Walker, and the recording facility where the picture was taken was Adams's own Pax-AM Studio in Hollywood. (Walker would go on to record his seventh solo album *Afraid of Ghosts* there, released in 2015.) After meeting for dinner they hit the studio and over two days laid down a series of brash, unhindered punk rock tracks, all recorded in one room with a minimum of takes and with Patrick singing live along with the rest of the band. If *Save Rock and Roll* had been a meticulously planned and executed assault on the mainstream, then these recordings were the band shooting from the hip, free of all expectation. Set up in the same formation in which they used to rehearse, Adams directed the sessions with an emphasis on spontaneity. On occasions the band would work their way through a song and then yell to Adams that they were ready to go for a take, only for Adams to tell them that he'd recorded the rehearsal, and that that was the version they should go with. It was, as Wentz told MTV, 'as close as our band ever gets to recorded improvisation.'

At first there was some doubt as to whether the recordings would ever see the light of day, but then in October 2013 the EP was finally released with the title *Pax AM Days*, and proudly sported an image of volcanic tennis maestro John McEnroe smashing a racquet on the cover. It was a perfect encapsulation of what the release contained: eight tracks of explosive, unbridled punk rock energy, all buzzsaw riffs and trashy drums. Opener 'We Were Doomed from the Start (The

King Is Dead)' lurches forward on chromatic riffing before its Misfits-esque chorus; 'Love, Sex, Death', recorded in a single take, sounds as if Trohman's guitar has been tethered to the back of freight train and recorded as it smashed against the sleepers; and closer 'Caffeine Cold' lets Stump's vocal take the lead as the palm-muted chords thump out an insistent rhythm behind him. Just because they had fought their way to the top of the radio rock food chain, they hadn't forgotten about the music they loved when they were teenagers – the snarl of Black Flag, the exuberance of the Descendents and the righteous anger of Minor Threat.

Since the band's return to the limelight, there seemed to have been a change in Wentz, too. In interviews he was calmer, more content to let other members of the band speak on his behalf, and in February 2014 there was happy news when he announced that he was expecting his second child with partner Meagan Camper, a model. Wentz and Camper had started dating in 2011 when they were introduced at a concert, but this time around he had been more eager to keep his private life private. Media attention, he felt, was not conducive to a healthy relationship, and he was also cautious about introducing any girlfriends to Bronx until he was sure that the relationship was serious.

Their son, Saint Lazslo Wentz, was born on 20 August – just over four months after Joe's wife, Marie, gave birth to their first daughter Ruby. On 15 October of the same year, Patrick's wife Elisa would give birth to their first son too, whom they named Declan. 'We're basically like Tusken Raiders, Sand People from *Star Wars*,' Wentz explained to *Rock Sound* about the challenges of being fathers as well as touring musicians. 'We're very mobile, our families are very mobile, and our kids can go on tour with us every summer.' Fall Out Boy had well and truly become a family band.

With all the demands of children arriving, and after a year-and-a-half of near constant touring that took the band all around the world, it's somewhat astonishing that they would be so keen to get back in the studio to work on a follow-up to *Save Rock and Roll*. After stints in Japan, South America and Europe, they'd spent the first half of 2014 on tour with Paramore on a run dubbed the 'Monumentour', a runaway success that took in dozens of arenas from coast to coast in the USA. But by mid-2014 they were writing again, determined to get the bulk of work done on a new album before the arrival of Stump's son in October. Stump is a perennial perfectionist, and even the record that had cemented their place in music history could not escape his critical gaze. 'One of my minor regrets over *Save Rock and Roll* was that it kind of wandered between styles,' he commented to *Alternative Press*. 'That kind of drove us to strive for something a little more together. Some albums are great for their capacity to bounce around. But then you have albums like David Bowie's *Low* or Elvis Costello's *This Year's Model*, where you pick any track and it sounds like it's from the same album.'

This time the band set to work with Jake Sinclair as well as Butch Walker, who was busy finishing up his record and touring with Ryan Adams. Sinclair had been a member of the NYC-based band The Films, whose second record had been produced by Walker; after the dissolution of the band Walker had taken Sinclair under his wing, and the pair had worked together on a variety of high-profile pop projects. Sinclair and Fall Out Boy had a bold vision for the album. Building on what Fall Out Boy had achieved on the last record, they wanted to realise a truly modern take on rock music, one that incorporated sampling and modern production methods and could appeal to young fans who also listen to hip-hop or EDM. Rock music has become a conservative form, stunted by narrow definitions of what is or isn't 'real music'. Asked about what the future of rock would be like, Wentz told *The New York Times*: 'The only way to do it is for kids to be able to see bands that are playing in arenas and amphitheatres that also have current songs being played on the radio. I can think of ten bands that can sell out arenas, but I'm not sure if kids are buying their music. The future of rock is going to come from kids that listen to Skrillex and to Kanye West.' Wentz made no bones about it: he wanted Fall Out Boy to be the biggest rock band in the world.

On the previous few records the band had utilised laptop recording methods to store ideas and demo skeletal versions of tracks, but with advances in technology they were realising that it was not always necessary to pay for expensive studio resources to re-record these parts – the demo versions could make it to the final album. With such a tight deadline to get the album finished, the band had to be fast and adaptable in making the record, and embracing the power of laptop and home recording enabled them to do it. It was, as Wentz joked to *Alternative Press*, 'like showing cavemen how to use an espresso machine'. Large amounts of Patrick's demo vocals or guitar work actually made it to the album mix, as did Joe's guitar parts, recorded at his home.

Joe would handle most of the guitar tracking on the record

this time around, imprinting the songs with his characterful, classic-rock influenced playing. But once again guitars were not going to characterise the sound of the album as the band moved ever further into a genre-bending space between rock and pop. 'Big Randy Rhoads guitar heroics were never a part of what Fall Out Boy was supposed to be about,' Joe had said to *Guitar World* in 2009. 'Our musical arrangements kind of defy categorisation. People used to call us 'punk' and 'emo', and lately they're calling us 'pop' and 'rock', which is fine. The truth is, we're a little bit of everything.' Those words are true now more than ever. Even Pete, who would typically go through various edits of his lyrics until he reached a place at which he was satisfied, was settling on a final version much sooner. The studio had evolved into a place for the band to meet and discuss the direction of songs rather than to lay down parts as such.

Momentum is an unmistakable thing, and when Fall Out Boy revealed the first cut from their new album on 8 September 2014, they made it clear to the world that they were on a roll. Premiering on Zane Lowe's Radio 1 show in the UK, it was entitled 'Centuries', and it was one of the most grandiose things they had ever written, like Queen reimagined for the Internet age. The track opens with a sample from 'Tom's Diner', a song first written by Suzanne Vega in 1981 that had come to be covered and sampled by a huge number of artists over the years. Stump had written it whilst on the Monumentour with Paramore, well before writing sessions had been completed on the album, but it was recorded and pushed out anyway with a plan to build the rest of the record around it. With its cascading piano figures, low-slung riffing and Stump's rallying cry of 'remember me for centuries!' it practically commands the hairs on the back of your neck to stand up, and it would be the band's most successful single since the release of 'This Ain't a Scene, It's an Arms Race'. Much like 'Sugar, We're Goin Down', it lingered on the singles charts for months, steadily gathering sales as it garnered more and more radio support. By the time the band were promoting and ready to release their new record, it had broken into the Top 10 of the Billboard 100 and become a genuine crossover hit.

American Beauty/American Psycho was released on 16 January 2015, and just as the band had promised in the run-up to its release, it gave the world a modern pop record that straddled dance music, upbeat radio anthems, hip-hop production and good old-fashioned punk-rock spirit. 'Irresistible' opens with a military reveille, a wake-up call announcing the dawn of this new era, and sees Stump delivering one of his most memorable verses in a while – a tongue-tripping salvo of syllables that almost flirts with rap without ever becoming it. The song had gone through more iterations than any other track on the record – over twenty – before reverting to its first version, and its urgency is undeniable. Driven by the horns and trap-influenced beats, there's very little about the song to define it as rock, and yet it's still undeniably Fall Out Boy. They had become a genre unto themselves.

The whole album is characterised by a gleeful hopping between different styles, pilfering sound bites from all over the musical spectrum. The title track is the album's most unpredictable, a collaboration with French producer Sebastian that sounds like an old Fall Out Boy song that's been dissected and reconfigured on some surgeon-come-DJ's operating turntable. Wentz was inspired to get in touch with Sebastian after hearing remixes of

Daft Punk's 'Human After All' and Rage Against the Machine's 'Killing in the Name', and the two started speaking over email. Sounds bleed together to the point that you can't be sure if you're hearing a mangled guitar or a rattling synth, and winding vocal melodies bump into shouted catchphrases. 'I'm an American', Stump yells over and again in such a way that it almost sounds as if he's saying 'I'm *un*-American'. It was also, in contrast to 'Irresistible', one of the album's easiest songs to write.

Surprising moments show up all over *American Beauty/American Psycho*. 'Uma Thurman' starts life as a club-ready banger with a house piano line, but completely wrong-foots the listener with the introduction of a surf-rock guitar riff fifteen seconds in. 'The Kids Aren't Alright' sounds like a crossbreed between doo-wop and Scandi-pop with a huge half-time rock chorus. 'Novocaine' has a distorted riff that recalls Kanye West's 'Black Skinhead' but mutates into a glossy dance-rock tune. And 'Immortals' – a song written specifically to soundtrack a scene in the Disney movie *Big Hero 6* – is a rousing anthem in the spirit of 'Centuries' that opens with the kind of sample RZA might have used on the Wu-Tang Clan's *Enter the Wu-Tang (36 Chambers)*.

It's not a flawless collection, however. 'Jet Pack Blues' and 'Favourite Record' fail to make much of an impression, but the album's strongest moments shine incredibly bright. Take album standout 'Fourth of July'. Opening with an evocative fluttering of woodwind cut with a chopped-up vocal sample, it builds into an agitated, mournful track that rushes towards an intense emotional climax. Older and wiser though he was, Wentz had not given up on exercising his old demons through his lyrics: 'You and I were fireworks that went off too soon / And I miss you in the June gloom, too,' Stump sings here, and you can't help but wonder if the words refer to his public but brief marriage.

When *American Beauty/American Psycho* was released, it outstripped even *Save Rock and Roll*'s unexpected smash success. It debuted at No.1 on the Billboard 200, at No.2 on the UK album chart, and No.3 on the Australian album chart. It was the band's third No.1 in the US, and first week sales were second only to that of *Infinity On High*, which had had the advantage of being released at a time when people still actually bought albums. It was an unqualified roaring success.

'The problem with modern rock is it isn't modern': the thoughts of *Rolling Stone*'s Brian Hiatt had distilled for Wentz exactly why guitar bands didn't get played on the radio any more. But Fall Out Boy had taken rock music and dragged it, kicking and screaming, into the modern age. From the day that Patrick had opened the door to Joe and Pete at his home in Chicago, nothing about Fall Out Boy's rise to the top had been predictable. They had a singer who didn't like the limelight and a motormouth bassist who had turned himself into an icon. They had been the most fiercely loved and widely hated band of a movement they didn't even claim to belong to, and Pete had endured the intense heat of public scrutiny whilst the rest of the band remained out of focus in the background. And they had all but retired from the game only to return at the eleventh hour and claim their greatest successes yet. It had brought them back from the brink of obscurity and made them one of the biggest bands in the world. When Patrick joined Fall Out Boy, all he wanted to do was to play the Metro in Chicago.